WRITTEN IN FLESH

A.D. WILDE

SWEETWATER SERIES BOOK 3

Cover Designer: Dark Woods Publishing

Developmental Editor: Kim Deacon

Editor: Kylie MacDougall

Third edition 2025

Author Website: www.authoradwilde.com

CONTENT WARNING

This book contains content that may be triggering to some readers. Please consider the following warning before reading.

This story is a dark military romance novel containing morally gray characters. There are descriptive scenes of graphic violence and gore, murder, dismemberment, disembowelment, drug abuse, suicide, sexual assault, stabbing, primal play, blood play, human/child trafficking, sex trafficking, child abandonment, PTSD, and somnambulism (sleep walking disorder).
This list is not inclusive, and there may be other content that some readers find disturbing.

YOUR MENTAL HEALTH MATTERS.

For all you nasty bitches who prefer your fictional men stabby,
unhinged, and hung like a horse.
This one's for you.

One

Alora

MY SKIN CURLS FROM my body like burning paper, the heated gazes of men scorching every inch of my exposed flesh as I close the space between me and my third mark of the night. Every cha-ching of the slots and boisterous laugh of men playing cards drives my dignity another inch beneath the surface. But I forge on, sauntering across the casino lounge and sliding onto the barstool beside the tall, well-dressed man I've been watching for the last two hours. I cross my legs and intentionally graze his knee with my bare one, ensuring my little red dress rides high up on my thighs. It sends an icy shiver rolling through me, but I stuff the feeling deep down where I keep my pride and self-respect boxed up.

Remember why you're doing this—to even the playing field. This asshole deserves it, just as the rest did.

But no matter how much I remind myself of these things, a slight twinge of guilt hits me dead center in the solar plexus. Because I'm a good person who does bad things. A little vigilante justice, if you will. And men who can afford expensive suits like this guy's can also afford the loss and to be taken down a peg. Besides, I have a strict rating system in place to ensure I'm only hustling men who are deserving of it. And on a scale from one to dickhead, this guy's ranking at douchebag—the type who's spent the entire evening ogling women and grabbing at the waitress's ass every time she serves drinks to his table. He's not afraid to flaunt his indiscretions, so in return, I'll exploit them.

Forcing my ruby-painted lips into a seductive smile, I angle my head and make eye contact with him. He beams back at me as if we share a special bond, adjusting the bulge at the front of his perfectly creased slacks, the silver watch strapped around his wrist winking at me beneath the dim lighting of the chandeliers hanging low over the bar. This casino isn't just some luxury establishment that serves high-end booze in fancy crystal glasses. It's opportunity disguised in flashing lights, dinging bells, and clanking poker chips.

It's my playground. One of many.

"Hello," I say sweetly, sprinkling on all the charm and batting my eyelashes for good measure. I sound like I have approximately four brain cells, but the dumber I act, the more they let their guard down.

My mark practically foams at the mouth, shooting another patron across the bar a glare. It's clear he's pissing all over his territory. But the joke's on him. Women like me cannot be possessed. But that doesn't mean men won't try to wrangle us into submission anyway. And that's fine by me because the ones here are all loaded down with cash and flashy timepieces.

"Well, hello," he responds flirtatiously, his words slightly slurred from too much alcohol. The backs of his knuckles drag over my bare leg, and I bite down on my tongue to suppress the colorful vocabulary I'm tempted to spew. He hooks his lips into a crooked grin and slides his palm over his balding head as if the five fucking hairs still surviving up there need to be tamed.

I release a tinkling laugh and boldly extend my hand.

"My name's Jessica," I lie.

His brows raise, the loose, leathery skin around his eyes crinkling in delight as he wraps his long, bony fingers around mine and shakes my hand. It feels a little like I'm introducing myself to Satan. Which is ironic because after the last two years, I'm definitely going to hell.

"It's a pleasure to meet you, Jessica," he says politely but avoids sharing his own name. I'm sure he thinks skipping a name will protect his identity after he takes me back to his hotel room and fucks me like the cheap hooker he assumes I am. It's adorable, really, because I won't be going anywhere with him. As soon as I get what I came for, I'll be gone in the blink of an eye.

"Well…" I drag my fingers down my throat and settle them at my collarbone. "I'm parched. How about a drink, baby?" It's a bold move, but I've always been a straight shooter.

A thick black wallet appears before my eyes as he waves the bartender down, counting out enough cash for two drinks plus a hefty tip. Forcing a smile, I avert my eyes from the stack of money.

His knuckles graze my thigh again, and I decide I'm going to need to bathe in battery acid after this interaction. The urge to slam my fist into his crotch is strong, but security around here is thick tonight, so I refrain and move on.

The bartender appears on the other side of the bar, her gaze narrowing on me suspiciously. I've done a damn good job of shoveling the makeup on tonight, contouring my cheekbones and weighing my eyelids down with lashes so thick a good gust of wind could carry me away. So the odds are in my favor. But this chick seems a little more observant than the last one. A little smarter. And that's bad news *pour moi*.

"A lemon drop martini, please," I say sweetly, grabbing the cash my mark laid down and thrusting it toward the skeptical woman in front of me. I shift uncomfortably in my seat, causing my G-string to ride so far up my ass I could chew on it. The thought of slipping the bill from the bottom of the stack into my purse crosses my mind, but then I'd technically be stealing from the bartender. And I have no intentions of robbing her of her hard-earned money.

My mark orders a whiskey from the top shelf and the bartender accepts the cash, shooting me one last suspicious glance before turning away to fetch our drinks. I smile at the man beside me as I smooth my long, caramel-colored wig down, ensuring it frames my face. I've learned over the last two years of hustling that the more features of my face I can camouflage, the better my odds of returning to the same establishment without being caught are.

Noting how late it is, I decide it's time I go in for the kill, wiggling my upper body just enough that the thin strap of my small purse slips off my shoulder and hits the floor with a gentle thud.

"Oops." I giggle, but internally, I'm laughing an evil, villainous laugh as my target reaches down and scoops my bag up like the perfect gentleman.

Sigh. So predictable.

"Here you go, honey." He offers me my purse and I accept it with both hands, my touch featherlight as my fingertips sweep over his watch, effortlessly unclasping it and sinking it into my bag.

Alora: three. Men: zero.

"My hero," I coo, plastering on a big, cheesy smile as I sling my purse back over my shoulder. I hate this shrill, obnoxious version of myself, but I have one more target in mind tonight, then I'm heading home to strip this glamorous faux costume off and sink into a bubble bath.

"Anything for you, Jessica," he tells me with a sly grin, an embarrassing shade of red creeping up his neck and into his cheeks.

The bartender reappears and sets our drinks in front of us. I reach for mine, but her hand coils tightly around the stem of the glass, halting me in my tracks.

"You," she says blandly. And I almost wish I had decided to skim a ten off her tip for being so fucking observant. "I recognize you from somewhere."

"Who? Me?" I stab my thumb into my chest and smile, then swat the air. "I'm not from around here. Surely you're mistaking me for someone else."

Her eyes pierce through me as she mulls something around in that bartender brain of hers, but she eventually releases the glass and steps away.

My nerves are rattled now, and I've gotten what I came here for. So instead of sticking around, I cut my losses and snatch my martini off the bar and throw it back, the alcohol stinging my nose on the way down. I slam the empty glass onto the bar top and swipe a dribble of liquid off my chin with the back of my hand as I slide not so gracefully off my stool. My victim's expression sours like he just sucked on a pickle as I pat him on the shoulder the way a familiar, old friend would.

"Welp ... It's been a slice. Thanks for the drink." I flash him a smile and turn to leave.

"Jessica. Wait," he starts, turning in his stool. But I'm already beelining it across the lounge, my ankles wobbling in my sky-scraper heels as I put enough space between us that his desperate pleas for me to return to his side are drowned by the chiming music from slot machines and the pounding of my poor old heart.

I disappear out the front door and hail a cab. I don't typically allow myself the luxury of a paid ride, but it's cold tonight and I had a profitable run. So I'll spare the change for a ride home instead of torturing my feet and waddling down the street in these godforsaken heels.

I slip into the back of the car, slam the door, and sink low in the seat, blurting out the address of my apartment in hopes the driver will step on it and get me the fuck out of here before one of the men I screwed over spots me.

I've been a thief for two years now, and although I'm doing it all in the name of getting even, the guilt is like coarse sandpaper, wearing me down and stripping me of my determination. Add that to the growing paranoia of being caught, and you've got yourself a hot-mess express.

But I've never been one to shy away from a challenge. And if I'm able to even the unfair scales of this patriarchal justice system ever so slightly, then I'll take my chances, consequences be damned, and return for a third and final night before I move onto the next location.

Those rich suckers with their fat wallets and slimy morals will never know what hit them.

Two

Liam

"Well, well, well," Sloane drawls, her eyes scanning me briefly as I stroll through the war room doors. "Look what the cat coughed up."

I shoot her a scowl and drop into my seat around the table.

Zak leans toward me and asks lowly, "You good, brother?"

"I'm fine."

He backs off, but I can feel his gaze on me from time to time, assessing me. Probably trying to gauge whether I'd rip his head off if he pushes me or if he should just keep quiet and let me stew in my own misery the way I prefer. The way I've been doing for years.

I pull my switchblade out of my pocket and begin mindlessly flipping it open and closed, drawing Zak's attention again.

But it's not just Zak studying me now. It's Sloane too. Today, her judgmental eyes are a vibrant turquoise from her tinted contacts, and they haven't left me since I walked in. I don't give her the satisfaction of glancing in her direction, but I know there's something brewing in that clever huntress mind of hers. Even as Mac, the head of Sweetwater, begins speaking, I can feel her assessment from the other side of the room. And it's making me twitchy and irritable. I've been this way for a while now, but the storm inside me is gaining power the closer we get to finishing off this mission once and for all. More specifically, finishing off the Petrovs, the human traffickers that stole my sister right out from under my nose and fucked her up six ways to Sunday.

"Well, boys," Mac drawls, and I swing my attention to him. "Thanks to Sloane, we have a lead on Ilya Petrov." My fidgeting hands stall, and he pauses a moment too long. "La Grandiosa Casino."

"A casino," I deadpan. When the popping sound of Sloane's gum intercepts the silence, I slide my gaze to her. As I suspected, she's staring directly at me, her jaw working as she chews thoughtfully on a wad of pink gum. Her arms are folded across her chest, her long fiery hair pulled back into two tight Dutch braids, an all-knowing smirk tugging at her lips.

"That's right," she chirps, snapping her gum between her teeth. "Ilya popped up on surveillance there. It seems the littlest Petrov has a bit of a gambling habit."

"When?" Joel asks from the other side of the table, his laser blue eyes narrowing on me briefly before shifting to Mac.

"Last night," Mac informs us, shaking his head. "But he vanished again. Sloane's working on tracking him down."

I ball my fists on my thighs as my blood grows itchy, scratching along the insides of my veins as it rolls through my body. Just when I thought I had my shit in check, the slow chant of my demons begins. I know that soon the violent monster caged up inside of me will wake from his slumber and require feeding.

The youngest Petrov is within reach. Which means his father, Ivan, and older brother, Viktor, could be somewhere close by.

I fucking hope they are.

It's been six years since we brought Rachel home. Six years that they've been flying under the radar and just out of our reach. They have too many friends in high places that have assisted them in remaining unfound.

But their time is coming to an end. The clock is running out.

"For now, we hang tight. Scope the casino out in case he decides to return."

I'm not satisfied with that plan, but I also realize there's not much else we can do right now.

We spend another hour going over intel. By the time we're finished, the chanting in my head is so loud, I can barely hear my own thoughts.

All of Sweetwater's missions are important to me. All deserve my full attention. But this one ... Nothing compares. The Petrovs are the unfortunate fucks that are going to make every one of my most depraved fantasies come true. Their spilled blood is the only thing that will make me whole again. The only blood that can finally euthanize my monster. Until they breathe their last breath, until their hearts no longer beat, he will continue to roar within me.

The rest of the team files out of the war room and I sit there a moment longer, quietly reeling in my fury. Just as I'm about to leave, Sloane appears in front of me with a cocky grin on her face. She kicks the door shut with her foot and stares up at me.

"What do you need, Sloane?"

"Oh, nothing," she says innocently, toying with the end of one of her braids as I scowl down at her.

Even in her lifted combat boots, the top of her head barely meets my chest. But despite her small stature, she's strong and capable and has been through the fucking ringer. She's a force to be reckoned with.

But it's not her physical abilities that make her invaluable to the team. It's her skillset and knowledge. She's our tech specialist and can hack into pretty much anything, anywhere. And she's as loyal as they come, albeit a little reckless at times.

She blows a bubble the size of my fist then sucks it back into her mouth. "You're looking a little twitchy, big guy."

"I'm always twitchy."

"Right." She shuffles on her feet and my scowl intensifies, the angry scar splicing through my brow crinkling tight.

"What's going on, Sloane?"

She stares up at me for a moment longer before spinning and walking out of the war room, gesturing for me to follow her. Groaning, I trail behind her to the parking lot. The headlights of her sports car flash twice as she presses the key fob and pops the trunk. I round the rear of the vehicle and stare down into the dark cavity.

"Liam, meet Ralph Philips. Old Ralphy here is a janitor at my niece's high school. He decided it would be fun to hide cameras in the vents in the gymnasium dressing rooms and sell the footage of underage girls getting changed on the internet."

I glare down at the unconscious man bound with plastic zip ties, his puffy ankles and wrists rubbed raw from his struggle against the restraints. His lip is busted and swollen, and he's sporting two black eyes and a broken nose. Other than that, he's in perfect condition and out cold. A blank canvas awaiting the paint of my fury. My palms tingle as something violent swirls in the pit of my stomach.

I glance down at Sloane again.

"How'd you get him here by yourself?"

She shrugs. "With the threat of a bullet to his crotch. Once he crawled into the trunk, I injected him with ketamine. He took the first dose like a champ, so I gave him a little extra to keep him down. He'll be out for a while."

She peeks up at me as I stand stock-still, new and thrilling ideas of how to make this particular loser pay for what he's done rolling through my mind.

I won't kill him. But I will make him wish he were dead.

"Was your niece one of the girls?"

She nods, her expression softening a fraction. And that's all the persuasion I need to do this.

I haul Ralph's body out of the trunk while Sloane holds doors open for me as we make our way through headquarters and down into my work area. I drop him to the cold cement floor and flip the lights on.

"Jesus," Sloane hisses, her eyes darting from the stainless steel surgical table bolted to the floor in the middle of the room, to the collection of torture devices hanging on a wall at the side. "It's been a hot minute since I've been down here. You're getting scarier by the day, my friend."

I don't bother responding as I drag Ralph over to the table and throw him on top of it, rolling him onto his back. Sloane takes a seat on a stool in the corner, her legs crossed and posture stiff, watching quietly as I cut his clothing off and secure his wrists, ankles, and head with the leather straps fastened to the table.

"What are you going to do to him?" she asks, her tone filled with apprehension and her expression stone-cold sober.

"Not sure yet," I answer honestly. "You plan on sticking around for it?"

I peek over at her as I finish securing the last of his limbs, noticing that her face has paled and she's gnawing anxiously on the inside of her cheek. Normally, she's poised and calm and more than a little irritating. But when it comes to family, even the strongest soldiers break.

"I'm ..." She hesitates and shakes her head as if clearing her thoughts from her brain. She straightens her spine and her shoulders snap into a tight line. "Yes," she says with finality. "I'm staying to watch. He deserves whatever you're about to do to him."

Nodding once, I stalk over to the wall of tools, selecting one that resembles an oversized fish hook. It's designed to be inserted into flesh with ease, then twisted and ripped back out.

I loom patiently over Ralph as he begins to wake, his glassy eyes rolling every direction to take in his surroundings. All sounds fade into the background, becoming white noise behind my chanting demons as I do what I was built to do.

Two hours pass as I torture the ever-living fuck out of him. By the time I'm done, he's been thoroughly castrated and his wounds have been cauterized, so sadly, he won't bleed out. It took an immense amount of restraint on my part to not end his life, but I suspect he'll suffer plenty in prison when Sloane submits all the evidence needed to put him behind bars.

Sloane and I dump him outside the emergency entrance of the local hospital before I head home for a quick shower and change of clothes.

I can't be bothered to sit around at home with my hand on my cock, waiting for a call with further intel on any of the Petrovs. So instead, I haul ass to La Grandiosa Casino and post up at a poker table, my head on a swivel as I search for anything out of the ordinary.

Chips clank. Machines sing. People laugh. I fucking hate places like this. They're overstimulating and reek of indiscretions.

A flash of blonde catches in my periphery, and I turn my attention to a woman seated at the bar. Her hair is a shade darker than platinum and cut into a short, blunt bob. Her back is to me, so I can't see her face, but I can see her black-painted fingernails drumming methodically on the bar top. She glances over her shoulder, affording me a slight glimpse of her profile.

Full, pouty red lips. Pert nose. High, angular cheekbones and large, round eyes rimmed in thick, dark liner.

Incredible.

Her fingers stall and her spine straightens, her shoulders snapping into a tight line as she stares at a man parked in front of a nearby slot machine. Her throat works as she swallows and steels her expression while she slides off the stool and tugs the hem of her dress down her thighs. I allow my eyes to roam freely over the tight black leather dress that clings to her narrow hips and round ass, down her lean, toned thighs, fixating on a small blue butterfly tattooed on the outside of her ankle. Normally, the ink would be innocent and feminine, but on her, it's sexy as hell.

She's petite and delicate, but there's an intensity about her that lures me in. A darkness that calls to me like a siren in the night.

The way she saunters across the floor and demurely seats herself at a nearby machine is mesmerizing. I still don't get a full shot of her face, but I can tell she's watching the man closely. Just as I am her.

She slides a coin into the slot and pulls the lever. When the machine lights up and begins singing, she claps her hands animatedly and bounces in her chair. It's not a big payout. Only a few bucks. So I know instantly that her excitement is fabricated. But it catches the eye of the man sitting a row away from her. The one she's baiting like a fucking fish.

The dealer at my table clears his throat, and I realize it's my turn. I slap a card down—no clue what it was because I'm distracted—and he slides me a new one. I scoop it up and nod once, signaling to move onto the player beside me. I peer back over at the woman at the machine and watch in amusement as the idiot she's luring into her web takes a seat beside her and throws his arm over the back of her chair. His knuckles graze her bare shoulder, and I can tell by the slight tension in her body that she's annoyed by the brazen contact. But she simply smiles and giggles, shoving her discomfort aside.

The sight of his hands on her makes my stomach churn.

But when she discretely shimmies her purse off her shoulder and lets the small bag hit the floor at her feet, I feel a tug of something unfamiliar in my chest. A heightened sense of curiosity, I suppose. She covers her mouth with her hand and laughs, her glossy black nails matching her overdone makeup and hair. The man leans down and snatches it up, offering it to her. She playfully touches his arm and ... fuck.

She giggles again, making a show of laughing at something he said as she touches his bicep with one hand and uses the other to unclasp his watch and slip it into her purse. The movement is so swift and practiced that there's not a chance in hell this was her first time.

Little thief.

My lip twitches in amusement and I take a swig of my bourbon, unable to peel my eyes off her.

When she's done flirting and passes the man a card—no doubt with a fake name and number on it—she scurries across the casino and heads straight toward the exit, pausing with her palm on the glass before she glances over her shoulder. Our gazes lock, her red lips parting on an exhale. Something resembling fear enters her expression. But it's quickly concealed behind a cold mask of indifference.

My cock chooses this moment to spring to life. She's more than just beautiful. She's tempting. Alluring and bold and fucking captivating.

She blinks. Once. Twice. Then pries her eyes off mine and pushes through the door. My gaze drops to her ass as she disappears beyond the tinted windows and into the night.

The nagging sensation in the pit of my gut tells me to go after her. Laying my cards down, I follow my natural instincts and storm across the casino, my heavy footfalls silent on the plush, carpeted floor. But by the time I'm through the doors, she's gone.

Three

Alora

THE SECOND THE CRISP evening air slaps against my heated skin, I suck in a lungful of oxygen, a cool mist of relief washing over me. Clutching the strap of my purse, I keep my nose directed at the cracked sidewalk as I jog down the street, slipping out of my heels along the way because, goddamn, my poor little toes hurt. It doesn't matter that I've been waltzing around in stilettos for the last two years. They still rub me in all the wrong places.

But tonight my pain is trumped by another feeling—unease.

I didn't catch an up-close view of the tall, dark, and dangerously handsome man at the poker table across the room. But from what I could tell, he was smirking at me, silently mocking me and my sticky fingers. He probably thinks I do it out of greed. Or that I'm too lazy to get a real job.

Judgmental dick.

But his judgment isn't entirely unjustified. Regardless of my good intentions, I'm still breaking the law.

Twenty minutes later, after a few internal pep talks about how I'll eventually give it up, I arrive at my apartment building on the east side of the city—the opposite side of the ritzy casinos and high-end clubs and fancy restaurants that serve caviar and champagne. The side of the city where degenerates like me thrive like the bottom-feeders we are. It isn't until I've locked all six dead bolts on my door that a melancholic sense of security settles in, and I drop my hands to my knees to catch my breath. Running from my problems has always been something I'm exceptional at. But running physically? No, thank you.

A gentle knock on my door startles me, and I jolt upright to peek through the peephole, my heart still pounding against my ribs from sprinting down the damn street like a track star in stilts.

I spot a mass of blonde hair and hot pink standing on the other side of the door and drop my shoulders from my ears.

"You okay, sweetie?" a soft, feminine voice filters through.

I open the door to greet Rose, my neighbor from across the hall, with a tight-lipped smile. She looks every bit the bubble gum Barbie doll that she is in her skin-tight pink dress and sparkly heels. Whereas most people are going to bed, Rose is getting ready for her shift at a swanky strip club that old, rich guys frequent after working their boring, mundane jobs.

But Rose isn't the innocent little lamb she pretends to be. Sure, she's incredibly sweet on the outside. But inside, she's determined and strong and takes care of the people she loves. She's also the person who taught me how to lift a watch. But what started as occasionally stealing from wealthy assholes has evolved into something else. And now my desire to relieve their wrists and wallets from them has morphed into an out-of-control hurricane of petty theft and hustling.

"I'm fine, Rose. Just a little tired."

There's a beat of silence. "Are you sure? I saw you running up the stairs and slamming your door shut like someone was chasing you."

I swat the air, feigning nonchalance. "I thought I left the stove on. Didn't want to burn the place down," I lie.

Actually, burning this dump to the ground would probably increase the property value. But that's neither here nor there.

Rose's expression softens and she huffs out a gentle laugh. "Well, at least you're lucky enough to have a stove that actually works."

I sweep a hand through the plasticky strands of my wig and angle my head at her. "Yours doesn't work?"

She shakes her head. "Nope. I've been complaining for months now that it wasn't working right, then just the other day it stopped turning on completely." She shrugs as if it's all no big deal. And since Rose farts sunshine and shits rainbows, her complaints will remain unheard and she'll slide to the bottom of the never-ending list of things that need repaired in this joint.

"Well, if you ever need to cook something, just come knocking and you can use my stove," I offer sincerely. This time, my smile is genuine. If I could ever keep friends, I would choose someone like Rose. Even though she scores a little high on the ditz-o-meter, she's incredibly caring and one of the few people who doesn't hide behind a false identity. But there's a faulty wire somewhere inside of me that prevents me from committing to anything beyond what's absolutely required to survive.

"Thanks, girl. I'd appreciate that."

Rose saunters back off to her own apartment across the hall. Just before she disappears inside, I stop her.

"Hey, Rose?"

She angles her head to peer at me over her shoulder. "Yeah?"

I rummage around in my bag and retrieve the watches I lifted tonight and hold them out to her. Rose's blue eyes flit to the expensive timepieces and back up to mine, a curious glimmer shining behind her irises.

"I know you want to do some good, Alora. But are you sure you want to keep doing it like this? It's risky business stealing the way you do. You could do some serious time for it if you get caught."

I snort. She's not wrong. But if I ever landed myself in hot water, my criminal defense lawyer of a stepfather would bail me out in a heartbeat. Not because he cares, but because he has a pretentious reputation to uphold and god forbid his beloved stepdaughter be charged and convicted of a felony. But I draw the line there, refusing to ask for Charles's help beyond legal support, if I ever need it. Otherwise, he's dead to me.

"Yeah, I'm sure." I urge her to accept the watches, confident she'll cave if I hold them out to her long enough.

Hesitation flickers across her face before she nods and accepts my offering, tucking the watches into her sparkly little crossbody bag.

"I taught you well," she says with a hint of amusement. "Where do you want the money to go this time?"

I consider that for a moment. The last time I asked Rose to sell the watches to the greasy contact she refuses to disclose the name of, I requested she use the sale proceeds to buy feminine hygiene products and baby supplies for the women and children's shelter a few blocks from here. And the time before that, the money went to a local mental health organization that's severely underfunded. Rose keeps a small cut that she uses to help pay for her grandmother's nursing home costs at the facility I volunteer at occasionally. But beyond that, everything goes to a cause, tipping the scales a fraction of a hair in the direction of people in need.

"You choose this time. I trust you."

Rose's painted lips turn up into a small smile. "I know just the place. Thanks, Al."

"You're welcome." A small stretch of silence trails on where Rose and I just stare at each other. Neither of us know much about the other, but there's an unspoken understanding between us, a silent agreement to not stab the other in the back. I've always had an impressive sense of character judgment, and Rose is all good on the inside. "Have a good night, Rose."

"You too."

I shut the door and relock all six dead bolts and press my spine to the cold wood, anxiety simmering on low beneath my surface.

My dirty, filthy soul could really use a thorough cleansing after the last week I've had.

Pulling my cell phone from my purse, I type out a quick message to Claudia, the recreational manager of the senior's home down the street where Rose's grandmother lives.

Me: Hi, Claudia. I have some free time tomorrow. Would love to host a class. Can you slot me in?

Stepping around the stacks of oil paintings propped against every wall in my tiny, one-bedroom apartment, I pad barefoot down the hall to my bedroom. I whip open the closet doors, cringing when the ungreased hinges groan loudly, and drop to my knees to pry a loose floorboard up with my fingers. I tuck the cash I stole inside with the rest of my savings, but my thumb grazes the smooth leather spine of the journal I keep hidden there, and I close my eyes, a heavy sadness weighing on my chest.

After my mother was buried, I snuck into her bedroom to retrieve the journal I knew she kept hidden in her sock drawer. A journal Charles knows nothing about because if he had, he'd have disposed of it the second the coroner removed her lifeless body from their bed.

I miss you, Mama.

Releasing a held breath, I drop the floorboard into place and sit back on my heels, staring blankly at my hanging clothing as I internally chastise myself for failing to see the signs of my mother's mental illness. Maybe if I had visited her more, I'd have noticed the subtle changes. Like how the twinkle in her eyes had slowly dimmed out. Or how her smile had grown more and more forced every time I saw her. Or how thin she'd gotten from not eating and drinking excessively.

My mother was sweet and soft and caring. But ultimately, she was weak and took the coward's way out of this world. Perhaps it's ignorant of me to believe that suicide is the easy option when life gets hard. But she left me behind when I needed her. And although I love her and miss her more than anything, I'll never forgive her for that.

Swallowing the boulder lodged in my throat, I give my head a shake and close the closet doors and head across the hall to my bathroom, switching on the single flickering bulb hanging over the mirror. I remove my wig and toss my long black hair loose, my scalp itching from the cheap hairpiece. I wet a tattered cloth and begin removing the mountains of makeup caked on my face, then crank the bath water all the way to hot, which is barely piss warm because the water heater in this place only works half the time. I squirt my favorite citrus bubble bath into the spray and sink beneath the surface and allow my aching muscles to finally relax after a long night of hustling.

My mind wanders back to my mother and the journal tucked beneath my closet floor. When she passed away, I read one entry per day until they ran out a year later. The last entry was the longest one of all and was written the night before she took her own life. She wrote about how much she loved me. How she was looking forward to our trip to Mexico together. But she also wrote about how tired she was of pretending to be something she wasn't. How she wished Charles would step back from his professional duties as a criminal defense lawyer and focus on doing something good with his wealth instead. I suppose the last few pages of her journal are a testament to how volatile one's mind can be when they're battling severe depression.

When I finished reading my mother's final words, I closed the book and stuffed it somewhere that I didn't have to look at it ever again. Sometimes I consider giving it another read-through, but then I remember that no good can come of me unearthing the emotions I've managed to bury deep down inside.

When the bath water turns cold, I drain the tub and slip into a pair of cotton panties that don't nearly split me in two and an oversized beer-branded T-shirt, and crawl into bed, the springs of my lumpy mattress digging into my back as I settle beneath the sheets and stare at the dingy popcorn-textured ceiling. The water stain from the leaking bathtub of the apartment one floor up looms over me like an apparition, the stain creeping a little further every day. I'm going to have to remind the superintendent for the thousandth time that it'll be much more expensive to fix when Mrs. Bell's bathtub falls straight through the floor and into my bedroom. I just pray the crotchety old bird isn't in it when it happens. And that I'm not lying in bed.

Because being squashed like a bug would be an embarrassing way to exit earth.

But if all goes as planned, I won't be around much longer, and someone else can worry about the sagging ceiling. Instead, I'll be in Mexico, living out my mother's dream of opening a local artisan shop where she'd sell her paintings and live a quaint, happy life. It was a dream Charles put an end to by tying her down with wifely duties and planning extravagant business parties for him and his associates.

My thoughts are cut short by my buzzing phone, and I reach over to pluck it off the nightstand and read the message.

Claudia: How does three o'clock sound?

Smiling now, I respond with a "perfect" and fall into a deep dream-filled sleep.

The next morning, I rise with the sun, a fresh perspective and clean slate to start the day.

I fix myself a quick breakfast, clean my apartment from top to bottom, then sink my feet into my sneakers and walk to the nursing home. The California sun is high and hot, the air is humid, and a fresh wave of excitement crashes through me.

Today is a good day.

When I make it to the nursing home, I ring the buzzer for a staff member to let me in but am greeted by an elderly man named Harvey, who never ceases to amaze me with his witty pickup lines.

"Hello, Alora," he says with a sly smile, his gray eyes twinkling as he grips the handles of his walker.

"Hey, Harv. How's it hanging?" I ask, knowing damn well it'll earn me a chuckle and ...

"A little to the left," he finishes my thought for me.

I laugh and banter with Harvey for a few more minutes before hunting down Claudia, who helps me set the recreation room up with jars of water, brushes, and paints that I donated with the proceeds of one of my evening's profits a few months back.

Three o'clock rolls around and seniors begin filtering into the room and taking their respective seats. I perch myself on a stool at the front of the class, a wooden easel and small canvas parked in front of me, and fall into what comes as naturally to me as it did my mother—painting.

But the warm, fuzzy feeling I get from volunteering soon subsides. And I mope back to my apartment to put my costume back on and tackle an evening of wrongdoing.

What's that saying? The road to hell is paved with good intentions.

Four

Liam

A LARGE MANILLA ENVELOPE appears on the table in front of me. I reach inside and retrieve a stack of papers, glaring down at the photo of Ilya Petrov seated in a dark booth with two rail-thin women in skimpy outfits glued to his side.

The chanting in my head begins, and I have to stomp down the urge to flip the fucking war room table over. But I don't so much as move. Because losing my temper won't help a goddamn thing.

Mac stares at me with scrunched brows, waiting for me to get my head straight. When I nod curtly at him, he begins speaking, and I ignore the demonic whispers and listen to every word my boss has to say.

"Ilya Petrov appears to be sticking around the area," he informs the team. "He turned up at a strip club last night."

Sloane pipes up next. "We've set surveillance up on the casino and the club in case he returns to either." She blows a bubble with her gum and pops it with her teeth. The sound makes me twitch.

"No evidence of any women or children going missing since he's been around?" Zak asks from beside me, his eyes shifting to me every so often.

"Not that we can see. But it's possible he's doing it under the radar. We all know how slimy these bastards are." Mac's gray eyes slide to mine. "We watch the area. *Quietly.* Do we have an understanding?"

I grunt out an agreement and drop the stack of papers onto the table, glancing over at Sloane. She flashes me a crooked smile and winks, knowing damn well my palms are twitching with the urge to feel bones cracking beneath my fists. The desire to watch blood bubble from the flesh of these soulless pricks causes every hair on the back of my neck to rise.

I rein it in and remind myself that the Petrovs will be worth the wait.

Another hour of bouncing intel around and I'm riding down the open highway, my Harley kicked into full gear as I book it to the club Sloane last tracked Ilya to. I'd love nothing more right now than to hunt the sick motherfucker down, drag him back to headquarters, and torture him until he cracks and gives me his father's and brother's locations. But I'm under strict orders to lie low. And as far as Sloane can tell, he's not picking up any victims right now. It doesn't make him any less deserving of the pain I want to inflict on him, but it makes it less urgent.

The moment my feet cross the threshold of the club, my lips curl in disgust. The place is packed, ninety percent of the crowd consisting of old men in suits, their ties loosened and tongues wagging. The kind of men with wallets lined with cash they withdrew from a bank account they hide from their wives, and ring fingers decorated with wedding bands they don't deserve to fucking wear. The other ten percent are barely legal girls in skimpy dresses, their bodies scarcely concealed by measly scraps of fabric smaller than the tag on my shirt.

A hand slaps my back and I flinch.

"Fuck, Davis. You look like you're about to tear this place apart with your bare hands."

I grind my back molars and glare at Zak. "What the hell are you doing here?"

"Keeping an eye on you, brother."

Sneering, I return my attention to the sight before me. Fuck, I hate these places. The loud music. The obnoxious laughs of drunken assholes copping feels when they should be keeping their hands to themselves. The bright strobe lights and rancid cocktail of cheap perfume, sweat, and booze.

"Welcome, gentlemen. Can I get you a booth?" I stare down at the brunette woman standing behind a small podium. She smiles sweetly and twirls a strand of hair around her finger, little dollar signs flashing in her eyes.

"Please," Zak responds politely before I have a chance to grunt out a less charming response. He gestures for the hostess to lead the way, and we trail behind her to a dark booth at the back corner of the lounge.

The girl's tinkling laugh grates on my nerves. Either she's a ditz or she's incredibly skilled at feigning stupidity. Either way, it's not my bag and I don't pay her any mind.

"What are we drinking tonight, boys?"

Zak and I order our drinks and the waitress disappears in a cloud of hair spray and body glitter. I sweep my eyes across the lounge in search of any signs of Ilya. I know I won't find him here, but it's in my nature to hunt, maim, and kill these fuckers, so my senses are all heightened.

A sudden boisterous laugh cuts through the blaring techno music, and I swing my gaze to the right to spot a man in his sixties with his head tipped back, a nearly naked girl who can't be more than nineteen perched on his lap. Zak's eyes follow my line of sight. I haven't a clue who he is, but the desire to whip my switchblade out and carve a path from his arrogant face all the way to his balls weighs heavy on me.

Zak's eyes dart back to me and he nudges my elbow. "Take 'er easy, man."

I snarl, the scar slashing through my brow crinkling and my fists balling so tight my arms ache.

The DJ's deeply animated voice bellows over the speakers, announcing the name of the next girl to perform on stage. But I can't be fucked to pay attention because right now, my retinas are searing a gaping hole straight through the strange man as he buries his face into the girl's hair. I don't need to hear their hushed conversation to know he's testing his limits with her. The way his hands keep wandering to her ass and tits even after she continues to swat him away ... It's infuriating. And as much as she's putting on a show, I can tell by the tension in her body and facial expression that she's annoyed by his persistence.

My mind flashes to the woman at the casino last night and the way she seemed irritated by the man's knuckles dragging over her shoulder. She persevered through it for a payday—a fucking watch of all things. But he was touching what he had no right to. And it made my stomach burn with rage, much like it is right now.

The song changes to a slower tempo, and I breathe through the thoughts of what this guy's cries for mercy would sound like if I strung him up and skinned him inch by agonizing inch.

"You're going to draw attention if you keep staring, man."

Reeling in my temper, I peel my eyes away and scan the crowd, my heart jackhammering violently against my rib cage. Normally, I'm not a hotheaded man. I don't blow up from the mere spark of something as small as getting a little too handsy with a stripper. But my temper's not exactly on a long fuse, either. I'm somewhere in between. It takes exactly the right combination of fuel and fire for me to explode. And right now, in this den of desperate assholes, I find myself fighting to keep the blaze under control.

The waitress reappears with a plastic tray and sets our glasses down on the table. She makes a show of arching her back and brushing her arm against my shoulder, her rock-hard tits like basketballs glued to her chest.

When I pull a fifty out of my wallet and slap it on the table, her eyes light up and she smiles brightly at me.

"Thank you, honey," she chimes, her long pink fingernails scraping the money off the sticky wooden surface. She doesn't bother asking if she should get me some change before disappearing again.

And just as one woman disappears, another slides in, this one bolder. More experienced.

"Hi, boys," the redhead chirps, pressing her palms to the table and leaning in toward me. Her false lashes are so fucking thick and long that I can't tell what color her eyes are, but I can see them dart between Zak and I as if assessing which one of us would be an easier kill. When she spots the wedding band on Zak's left hand, she turns her attention to him and asks if he'd like a private dance.

I'm not surprised that she assumes he's in a sexless marriage and frequents clubs to find strange pussy to get his dick wet. Little does she know, the feisty blonde he's shackled to would rip her to shreds.

Zak puts a palm in the air and shakes his head. "No, thank you. Happily married and I'd like to keep it that way," he tells her with a soft chuckle, forever the gentleman.

I, on the other hand, can't be fucked to give this woman an ounce of my energy. So, instead of declining politely, I avert my eyes and ignore her completely.

Her thin lips pucker into a tight scowl and she stands to her full height, her bony hips protruding from her body and her loud lime-green bikini causing me to grow twitchy. She's probably in her early twenties, but her lifestyle has aged her far beyond that.

When she decides she's not getting anywhere with either of us, she vanishes into the sea of suits, making her way through the crowd to scope out her next victim. The song changes, and I return my attention to the man in the booth. There are two women with him now.

I take a swig of my bourbon and force myself to look away, the alcohol failing to loosen the tight knot of irritation in the pit of my gut.

Zak turns his attention to the bar while I stare straight past the naked girl swinging around the pole on stage, thinking of all the ways women who work in places like this put themselves at risk. How my sister was nabbed up on her way home from bartending at a club not much different from this one. How statistically, one in every five of the men in this joint enjoy getting rough with the women they're screwing on the side.

"How's Rachel doing?" Zak asks, catching me off guard. I know what he's doing. Offering me a distraction.

I exhale a frustrated breath and take the bait. "She tried dating again."

Zak's brows shoot high, and he huffs out a dry laugh. "No shit. How'd that go?"

I shake my head. "Fucking terrible."

"What happened?"

My lip twitches as I replay the phone call from Rachel in my head, the disappointment in her voice all while she insisted she was fine and could handle herself.

"He was flirting with the waitress the whole night. Then left Rach at the bar alone after calling a cab for himself because he had too much to drink to drive either of them home."

"Jesus," Zak hisses, then narrows his eyes on me. "Tell me the idiot's still breathing."

I side-eye him and nod once. "He's still breathing."

A slight look of relief washes over him.

Downing the rest of the liquid in my glass, I slam the empty tumbler down. On cue, the waitress appears again.

"Another round?" she asks coyly.

"No," I respond bluntly. "I'm driving."

Her lips press into a flat line before she scuttles off.

"He's on the move," Zak says, and I watch as the man in the booth rises from his seat, the two girls clinging to his side. They disappear down a hall and into a private room. At least with him out of sight, I can focus a little.

Zak and I spend the next couple hours making useless small talk and hoping the waste of flesh I want to peel like a banana decides to show his ugly mug.

Just as I stand to head to the men's room to take a leak, a wave of heat settles low in my back and I freeze, angling my head to peer across the lounge. My eyes immediately lock on the woman sitting alone at the end of the bar.

Platinum blonde bob cut that I can now tell is obviously a wig illuminated by the strobe lights. Short black fingernails. Blue butterfly tattoo on the outside of her ankle.

It's her. The little thief from the casino last night. What are the odds of bumping into her again in the same place we've tracked Ilya Petrov to?

Slim to none.

Tonight she's dressed in a shimmery gold dress that clings to her every lithe curve. The neckline dips low between her small, perky tits, the fabric cinching in around her belly button. And the back is basically nonexistent, showing off smooth skin and two small dimples low on her back on either side of her spine. Her fingers drum on the wooden surface as she glances around in search of something. Or *someone*. Another target, I presume. When she finishes the drink beside her and spins around, our gazes clash. She falters, her expression sobering completely. That pretty, fake smile she wears so well vanishes from her made-up face.

Just when I think she's going to come over and talk to me, she turns and bolts down the hall toward the ladies' room.

I calmly saunter down the hall behind her, refusing to let her go for the second time. My plan after I catch her? Not a fucking clue. But my instincts have kicked in, and I can't help but naturally gravitate toward her. It's as if she's magnetic.

She glances over her shoulder at me more than once, fear leeching into her expression. I hate myself for scaring her. But my curiosity is unusually piqued. Her timing seems a little too convenient for my liking. And I'm not sure if I believe it to be a coincidence or not.

The bathroom door slams shut and I pace the hall for a brief moment, considering my options. Barge in and question her? Or hover out here like a fucking creep?

When a brunette woman bursts through the door and shoots me an all-knowing smirk, my decision is made for me, and I slip quietly inside, groaning in irritation when I find myself standing in an empty restroom. My eyes slide to the mirror over the sinks.

Kick rocks, stalker is scribbled in bold red that matches the color of the thief's ruby lips.

An unexpected gust of fresh air swirls around me, and I glare up at the small window above the toilet in one of the individual stalls. The pane is propped up, the opening just large enough for her to squeeze through if she were desperate enough. My lip twitches in amusement, and a sick thrill moves through me.

You can run, little thief. But you can't hide.

⚫

The flashbacks have been coming more frequently. Memories of walking into Rachel's apartment to find it empty. Of the frigid Russian air burning my lungs as I ran toward the bunker we found her in. Of her malnourished body, littered with infected cuts and bruises and track marks from where her captors injected the drugs into her system day after fucking day until she was so addicted, she'd do anything for another hit.

Banishing the thoughts from my head, I open my eyes and find Sloane's from across the table. She stares back at me with empathy and concern in her expression and asks, "You good, big guy?"

I nod once, but I'm anything but good. Disturbing memories continue to creep out from the dark corners of my mind ever since Mac informed us that Ilya's in the area. The hollow ache that consumed me from the moment I realized my sister was gone to the moment I laid eyes on her will haunt me for the rest of my miserable fucking life.

Sloane returns her attention to her laptop and begins tapping away on keys as I fiddle with my switchblade, silently waiting for her to dig up the information I've requested.

She eventually turns the screen to face me, and I narrow my eyes on the image of a woman in a skimpy gold dress running down the street in the opposite direction of the club I last saw her in.

"This her?" Sloane asks.

"That's her."

Sloane's lips turn up into a crooked grin as she resumes doing whatever the fuck it is she does to hunt people down. It feels like hours roll by at the pace of molasses in wintertime, but it's probably only seconds before Sloane's wheeling her chair around the table and taking a seat beside me so I can see her screen more clearly.

"Her name's Alora Berkley. Twenty-six years old," she tells me as I stare at the picture of a woman with long ebony locks and daring green eyes. She's even more incredible in her raw, natural state. All dark hair and vivid emerald orbs that remind me of the lush, rolling hills of Ireland. A light smattering of freckles dot her pert nose and cheeks.

But even without all the makeup, she still has the same intensity that first lured me in. Sharp edges and a darkness that speaks to me.

"Kind of a drifter by the looks of it. Not much family and no friends. No reports of a job or a fixed address. She does have a cell phone, though, which I've tracked to an apartment building on the east side."

"Parents?"

"Her father was a deadbeat from day one, so he's out of the picture. Her mother raised her most of her childhood until she married Alora's stepfather, Charles Gregory, when Alora was fifteen. Her mother committed suicide two years ago and Alora took off, leaving her stepfather behind. There hasn't been any form of contact that I can see here since she moved."

Sloane pops her gum in my ear, and I glare at her. "Do you mind?"

She beams at me, blows a bubble, then sucks it back in. "Not at all." Thankfully, she tones down the gum chewing and flips through more intel on Alora. The deeper we get into her life, the more questions I have.

"She's living in the slums but has a wealthy stepfather," Sloane acquiesces. "Seems a little unusual if you ask me."

"I want her location on my GPS."

Sloane extends her hand, and I set my phone in her palm. When she hands it back, I glare down at the little red dot on my screen that indicates the location of Alora's cell phone.

And I know without an ounce of doubt that this is the beginning of something long and tumultuous.

Five

Alora

I STARE OUT AT the glistening water, the rippling surface a mirror image of the setting sun. A little white sailboat bobs in the distance while seagulls squawk overhead and a gentle breeze drifts in off the water. It would be the perfect scene to paint. But other than the silly little classes I volunteer to teach at the nursing home, I can't find the ambition to pick a paintbrush back up and create a piece out of pure pleasure. Not since my mother died. It's as if my passion for the visual arts was buried right alongside her.

The air is salty and warm, but the temperature is quickly plummeting as the evening settles in. Goosebumps pepper my bare legs as icy waves slosh against my ankles, washing away my footprints in the sand as I stroll down the beach, sneakers dangling from my fingers. I glance back at my trail. It's as if I were never here at all—a thought that amuses me.

I pick up the pace into a light jog until I reach the boardwalk, then dust off the wet sand from my toes and stuff my bare feet back into my sneakers. Untying my sweater from around my waist, I pull it on, flip the hood up, stuff my hands into the pockets, and head home. I keep my face pointed to the sidewalk as I always do, counting the cracked concrete tiles as they pass. The back of my skull tingles every so often as if someone's watching me. But when I glance over my shoulder, nobody's there.

It's an eerie feeling I've grown accustomed to over the last few weeks. One I have no reason to feel, but I find it creeping up on me more frequently than I'd care to admit.

When the scuzzy yellow brick building I call home comes into view, I release a held breath and slip inside, the busted front door slamming shut behind me. The state of the secured entrance is another thing I've been complaining about, but just like Mrs. Bell's leaking bathtub and Rose's broken stove, the superintendent, who's as useless as tits on a bull, refuses to fix it.

I take the stairs two at a time to the third floor and lock myself in my apartment, ensuring the series of dead bolts are engaged before kicking my sandy sneakers off at the door.

Padding over to my bedroom closet, I whip the doors open and drop to my knees and pry the single loose floorboard up, reaching down into the dark cavity and fishing around. When my fingertips graze the edge of the envelope, I latch onto it and pull it out of my makeshift vault.

I count out the cash right there on the floor and decide with finality that it's time I purchase a vehicle. Which means my stack of stolen money is about to dwindle before my eyes. Biting my lip, I stuff the cash back into its envelope and saunter to the kitchen in search of something to eat, settling on an expired granola bar. I take a seat at the kitchen table and flip open my laptop and search for used cars online, cringing as I scan the prices.

Fucking highway robbery.

But if I plan on driving down to Mexico, a set of wheels is necessary, so I'll have to make it work.

My attention snags on a 1979 Chevrolet Corvette. The interior is littered with cigarette burns and other unidentified stains. The original red body paint is faded from years of abuse beneath the California sun. And there's some surface rust on the front bumper. But it reminds me of the Corvette my grandpa and I refurbished when I was a teenager, and that warms my heart with nostalgia.

The ad says *as is*, but that it's in good working condition and was well cared for.

Typing out a quick message to the seller, I wiggle my toes and anxiously await a response, pleasantly surprised when one comes almost immediately.

Jimmy: Hi there. Still available if you'd like to come check her out. I'm home all afternoon. The address is listed below.

Scrolling frantically, I find the address and pull it up on Google Maps.

By car, it's nearly an hour out of the city.

Gnawing anxiously on my thumbnail, I think things through. A cab or Uber will cost me a small fortune, but reliable vehicles within my price range are hard to come by.

Sucking on my bottom lip, I type out a response.

Me: Be there in an hour.

Tires crunch on gravel as the cab pulls into a laneway leading up to an old farmhouse surrounded by nothing but fields and trees. The white siding is stained from years of neglect, the weeds surrounding the foundation overgrown and strangling the life out of the place. And there's a wooden door, presumably a storm cellar, flipped open at the side of the building. I press my nose to the glass and glance around to take it all in. The place looks like it was dropped straight out of an apocalyptic sci-fi film. It's creepy and dirty and exactly what I imagine a serial killer living in.

"Do you mind waiting a few minutes?" I ask the cab driver after he parks. He stares at me through the rearview mirror, nods once, then pulls out his phone and starts scrolling.

I clamber out of the back seat and walk up the crooked wooden stairs to the front door, knocking three times and glancing around for any signs of life. I'm in the middle of buttfuck nowhere, and I have a sneaking suspicion that the barn with the sagging roof perched at the back of the property is where the car is being stored.

Or a meth lab. Or bodies. Or both.

When the front door swings open and a balding man in his sixties with filthy jeans and a ripped tee that barely conceals his overhanging gut stares down at me, I tighten my grip on the strap of my bag.

"Hello. I'm here about the car. We exchanged messages earlier."

A set of beady eyes rake over my body, and I have to suppress the urge to kick this guy in the balls and make a run for it.

"That's right. Name's Jimmy," he responds with a grunt.

I don't love the idea of being out here alone with a stranger. Especially one who looks like he skins dead animals and leaves them to hang from the rafters in his basement. But logic tells me I need a vehicle, and Jimmy looks like he may be easy to convince to lower the asking price by at least ten percent. He also looks easy to outrun.

So instead of bolting, I smile and say, "Great. Can I take a peek?"

Waving the cab off, I trail behind Jimmy to the barn, my eyes and ears on alert in case a masked man wielding a chain saw pops out of nowhere. We stop at the barn, the large rickety wooden door squeaking loudly as Jimmy slides it across the rusted track. He gestures for me to follow him inside, and I straighten my spine and remind myself that most people are good.

"Here she is," he says proudly, a dark blue tarp gliding over the hood and off the back of the car. "She ain't much to look at. But she's reliable."

My eyes skim over the classically sleek angles of the body, a little bubble of excitement building deep in my stomach.

"Mind popping the hood?"

Jimmy quirks a dark bushy brow. "You know what you're looking for under there, darlin'?"

I shrug and respond coyly, "I know some things."

Reluctantly, he circles the car and pops the hood. I peer down into the bowels of the vehicle I've already decided I'm going to purchase while Jimmy breathes heavily down my neck. He reeks of stale cigarettes, body odor, and smoked meat.

Without looking back at him, I singsong, "Nobody likes a mouth breather, Jimmy."

He grunts and backs off, providing me just enough space to move around without bumping into him. Adjusting my bag on my shoulder, I reach into the engine and feel around. Then I drop to my knees and peek under the front bumper, spotting some damage to the radiator.

I climb to my feet and dust my jeans off, finding Jimmy staring at me with his arms folded across his barrel-shaped chest.

"The rad's cracked. Does it leak?"

"What do you know about radiators?" he asks, a hint of irritation sharpening his tone.

"Only that they shouldn't leak. And that this one is missing some fins, likely from hitting a small animal on the highway."

"Hmm," he hums, a curious glimmer in his eyes as he scratches his short gray beard with his thick, hairy knuckles. "Here." He tosses me a key. "If you can figure out how to start it, *then* I'll be impressed."

Smirking, I open the driver's door and slide behind the wheel. My fingers itch with anticipation as I jam the key into the ignition, press my left foot to the clutch and right to the brake, and fire it up. The engine roars to life beneath me, the steering wheel vibrating in my grip as I release a held breath, refraining from squealing in excitement.

Hopping out, I watch the engine work while Jimmy stands beside me, his gaze boring into the side of my face.

Without sparing him a glance, I chirp, "Not just a pretty face, Jimmy." He shuffles awkwardly on his feet, obviously surprised by my mechanical knowledge. "She needs new sparkplugs and an oil change. And I imagine the brakes are seized up from sitting for so long. And the radiator will need to be replaced at some point, too. That's a big expense for a broke girl like me."

"The ad says as is," he reminds me.

Shutting the hood, I match his stance and flash him a smile. "I never said I needed you to fix it, Jimmy. What I'm asking is if there's room for negotiation on the price considering I'm going to have to put some money into her to get her roadworthy."

Jimmy rakes his eyes over me once more, and I decide now's the time to play him like a fiddle.

"Or, you know … I could go find a car somewhere else. I'm sure you have *tons* of other interested buyers." No he doesn't. The car's a heap of junk and he knows it. And I happened to notice his ad has been active for more than six months, which means he's having a hard time making the sale.

Scoffing, Jimmy takes a step forward. But I don't back away. Instead, I remain perfectly poised and bat my eyelashes at him.

"Make me an offer."

Jimmy and I haggle it out, and I manage to chew him down well below asking. So much so that a good chunk of the repairs I need to make can be covered with the savings off the asking price.

I count out the cash and he signs the ownership over to me.

When we're finished in the shed, Jimmy leads me back toward the house and I take a seat on the front step and call for a cab. I could have just left the one I had to sit idling, but they're on a clock and I can't afford to pay someone to scroll their phone while I swindle a deal.

When the cab arrives, I let my new pal Jimmy know I'll be back in a few days to start working on the car. I slide into the back seat of the cab, pride inflating in my chest like a hot-air balloon preparing for flight.

Purchase a vehicle. *Check.*

I ask the driver to drop me off at an auto parts store near my apartment. A young man with a wide smile and thick glasses taps away on the keyboard as I rhyme out the year, make, and model of the car and the parts I need to order. They have some in stock, but others need to be located and shipped in. He informs me they'll arrive within five to ten business days, and I slap the cash down on the counter to pay, collecting every red cent of change and stuffing it back inside my bag, recalling one of my grandpa's most valuable lessons to me.

Those who don't appreciate a penny, don't deserve a dollar.

Six

Alora

A KALEIDOSCOPE OF COLORS reflect off the polished bar as I spin my glass in front of me, subtly peeking around the buzzing lounge for my first target of the night. I'm at the club Rose works at—The Afterlife—scoping the place out. It's the first time I've ever stepped foot in here, and it's obvious that it's oozing with wealthy businessmen who struggle to keep the snake in its cage, so I know I've made a good choice.

Just as I'm setting my sights on a lonely man on the other side of the room, a soft, feminine voice rips me away.

"Hey, girl."

I spin to find Rose standing behind me dressed in nothing more than a white lacy bra and thong. Her naturally blonde hair is curled and hanging down to the middle of her back. Her makeup is flawless and bold. It's like staring directly at the sun—you know it'll hurt your eyes, but it's just so darn pretty to look at.

"Hey, Rose. I thought you were off tonight." I bring my lemon drop martini to my lips and take a sip.

"I was. But Candy called in sick, so I picked up an extra shift. Can always use the cash, ya know?"

I force a smile, but deep down, I'm hesitant to stick around now that I know Rose is working. The last thing I want is to bring heat on her when I'm the one with the thirst for misplaced revenge.

Rose opens her mouth to speak, but a large man appears between us, his round belly and overwhelming cologne invading my personal space.

"Rose," he snaps. "Get your ass on stage."

Rose's shoulders slump, and my desire to kick this guy in the shin for being rude to her rises to the surface. Nobody talks to sweet, innocent Rose like that.

"Sorry, Stan. I was just talking to a cust—"

"Now," he bellows, his face turning beet red as he points a fat, hairy finger at the empty stage.

I'm not entirely sure if this is the club manager or bouncer, but judging by the veins popping in his thick neck and weathered forehead, he could use some blood pressure pills and a vacation.

Rose offers me a shy smile and pats me on the arm. "I'll catch up with you later, Alora," she tells me, then quietly saunters off to the stage to begin her performance.

The man I now know as Stan casts a large shadow as he glowers down at me. He rakes his eyes over my little red dress and grunts in dissatisfaction.

"Can I help you?" I ask boldly, straightening in my seat and glaring back at him.

"You've been requested," he tells me gruffly.

"I don't work here," I snip out.

"I'm aware. Come with me."

I tuck my faux hair behind my ear and jut my chin out. "I'm sorry." *No I'm not.* "But I have to decline—"

He cuts me off with a frustrated sigh. "You'll be compensated for your time. Now follow me. We're headed back to the Champagne Room."

I glance around the dimly lit bar. Nothing seems out of the ordinary. And well ... if I'm being compensated, say no more. Besides, I've always been a curious kitten.

I slide off the stool and smooth my dress down my body. My fingers keep a firm grip on the strap of my purse as I confidently follow Stan down a long, dark hallway. It's cooler back here, the air a little lighter and less stuffy than the more populated part of the club. We pass several doors, a black plaque engraved with "private" on each of them.

My heels sink silently into the plush burgundy carpet as I trail closely behind, my heartbeat picking up speed the closer we get to the steel door with a gold plaque—not black—that indicates this is the Champagne Room. Stan opens the door, and I take a calming breath and step over the threshold.

"All yours, sir," Stan says from behind me, the door clicking shut as he lets himself out.

Two large, well-worn brown leather boots the size of skis appear before my eyes. And my eyesight travels north—way north—latching onto a pair of warm amber irises, their hunger rivaling that of a starving wolf. But it's not his size or the intensity of his gaze that makes him unapproachable. It's the angry scar ripping through his brow that unnerves me.

Instantly, I recognize him. And all the blood drains from my face. Because the very man I suspected was stalking me is now here, staring down at me like I'm his next meal. Seeing him twice can be chalked up to a coincidence. But three times? Not a fucking chance.

My cheeks burn so hot you could cook eggs on them as my body temperature rises to a balmy degree. Sure, I taunted him with my cute little message on the mirror last night, but I just couldn't help myself. Being a well-behaved shy girl has never been my modus operandi. I'm a rebel through and through. And if this guy thinks he can scare me, he's in for a special treat.

Peeling my tongue from the roof of my desert mouth, I rasp out, "So, we meet again."

"That we do."

Jesus. Even his voice is big. And I'm willing to bet the wad of grimy cash beneath the floorboards of my closet that this guy's dick matches the rest of him.

Don't look. Don't look. Don't look.

I look. Shit. Yup. He's packing. A sudden flood of heat crashes over me like violent coastal waves kissing the cliffside, corroding my resolve until all that's left is nothing but microscopic grains of sand.

When I lift my lashes again, I realize he's smirking at me, one corner of his mouth hooked into a cocky grin.

He looks ... gulp ... terrifying. Why does that intrigue me? Why are my underpants growing damp?

I must be sick.

Shaking my head, I blink several times in hopes this is all in my very wild—very vivid—imagination. Surely I've conjured this guy up from one of my wet dreams. When I open my eyes, I sigh in defeat.

Still here. Awesome.

Correcting my posture and tone, I ask, "And what is it you'd like?"

He quirks a brow, that scar of his warning me to run. Fast. Far. Hard. Fast. I know I already said fast, but it deserved a second mention because this guy looks lethal.

He turns and saunters to the sofa, and I watch in awe as all those big muscles of his flex beneath the tightly stretched fabric of his black cotton T-shirt. Holy mother of mayhem. There are mountains less solid than him.

He takes a seat, the leather couch groaning beneath his weight, which I'm certain is at least a thousand fucking pounds. He stares at me expectantly, and all the little alarms in my head begin wailing. But I keep my feet firmly planted, refusing to show any signs of distress. If this guy thinks he's going to get me to take off running again so he can enjoy the chase, well ... that may be exactly what happens.

"I'm sorry. I guess I missed the part where you answered my question." The words are out before I have a chance to stop them.

His lip twitches in amusement.

Oh boy, Al. You've done it again. You've fucked up. Tested the waters when you should have stayed on shore.

"I'd like a bourbon," he says smoothly.

I do some weird, awkward version of a curtsy that was meant to be ironic but probably looked ridiculous because I'm wearing a slutty dress and a thong that I think might be permanently imbedded between my butt cheeks. I strut over to the table where the bottles of alcohol are neatly lined up and pour him a glass of bourbon. It's moments like this where I wish I carried laxatives in my purse because I'd love nothing more than to spike his drink and take him down a peg or two.

I saunter back over to him and hand him the glass, our fingers brushing lightly as he accepts it from me. The contact sends static electricity coursing through me, starting from the tips of my fingers and traveling all the way down to my clit.

Get a grip on yourself, you horndog.

"Thank you," he murmurs, but it comes out deep and rough. I bet he snacks on gravel and drywall screws. He pats the leather sofa beside him. "Sit."

I'm not normally one to obey men's silly little orders. And I'm not about to start now. Instead, I cross my arms and pop a hip.

"Say *please*."

His lips curl into a snarl, baring a set of straight white teeth. It looks like it takes massive amounts of effort on his part, but he eventually obliges, grating out, "Please," through a clenched jaw.

"Since you asked so nicely." I flash him a smile and seat myself next to him, crossing my legs like the lady I pretend to be and forcing every inch of space between us to a maximum. But our thighs brush, and the rough fabric of his jeans crackles against my bare knee. I'm hypersensitive right now, and that means I'm also in no frame of mind to be making important decisions. Like whether to stay here in this room with a man who looks like a big, hungry wolf ready to pounce on an innocent, little creature, or to run for my fucking life.

He takes a sip of his bourbon and sets the glass down on the table, licking the remnants of liquid from his lips. If that's not erotic, then I don't know what is. He sits back, stretching his arms over the back of the couch like a king, and I take a moment to appreciate the impressively wide span of his chest and shoulders.

And the tattoos ... I noticed them before, but I didn't pay them any mind. But now? Yes. Yes, I certainly do. His arms are a work of art, ink crawling over his hands and dusting his knuckles. There's a rose on the back of one of his hands and a cross on the other. Something else peeks out of the collar of his shirt, but I can't quite make it out.

Wetting my lips, I repeat my earlier question in hopes of receiving a legitimate response. "What do you want from me?"

His response comes quick and without hesitation. "What do you offer?"

I shift in my seat, the leather cushion sticking to the backs of my sweaty thighs. I recite the rules of the club that Rose shared with me when she asked to use my stove before her shift tonight. "Dances. Twenty a song. Payment first. No touching."

The mountain of a man nods at the thick white envelope on the coffee table. "Payment is there."

I flash him another smile and reach for the envelope, slipping out the wad of cash. Satisfaction burns through me as I count it out. It's more than a month's rent. Stuffing the bills back inside, I clear my throat and stand, suddenly very aware of my hands.

What the hell am I supposed to do with them?

A set of long, muscular legs stretch out before him as I stare at the bulge in the front of his jeans. I don't want to know if he's hard or not because it really wouldn't matter. That thing is gigantic and could cause some serious internal damage, flaccid or not.

Positioning myself between his knees, I repeat rule number three. "No touching."

"I can follow simple instructions, sweetheart."

Gripping his hard thighs, I drop to my haunches and make a show of swiveling my hips and working my way back up to the beat of the music playing lowly in the background. The muscles in his arms flex, his fingers digging into the back of the couch until they bleach white. He wants to touch me, of that I'm sure. But why it sends a sick thrill through me is something I'm not ready to unpack right now.

"So ..." I drawl, spinning around and grinding my ass on his lap, "do I get to know my stalker's name?"

A low rumble vibrates from his chest. "I'm not stalking you."

I roll my eyes. "Sure, you're not. Anyways ... your name?"

"You first."

"Jessica," I tell him shyly.

"Your real name."

I lift my butt from his thighs and turn around to face him again. "You and I both know I'm not going to tell you that."

"Yes you are."

I angle my head at him. "You must really think I'm dumb, huh?"

Gripping his shoulders, which feel a little like granite, I climb onto his lap and straddle him, my dress riding up and stretching around my hips. He releases his grip on the back of the couch, his large, rough palms splaying over my bare thighs.

I suck in a sharp breath and freeze. "No. Touching," I grit out, my jaw clenched tight and nails biting into his shoulders.

But he doesn't remove his hands from my thighs. Just stares at me with a hungry glimmer in his wolf eyes.

His touch is gentle at first, his wandering hands drifting slowly up my legs, his searing gaze never leaving mine. I hiss when his fingertips dig into the soft flesh of my hips. He releases a low groan as he drags me forward in one quick motion, my breath hitching when he tugs me down, coaxing me to grind against him. I comply, rocking my now trembling body against his and relishing in the friction of his jeans against my throbbing clit.

Stupid hormones.

"You're breaking the rules," I warn him, but it's barely a whisper, my voice raspy from arousal I definitely shouldn't be feeling right now.

He brings his mouth to my ear, his breath minty and hot with just a hint of bourbon lingering on it. It clings to my neck like honey, thick and warm and entirely too enticing.

"I remember the rules, sweetheart. But you know better than anyone that rules were made to be broken."

Welp, he's got me there.

"Not these ones."

"Hmm," he hums, retreating and pressing his back into the sofa again. He removes his hands from my hips. But the heat of his touch lingers there. "I suppose you're right."

"I'm always right," I say with a playful grin.

Deciding it's far too dangerous to be facing him, I climb off his lap and spin around again, repositioning myself with my hands gripping his thighs for support as I dip and roll and tease him until that bulge in his jeans has doubled in size. I wasn't sure if I was doing a good job or not, but his erection is like receiving a gold star, and I'm feeling a little proud of myself for it.

"So, since I told you my name—"

He cuts me off. "You didn't."

"Right. Anyway," I press on, flipping my hair and seating all of my weight on his thigh. "What's your name, baby?"

He's quiet for a long, tense moment. When his hand snakes beneath the front hem of my dress and settles on my bare stomach, every muscle in my body galvanizes. He guides me back against him, the strong, rhythmic beat of his heart clashing against my frantic one. His free hand gently cups my jaw, tilting my head back to rest on his shoulder as his thumb slides back and forth over the ribs just beneath my breast, his pinky skimming the lace edge of my panties.

God, he's so hard. Everywhere. And warm, his body radiating heat like a giant furnace running at full blast.

The words "just a little lower" dangle on the tip of my tongue, but I swallow them back, thinking wiser of poking this very large and dangerous bear.

"Do you call them all baby?" he asks hotly, his lips grazing the shell of my ear.

"Them all?"

"The men you steal from. Do you call them all that?"

I'm not sure what possesses me to do it, but I respond honestly. "Yes."

The energy in the room thickens, and his core temperature rises, searing my back and causing my body to break out in a sweat.

"Then don't ever call me baby again, got it?"

I wet my lips, and his eyes track the movement. "Then what should I call you?"

"Liam," he growls lowly.

"Liam," I echo, testing the syllables on my tongue. "It's nice to meet you, Liam."

He drags the tip of his nose up and down my shoulder, inhaling deeply when he reaches my hairline. A sudden shiver racks my body, and my sweat turns feverish and cold. A satisfied hum vibrates against my back, and I pinch my knees together, feeling myself grow slick with arousal.

"Lemons," he growls. "Of course you smell like lemons."

"Do you not like lemons?"

The warm hand on my jaw glides down my throat. He wraps his fingers around my neck and presses his thumb upward against my pulse. He's holding me so close and tight, yet somehow his touch is gentle. It's confusing and terrifying and I find myself desperately wanting more of it.

"Oh, sweetheart. I fucking love lemons."

A strangled whimper escapes me. If he keeps holding me like this, making my heart palpitate and pussy ache for something I shouldn't want from him, I'm going to require serious medical intervention.

He gives my body a subtle squeeze then releases me. I stand abruptly on wobbly legs and turn and back away from him, desperate to put some space between us. Desperate to get the hell out of here so I can breathe again. My lungs have been deprived of oxygen. Not because he choked me. But because I forgot how to do something that comes naturally to humans—breathe.

Giving my lungs a swift kick in the ass, I finally inhale, my head light and ears ringing.

Liam stands and stalks toward me, backing me up until my shoulders bump the drywall. His hands come flat on either side of my head, caging me in with his strong arms. He dips his gaze, his nose brushing the tip of mine as he stares straight through my bitter soul. I recoil slightly, and he doesn't miss it, backing off just enough that I don't go cross-eyed while looking up into his flaring hot coals.

"I'll be seeing you around, little thief." He says it tauntingly, and I know there's a threat lying somewhere beneath his statement. No. Not a threat. A promise.

God, I hope he keeps that promise.

He stands to his full height and walks out the door, leaving me plastered to the wall like fucking wallpaper as I struggle to get a grip on my composure.

Someone needs to bring a mop and a bucket because I'm a wanton mess right now.

Seven

Liam

I KNEW I COULDN'T stay away. From the moment I witnessed her lift a watch off the man at the casino, she had me in a chokehold. And when I finally saw her up close and in the flesh, with those emerald orbs of hers shining so bright against her flawless pale skin, with her flushed cheeks and plump red lips begging to be devoured, I felt a rush of adrenaline like never before, followed by an overwhelming sense of quiet that I haven't felt in years.

And even now, with my left wrist relieved of my beloved Rolex—which I felt her unclasp and slip between the couch cushions last night while she was grinding her hot little cunt on my lap—I realize that nothing can hold a candle to the relief I felt while staring down at her beautiful face. The girl's a wet dream. One designed to haunt me for every waking moment until I finally cave and hunt her down again. Just to see her eyes flicker with defiance.

To see her pulse jump in her throat when our gazes lock. To see the small bead of sweat that forms on her upper lip when she's nervous. I want to see the rest of her body sweat like that. And I want to lick every drop of it from her heated skin.

For whatever reason, she doesn't seem to fear me, and that turns me the fuck on. That fiery attitude of hers only heightens my desire to sink inside her. She's a venomous little thing, and I'm ill from the lethal dose of obsession she's injected into my veins.

Leaning against my Harley, I watch as Alora strolls through the busted front door of her apartment building, her long, naturally black hair spilling out of the hood pulled over her head and cascading in soft waves down the front of her oversized sweater. She stuffs her hands into her pockets and takes off down the sidewalk, a large, saggy duffel bag slung over her shoulder.

She crosses the street and vanishes around a corner, and I hop on my bike to follow her, watching from a safe distance so I don't set off any of her well-honed instincts.

What are you up to, little thief?

She walks for another ten minutes before disappearing into an auto parts store. I park down the street and wait patiently for her to reemerge from the building. When she does, her duffel bag is weighed down and she's carrying two jugs of fully synthetic motor oil. She sets them on the sidewalk and glances around, anxiously shifting her weight from side to side. When a breeze blows past and her hood flies off, I get a good look at her face. She's free of makeup, and fuck if her natural state isn't the most beautiful version of her. But her eyes are rimmed in darkness and her complexion is ghostly.

She looks as if she hasn't slept in days. And I want nothing more than to drag her back to my bedroom and fuck the rebellion out of her, only to watch her sleep off whatever demons are ailing her.

A cab rolls up moments later and she climbs into the back seat with her bag and oil. I follow the car an hour out of the city to a dumpy old farmhouse surrounded by nothing but fields and trees. I pull in and circle around, facing the cab head on. Alora hops out and stands beside the car, her ebony hair catching in the breeze and dancing in the wind. She glares at me and balls her fists at her sides. Her sweater is tied around her waist now, her tank top exposing her shoulders and arms. That's when I catch sight of the black Rolex hanging around her forearm—*my* Rolex. It's far too large for her, but fuck if seeing her wearing something that belongs to me doesn't make my dick lengthen and a sick possessiveness to take hold.

"Why are you following me?" she shouts over at me, frustration bleeding into her tone.

I slide my helmet off so she can see my face.

Something resembling anger—not fear—ignites in her eyes.

"Speak," she demands harshly.

I dismount my bike and prowl toward her, pausing several feet away. I had intentions of interrogating her last night at the club. Of asking her why she seems to be popping up in every location we've connected Ilya Petrov to. But I couldn't bring myself to do that while she was grinding all over me and making me hard as fuck.

The fact she makes no move to retreat or cower makes me question her sanity. I'm a large man—a scary one that most people cross the street to avoid. And I'll admit I'm slightly unhinged at times. Yet she doesn't fear me. Which means she's either incredibly brave or really fucking stupid. Perhaps a little of both.

The driver pipes up before I can respond. "Clock's still running, miss. Am I waiting or leaving?"

Alora's eyelashes flutter for a second as she sucks in a deep breath then releases it slowly as she considers the situation. Send the cab on its way and risk being caught alone with a strange man that's been following her? Or let it idle and rack up the bill? She reaches into her back pocket and pulls out a thin stack of cash and counts out the exact amount shown on the meter on the dash, plus a couple bucks for a tip. Then she reaches into the back seat and retrieves her bag and the jugs of oil, slams the cab door shut, and stares at me while the cab backs out of the driveway, the sound of gravel crunching beneath the tires breaking through the tense silence.

She glances at my bike. "I suggest you hop back on that pretty little Harley of yours and peel a strip off the white line. Because I don't have time for a stalker."

There's that term again: stalker.

"I'm not a stalker."

She cocks a brow, and I stroke my beard with my knuckles and narrow my gaze at her. Fuck, she's an unusual creature.

"I'm not a threat to you," I tell her honestly.

She all but scoffs. When I don't respond, her lips press into a firm line and a tiny crease forms between her furrowed brows.

She lowers her tone as if the open fields surrounding us have ears. "Look. Whatever it is you want from me, I don't have it. You're barking up the wrong tree."

I take a step forward and angle my head at her. "For starters, I want my Rolex back."

She rolls her eyes. "Finders keepers."

I take another step and her jaw clicks shut. Her posture stiffens. Perhaps I was wrong. She does fear me. She just refuses to show it.

"Take another step closer and I'll scream," she warns, matching my advance with one large step back.

"I already told you I'm not going to hurt you."

"And I'm supposed to believe the big, terrifying man who's been following me?"

"I don't lie."

"Sure," she deadpans. "Says every man ever." She adjusts her grip on the handles of the jugs weighing her arms down, her knuckles bleaching white as the pulse in her throat picks up speed.

Glancing around the desolate landscape, I ask, "What are you doing out here alone?"

"Burying the body of the last guy who crossed me," she snips out.

The attitude on this woman.

Two long strides close the space between us, and I scowl down at her, the scar through my brow crinkling. Her shoulders snap into a tight line and she stares up at me unblinking, refusing to show weakness.

Her nostrils flare in defiance, her green eyes darting back and forth between mine. Just as she opens her mouth to speak, the door of the house whips open and a burly old man steps out, his clothing in disarray, his large gut hanging over the top of his baggy, worn-out jeans. His boots come to a standstill as he stares at us. Alora doesn't spare him a glance. Instead, she focuses all her energy into burning a hole through my face.

"I see you brought help," the man calls out, his tone slightly smug but laced with disappointment.

"Help for what?" I ask lowly, keeping my gaze pinned on the creepy old fucker. The way his eyes roam over her backside tells me he's not a relative of hers. So who the hell is he and why is she alone out here with him?

She stands stock-still, the gears in her head turning over. Just when I think she's about to tell me to kick rocks again, she thrusts the jugs into my chest, my watch sliding almost all the way up to her elbow, and says, "You seem like the type of man who knows his way around an engine. If you're going to follow me around like a lost puppy, you might as well make yourself useful."

She spins on a heel and stomps up the laneway, waving at the man as we pass by the house. "Hey, Jimmy. We'll just be a couple hours, then we'll be out of your hair."

I glance back at Jimmy and shoot him a warning look before following Alora to the barn behind the house. Even in a pair of loose-fitting jeans with a hoodie tied around her waist, the sway of her hips is mesmerizing, and I find myself thinking about what it might be like to bite into the soft flesh of her ass.

When we get to the barn, she drops her duffel bag to the ground and presses her shoulder into the door, the squeaky wheels grinding on the metal track as the slab of wood slides to the side. She scoops her bag up again and strolls inside the building as if she owns the place.

I set the jugs down on the uneven floor and watch in rapture as she slides a tarp off the car parked in the center of the small building.

I circle the 1979 Corvette, taking in its wide slicks and original red body paint. "This yours?"

"Nope. It's Santa's. He stuffs all the presents in the back seat and uses the light from Rudolf's nose to power the engine," she quips dryly, popping the hood with ease.

She props the slab of metal open and removes the sweater from her waist, dropping it onto a workbench along the far wall. She turns to face me, and I have to bite back a groan. She's wearing nothing but worn-out jeans with tears in the knees and a tight black tank top, her pert nipples visible through the thin cotton. But it's no less erotic than if she were in nothing at all, an image I've conjured up more than a handful of times while fucking my fist.

As she's walking toward the car, she gathers her hair up and uses an elastic to secure it into a high ponytail.

"There's a jack on the workbench," she tells me, grabbing a wrench from a nearby toolbox and leaning over the side of the car, her back arching as she reaches beneath the reverse hood. "Mind grabbing it for me?"

I fold my arms over my chest and glower at her. "You're pretty bossy for a such tiny thing."

She peeks up at me as she locates whatever she's searching for and begins cranking her hand, loosening something. "You said you'd help." She shrugs. "So I'm putting you to work."

"I didn't say I'd help."

"Yet here you are." She removes a rusted nut and bolt and sets them on top of the engine block, then sinks her hand back down inside and repeats the process.

I come up behind her, her ass bristling against the fronts of my jeaned thighs. She slowly stands to her full height and stares forward, the top of her high ponytail tickling my chin as her shoulders rise and fall with each breath she takes.

She grips the wrench in her hand tight, preparing to use it as a weapon.

"Back up," she grates out through clenched teeth.

But I ignore her request and step further into her, pressing my body into the back of hers, relishing how small she is in comparison to me. She spins and raises the wrench high, but I stop her before she can swing, her tiny wrist completely engulfed by my hand, my watch winking at me tauntingly. The contact is unexpected and sends a disturbing satisfaction rolling through me, straight to my rock-hard dick.

"I don't take too kindly to being ordered around, sweetheart."

Her eyes light with fury. "And I don't take too kindly to being touched without permission."

"You didn't seem to mind last night when you were grinding your ass on my lap."

Her eyes widen and a look of fury enters her expression. Reluctantly, I release her and back away, but only because I suspect Jimmy will come running if she starts screaming for help, and frightening women isn't my bag. Although that's exactly what this girl needs—a good scare to snap her back to reality.

"What do you want from me, Liam?"

"I already told you. I want my watch back."

She narrows her gaze on me. "You've been following me since before I took your beloved watch. Besides, I already told you I'm keeping it."

"No, you're not."

She snorts and rolls her eyes. "Okay."

When I say nothing, she tucks a free strand of hair behind her ear, her fingers leaving a small smudge of grease on her face. Seeing her smeared in filth is incredibly sexy. My dick strains against the inside of my boxers, and I will away my erection.

We stand there in silence for a few seconds before she releases a long, frustrated sigh. I imagine I'd take great pleasure in fucking the snark out of her.

Instead of firing off a line of questions, I decide to change the subject, crowding her until the backs of her legs are flush with the cold metal of her car.

"Interesting choice of vehicle for such a dainty little woman."

She wets her lips and flicks her gaze over my chest and arms. "I guess you could say I'm a fan of all-American muscle."

"Is that so?"

"Mhm."

I go to snatch the wrench out of her hand, but she swiftly raises it above her head in an attempt to put it out of reach. I suppress my amusement. I could easily take it from her. But it occurs to me that she needs to feel in control. She needs to feel as if she can defend herself. Perhaps that's why she faces danger head-on rather than turning her back and running from it.

"Has anyone ever told you you're kind of an ass?" she asks blatantly.

"Has anyone told you you're kind of stubborn?"

"All the time, actually," she responds with a smirk. "It's one of my finest qualities."

We stand there staring for a beat before I cautiously reach out and rub the pad of my thumb over the smudge of grease on her cheek. Her plump lips part on an exhale and her eyes flutter shut, her long, dark lashes fanning over her cheekbones. Touching her feels ... cathartic, in the most fucked-up sense of the word. When I spot the pulse in her throat jumping erratically, I stuff my hand in my pocket and step away before I'm tempted to touch more of her. Because if there's one thing I know for certain, it's that I want to touch every fucking inch of her. I want to reach deep down inside of her and wrap the blackened fragments of my soul around her sweet, delicate one, shielding her innocence from the evil surrounding her. Protecting her from the demons lurking in every dark corner of the world.

It's in this moment that I decide she's mine. And for the first time in a long time, I feel a spark of something fiery and hot inside my chest. A small flicker of hope in an otherwise dark, desolate space.

Perhaps my monster can be tamed after all.

Eight

Alora

LIAM IS A DANGEROUS force. He's intimidating, strong, and all around a walking red flag. I fear him, but not in the usual sense of the word. I fear the way he makes me feel: all small, delicate, and dainty. Things I've never really felt before. Besides, if he wanted to rape and kill me, he'd have done it by now. So my stubborn feet remain firmly cemented to the floor as I watch him slide the jack beneath the chassis of my car and crank the lever to raise the front end off the ground, although I'm sure he could simply lift it with his pinky finger and not even break a sweat. The muscles in his inked forearms flex with every revolution, and I swallow the drool gathering at the corners of my mouth. I could do this by myself. I'm capable of changing my own oil, thanks to my grandpa's hand in raising me. But watching Liam do it is much more interesting.

I'll log these memories up in my spank bank for nights in Mexico when I'm lonely and horny. Because god knows there will be plenty of those. Besides, men like Liam are a rare find. He's rough and dangerous on the outside, but there's something about him that's different. And I want to know exactly what it is that makes him tick.

When he stands to his full height and swings his amber eyes my direction, I clear my throat and snap my attention to Jimmy's toolbox and begin rummaging around inside for the right-sized wrench to remove the oil filter. When I find what I'm looking for, I grab a tray from the corner of the shop and round the car and drop to my knees, sliding it under the oil reserve. I feel Liam's heated gaze on me the entire time as I putter around, and I pretend I don't notice him watching me.

He's not exactly discrete about checking me out. But I'd be lying if I said I hate it.

When I rise to my feet and dust my knees off, Liam towers in front of me and orders, "Go sit down. Women shouldn't have to do this shit."

I snort. "So, we've established in addition to being a stalker, you're also definitely not a feminist."

"I never said they couldn't do it. I said they shouldn't have to."

"But they can," I volley with a smirk.

He grunts and picks up where I left off on the oil change. *Alora: one. Liam: zero.*

"You need a new radiator," he tells me from the ground.

"I know. It's on back order."

He glances up at me. "How long?"

I shrug a shoulder. "Another week or two."

"I can get one in a day."

I huff out a laugh. "I appreciate the offer, but it's fine. I've already paid for it."

His phone dings and he stands and pulls it out of his pocket, his big, rough hands now smudged in grease. My memory flashes to how tender his touch was when he held me against him in the Champagne Room of The Afterlife. How the pad of his thumb gently stroked my stomach until I was ready to spontaneously combust.

He glances at me for a beat, then shifts his focus back to his phone, types out an angry message, and stuffs the device back into his pocket.

"Someone wondering where you are?" I try to sound nonchalant, but it's entirely too difficult to do when Liam's powerful pheromones have highjacked my brain. Because now all I can think about is what it might be like if he ripped off all my clothes and bent me over the hood of my car and shoved that monster dick inside of me.

"No. Just my boss."

"Let me guess," I drawl, tapping my chin and feigning thought. "He's disappointed with your performance."

"I can assure you, sweetheart, my performance is just fine."

Phew. If that's not a double entendre, then I don't know what is.

It's time I move this conversation along and get him out of my hair. He's a distraction. One that's making me lose track of why I'm here in the first place. And his presence seems to give me some form of temporary amnesia, because the last thing on my mind is the fact that he's been stalking me and I'm currently alone with him in the middle of fucking nowhere.

It's time I put an end to this lengthy highway of poor decisions I've been speeding down.

"Welp." I slap my thighs and straighten my spine, focusing on the space between his eyes. "This has been fun, but I think it's time you leave."

If it weren't for the subtle tightening of his scar, his expression would remain completely impassive. He leans against the side of the car, hooking one ankle over the other and folding his tree-trunk arms over his chest. He studies me for a moment too long, his intense gaze causing discomfort to press against the inside of my stomach.

Just when I'm about to burst into flames, he says, "I'm not leaving."

I narrow my eyes to slits. More silence.

"Okay then. So it's settled. You're not leaving. But I have a car to fix, then work later. So, if you don't mind ..." I gesture for him to move away from my vehicle so I can change the spark plugs.

That causes a domino-like reaction. At first, he looks surprised, but then his brows furrow. His jaw ticks. He unfolds his arms and legs and takes a step toward me. God, how his presence is all-consuming. He's all tall, dark, and ruggedly handsome with eyes so piercing they could cut glass. But there's more to him than that. I get the sense he's intelligent in a dangerous sort of way. The strong, quiet type who prefers to listen rather than speak. I bet he's super anal too. He probably keeps his collection of movies or books or whatever he fancies in alphabetical order. Or worse … he collects pinky toes or belly buttons or other small body parts that he soaks in formaldehyde and stores in jars in his kitchen.

I'm snapped out of my disturbing thoughts when he reminds me, "Stealing isn't a job, little thief."

"Nope. But it pays the bills."

He strokes his dark beard with his knuckles, his heated gaze sweeping over my curves and taking a blowtorch to every nerve in my body. "Why do you do it?"

The answer is simple. "Because a girl's gotta eat. And they deserve it."

"Who deserves it?"

Sighing, I say plainly, "Rich assholes who can't keep their dicks in their pants."

"You've been hurt before," he acquiesces.

I shake my head. I haven't been hurt before. Not in the way he's suggesting. But my mother was. Over and over again by my stepfather—a man no different than the ones I steal from.

"Then you do it for the thrill."

I make the sound of an angry buzzer. "Wrong."

We stew in another moment of tense silence before he tells me, "What you do, who you steal from, is dangerous. And I don't want to have to murder every prick that glances in your direction."

"Because you're jealous," I deadpan.

Liam's gaze darkens, his amber eyes flaring like two hot coals in the night. "Dangerously so."

I swear I hear tires screeching to a halt somewhere off in the distance. I'm not sure what I expected him to say, but it certainly wasn't an admission to jealousy.

I garble out a "shocker," but it sounds more like the sound a donkey makes when it's startled.

When he grins, I decide I officially want to die. Without another word, he returns to my vehicle and finishes my oil change. When he's all done, he lowers the car back to the ground and returns the jack to the bench, grabs a rag from somewhere over by Jimmy's toolbox, and wipes the grease off his hands.

"Spark plugs," he says.

"What about them?"

"You brought them along. I'll change them for you."

"How do you know I brought spark plugs?"

"I had a friend hack into the part store's database. You picked up an oil filter, two jugs of fully synthetic, and new spark plugs."

"Jesus," I hiss, striding over to my duffle bag. "Creepy much?"

Liam watches quietly as I rummage around my bag before handing him the spark plugs.

"Do you have a ride home?" he asks as he begins skillfully replacing the plugs.

"I'll call a cab."

"No you won't. I'll give you a ride back."

My eyebrows shoot to my hairline, and I laugh softly. "I'm not stupid enough to accept that offer."

"Never said you were. But you need a ride, and I'm headed that direction anyway."

"Of course you are."

His expression hardens, and I get the sense this absolute hoot of a conversation is about to take a nosedive.

"Women go missing from cabs all the time."

Aaand cue the nosedive.

"I'll take my chances. Besides, it's far less dangerous than getting on the back of a motorcycle with my stalker."

His jaw slides. "Call me a stalker one more time ..."

"And what? You'll spank me?"

"Yes." There isn't a hint of amusement in his tone.

I angle my head at him. "Is it fun bullying innocent women?"

"You're not innocent."

Narrowing my eyes on him, I respond boldly, "I'm a fucking angel."

He grunts and closes the last few inches between us. If I inhale deeply, my nipples will brush his stomach. It's tempting. It really is. All my senses are heightened, and there's a growing wet spot in my panties that tells me if I feel even the slightest bit of friction, I'll likely orgasm right on the spot. So, I do the wise thing and stop breathing all together.

"You're impossible," he tells me, as if I didn't already know that.

Glaring up at him, I warn, "And your balls are within kneeing distance."

"I'd like to see you try."

"Don't tempt me."

He chuckles. The sound is so deep and beautiful and makes my insides feel funny. I'm going to need a stiff drink after this interaction.

"I'd like to do more to you than tempt you, sweetheart."

I snort. It's unladylike, but since when do I care what men think?

His lips hook into a subtle grin. I bet his smile could charm the pants off a nun. Probably best I never see it.

We face off for a moment too long. As much as I appear confident and brave on the outside, I'm a weeping, trembling mess on the inside. This man is unnerving, to say the least, but I'm not going to give him the satisfaction of showing just how nervous I am around him. Because I get the sense he would feed off my anxiety like a starving lion would feed off an innocent little dear.

When he makes no move to prove me wrong, I back off, slam the hood of my car shut, gather up my belongings, and book it out of the barn and down the laneway in record speed. My departure is abrupt, but fuck the spark plugs. I'll come back to finish changing them another day. Heavy footfalls pound behind me, shaking me to my very core. I don't need to turn around to know Liam's hot on my tracks.

Jimmy must have been watching out a window, because he appears at the front door almost instantly. He takes one look at me and frowns.

"Hey, darlin'," he drawls. "You alright?"

"Just peachy." I retrieve my cell from my back pocket and glare at it, cursing under my breath at the dead battery. "Can I borrow your phone, Jimmy?"

"Of course. Just inside the door on the wall," he tells me as I stomp past him into his house, beelining it for the telephone. I need the hell out of here and away from Liam and whatever it is about him that makes me act so fucking reckless.

I glance out the window at the tyrant himself. He looks like he's about to blow a gasket and mow Jimmy down, but instead he just paces the gravel laneway like a large, pissed-off panther while he waits for me to return. When I've called for a cab and go back outside, he shoots me a glare so intense, it could melt steel.

"You can go," I tell him. "My ride will be here shortly."

Jimmy glances between Liam and I, obviously sensing the tension. I'm not particularly fond of the idea of being left alone with either of these men. But at least I'd have a chance at fighting the old man off. Liam, though? No way in hell would I win.

"You sure you're alright, darlin'?"

"I'm good. I'll be back in a few days to finish up if that's alright with you?"

"Course it is. Come by anytime."

I shoot Jimmy a tight-lipped smile and he disappears inside the house while Liam stands at the bottom of the porch stairs, stance wide and fists balled. The scar through his brow looks angrier than usual. And his warm amber eyes are molten lava, hot enough to burn the entire world down.

I have no doubt I'm going to pay for my defiance. But he's not the boss of me. *I'm* the boss of me. And I'm making the right decision for my own safety. I may be careless at times, but I'm not stupid or naive.

Tires crunch on gravel as I grip the strap of my duffel bag tight and pad down the stairs toward the waiting cab. But when I pass Liam, his large, rough hand wraps snuggly around my bicep and halts me. I glare down at it, wincing when I see how pathetically small he makes my arm look. He could snap it like a twig if he wanted to. But he won't. Not here, anyway. Not in front of a witness.

Seething, I shoot my gaze north and snip out, "Hands off, pal."

Just when I thought he couldn't be more intimidating, he leans in, his warm breath fanning the loose hairs around my ear, his thumb sliding over the face of his watch on my wrist. When my brain finally reminds my lungs they have a job to do, I inhale. It was a mistake. I shouldn't have done it. Because now I'm drunk off the intoxicating combination of spearmint, something woodsy, and just a hint of leather. A flush of heat creeps up my neck and into my cheeks. Fuck him for smelling as good as he looks.

His facial hair tickles my jaw, his lips grazing the shell of my ear. "I'll see you soon, little thief."

He releases me and I stumble back from him, my eyes wide and heart throbbing in my chest. Swallowing hard, I snap my mouth shut and spin on a heel, then crawl into the back seat of the cab and shrink down to approximately three inches tall. The cab backs out of the driveway and takes off down the highway. I glance out the back window several times throughout the hour-long drive, spotting Liam tailing us on his motorcycle.

A million thoughts flip through my mind. But the one that seems to stick is that even when given the perfect opportunity to take his watch back, it's still hanging limply from my arm. I don't normally wear the pieces I've lifted, but for some stupid reason, I decided to try it on.

And then I just never took it off.

Nine

Alora

APPLYING MY MAKEUP WITH extra care, I slip into my outfit for the evening. It's a royal-blue wraparound dress that falls mid-thigh. The back is all lace, carved into the shape of a butterfly, its wings spanning the width of my shoulders and tying in at the sides of my waist. My wig goes on last, and I stand in front of the mirror staring at myself, my hands a little shaky and my heart rate elevated.

I've always had impeccable instincts, something I must have inherited from my estranged father because I definitely didn't get them from my mother. She was intelligent but too soft and caring. Always saw the best in people even when there wasn't an ounce of good there. Her naivety led her to Charles, and his disgusting behavior led to her depression and ultimately her demise.

But the instincts I've homed in on are firing on all cylinders tonight. Something bad is going to happen. I can feel it in my bones. And since history tends to repeat itself, I know that staying home won't prevent it. One way or another, trouble is coming for me. There's no escaping it. So instead of cowering and hiding out in my apartment, I'm going back to The Afterlife to try my luck for a second night.

Maybe Liam will be there.

I blow out a ragged breath and hook my purse over my shoulder, internally chastising myself for thinking of my stalker at a time like this.

"You've got this, Al. Chin up. Shoulders back. Mind sharp."

I make the twenty-minute trek to the club, my feet already aching in my heels, promising a night of discomfort. When I pass through the front entrance and glance around, a strange fizzing sensation crackles through me. The club is unusually packed tonight. Men in suits line every booth, table, and stool at the bar. Several stand huddled in dark corners with drinks in their hands, their gazes swinging from one set of tits to the next. If I didn't know any better, I'd say it looks like there's some sort of special event taking place here. But that's not the case because Rose would have mentioned it to me earlier when I told her I was going to swing by for a drink.

The back of my skull tingles, a million pins and needles pricking at my nerve endings. The feeling of being watched comes rushing in, and I just about spin around and walk right back out.

"You," a gruff voice startles me, and I turn around to find Stan lurking behind me, his arms crossed and judgmental eyes glaring down at me over the bridge of his wide nose.

"Yes," I rush out, despite the fact that I don't fucking work here and this big meatball knows it. But that's fine by me because the last time he summoned me, I wound up in the Champagne Room with Liam and left a wad of cash and a Rolex richer. A Rolex I've decided wise to leave at home tonight, tucked safely under my floorboard with the rest of my limited prized possessions.

"Let's go."

"Where?"

"Champagne Room."

I swallow my nerves and grip the strap of my purse tight, following Stan through the lounge and down the hall to the Champagne Room. My heels sink silently into the plush carpet just as they had last night, and with every step I take, the anxiety mixed with adrenaline rising in my chest thickens like sap in the winter.

The door to the Champagne Room swings open, and I steel my spine and cross over the threshold. It's darker than I remember, the room bathed in black light that illuminates every color and speck of white. The slab of steel clicks shut behind me, and I stare at the man lounging on the couch, a renewed sense of unease crashing over me.

Not Liam.

"Good evening," the stranger greets me, his eyes raking slowly over my body as if he's appraising my worth. I suppose in a way that's exactly what he's doing. Calculating whether I'm worth his spend tonight.

Familiarity stabs at my guts, and I find myself wondering where I've seen this man before.

"Hello," I respond hoarsely, my throat suddenly tight and mouth bone dry. Instinctively, I glance at his wrist. No watch. Damn it.

I swallow my anxiety like an oversized pill and straighten my posture, feigning confidence that doesn't exist. There's an eerie aura surrounding him, an inky murkiness that creeps toward me, seeping into my skin and chilling me to the bone. This man is darkness personified. And not in the sexy kind of way. More like he's the scary monster hiding under the bed, and I'm about to plant my feet on the floor, offering myself up for him to sink his claws into and drag me under where he'll rip me limb from limb with his razor-sharp teeth.

He stands and stalks to the table where the liquor is lined up and two crystal glasses sit ready for use. He pours two drinks and offers me one.

But I don't accept drinks poured by strange men. Especially ones like this.

"Do you mind if I pour my own?" I ask politely, forcing a smile and batting my lashes.

Something resembling irritation flickers behind his coal eyes, and I know I've insulted him. But I'm street smart and won't be taken advantage of. He nods in approval, and I saunter to the table to pour myself a finger from the same bottle he poured his own drink from, just in case.

"Thank you," I rasp, taking a sip only after I've seen him drink some, the alcohol burning on the way down and causing the fiery ball in the pit of my stomach to flare.

"Have a seat. Let's chat," he instructs gruffly, and that's when I detect a hint of an accent. Russian, perhaps?

Another pang of familiarity.

He gestures for me to join him on the couch, and I hesitantly oblige, cautiously seating myself and crossing my legs. The sofa dips with his weight beside me and he clears his throat and stares at me. His gaze is cold and soulless, and it makes my skin crawl with a thousand tiny bugs.

He leans back, lazily running his knuckle down my bare thigh. Every cell in my body is screaming at the top of their tiny cell lungs to get as far away from this guy as possible.

Drumming my fingers on my glass, I sit still as a statue, weighing out my options. Surely there are security cameras throughout the club. And the only door in this room leads out into the hallway, so it would be incredibly difficult for him to kidnap me without anyone noticing.

"Such a pretty little thing," he says as if it's a shame, a malicious undertone lying deep beneath the compliment.

I shiver in response. And suddenly, it's as if barbed wire has cinched itself around my lungs, squeezing until all I can manage is tiny, labored breaths. The lack of oxygen is causing me to grow dizzy, and I take another swig of alcohol.

A wicked grin splits across his face, his gaze clouding with something terrifying. The dizziness grows stronger, and I find myself struggling to not leap to my feet and bolt for the door. He watches me closely as I fight to maintain my composure.

Normally, I don't fear men. They just sort of ... exist. Like dust particles floating around in the air. Kind of useless and a little annoying. But occasionally you inhale a big one and choke.

This is one of those times.

Thick fingers curl around the top of my thigh, squeezing painfully. I hiss and try to swat his hand away, but he tightens his grip and snarls, "Don't you fucking move."

I glare at him, my breaths coming short and fast and my heart slamming against my ribs.

"Remove your greasy hand from my body," I demand, no longer playing the sweet, innocent act. It's time to move this thing along so I can get the hell out of here.

His obsidian eyes pierce through me like knives ripping into my soul. He wets his lips, and I suppress the whimper lodged in my throat.

Angling his head at me, he asks lowly, "You really don't remember me, do you?"

"No. Should I?"

He releases my thigh and eases back into his seat. But my skin burns from his touch, and I know there will be bruises in the morning.

The panic finally bubbles over, and I go to stand and leave. But a cold, rough hand snatches my wrist and drags me back down onto the couch. I lose my grip on my drink, and the glass clatters to the floor, alcohol spilling and absorbing into the carpet at my feet.

"I told you not to fucking move," he snaps, throwing his weight at me and pinning me down on the couch.

"Let me go," I scream, digging my nails into any bare flesh I can find and ripping at his dress shirt in an attempt to remove his hands from my body. My legs fly up and I knee him in the crotch. He flinches and groans, but it only infuriates him further.

His arm rears back and his hand comes down across my face. White-hot pain scorches my cheek as my head whips to the side. Stars dot my peripherals and I blink several times in complete shock.

When my vision comes back into focus, I glare viciously up at him as he grips my jaw, squeezing so hard I think it might crack. He pins my wrists between us in his other hand and I struggle against his restraint, but he's much larger than I am and has me flattened uncomfortably beneath him.

Hot, acidic breath assaults my face as he brings his mouth within an inch of mine. "You stole from me, bitch. And now you're going to pay."

A memory floods my system as I stare in shock at one of the men I robbed a week or so ago at a casino. It was a gold Breitling, if I remember correctly. And worth more than my entire existence.

But instead of admitting it, I lie like a rug.

"You've got the wrong girl. Now let. Me. Go," I seethe, bucking my hips in an attempt at derailing him.

He rears back and laughs maniacally, and I take my shot, jerking my face to the side and snatching his thumb between my teeth. And I fucking bite. Hard.

Blood spurts from the wound, and the taste of copper floods my mouth and seeps down my throat. I gag at the intrusion and release his hand. He wails in pain and loosens his grip on my wrists, and I take the opportunity to reach up and grab his head, shoving my thumbs into his eye sockets as hard as I can. I may be small, and this guy may have a solid seventy pounds on me, but I'm vicious.

He screams and rips himself away from me, tumbling off the couch and onto his ass on the floor. He rolls onto his knees, turning his back to me. And that's when I spot the handgun sticking out of the back of his waistband. I bolt toward him, snatching his gun before he has a chance to react. I could switch the safety and cock the hammer and put a bullet in his head, but that would be murder—a crime I'm not quite prepared to commit.

So instead, I grip the gun tight and turn for the door, reaching for the handle. But he's faster, snaking his arm around my waist and hauling me back. I cry out for help as he tosses us both to the floor, the carpet burning my exposed flesh as I'm thrown against the coffee table. The gun flies from my hand, and he rolls me onto my back and straddles me.

I don't give up. I kick and scream and fight for my fucking life because I realize now that it depends on it. This guy wasn't just going to smack me around a little for stealing his precious watch. He's out for cold-blooded revenge.

But every muscle in my body aches from the impact, and my strength begins to wane. He palms my face and slams my head back, my skull bouncing off the floor with a nauseating thud. My vision blurs and there's a buzzing so loud in my ears that it feels like my brain is being drilled into.

I pry my eyes open just as something cold and clammy touches my arm and the room spins off its axis. Around and around and around I go.

There's grunting and groaning, something sticky coating my lips and mouth. Blood. His blood. And probably a little of mine.

"You stupid fucking cunt. He warned us you'd be a pain in the ass. So I'm going to fuck you until you're no longer of use to me. Then I'm going to sell your used-up pussy to the lowest fucking bidder. Because if there's one thing I've learned, it's that the ones willing to pay the least are the cruelest."

Lowest bidder. Willing to pay. What …

He's unzipping his trousers, his hips pressed between my legs as he tears at my panties and lines himself up with me. I use every ounce of remaining energy in my body to hike my leg back and jam my heel into his stomach. I feel the stiletto break the skin between two of his ribs, and I roll away from him and crawl on all fours toward the discarded gun lying under the sofa.

But just as my fingertips are grazing the cold metal, there's a loud crashing sound and my head whips toward the door being busted open. Rage-fueled amber eyes meet mine for all of a nanosecond before sliding to the howling prick on the other side of the room.

Liam charges at lightning speed and tackles my assaulter. Just as I open my mouth to scream, something warm spatters my face and chest, silencing me. Not once. Not twice. Not five times. It feels like the world slows and time ticks on at a sluggish pace. I lose count as the splattering ebbs, and I come out of the terrifying nightmare I've convinced myself I'm having.

But as I blink my vision into focus, I realize it's not a nightmare at all. It's very much real life. And I'm still sitting here in a daze, completely defenseless and in shock. I search my surroundings, trailing drops of red on the walls illuminated by the black light. Smears of it on the couch and floor. A body—his body—slashed and shredded and drowning in a pool of crimson as blood oozes from the countless holes littering his torso, chest, and neck.

My stomach roils as bile rises in my throat, stinging my nostrils and burning my eyes. My body lurches but nothing comes out.

I blink again, my instincts finally kicking in.

Fight or flight.

I choose flight, grab the gun from under the couch, and I fucking run.

Ten

Liam

I STAND LOOMING OVER Ilya Petrov's lifeless body like the blood-soaked grim reaper that I am. Red paints every surface in the room, the essence of life speckling the walls and furniture. I'll admit this isn't my finest moment. But my self-control slipped away. And how satisfying it was to shred him to pieces with my knife. To sink my blade into his flesh and carve him up like the useless slab of rotten meat he was. To finally give in to the chanting that's always playing on low in the back of my head.

It wasn't supposed to happen like this. Alora shouldn't have been here. But when I rolled into the war room and Sloane informed us that she uncovered that the Petrovs own The Afterlife through a well-layered shell company, and that they were using the business to launder money, I snapped. And when both Ilya's and Alora's faces registered on the club's surveillance cameras, I gave my monster free rein. After years of feeding him measly crumbs, just enough to keep him alive, I finally allowed him to feast. To devour Ilya Petrov and take the revenge I've been craving for years.

But this is just the beginning. Because now my monster is roaring within me, slamming against his cage, pounding his fists, and gnashing his teeth. He's had a taste of Petrov blood, and there's no way I can control him. He's unhinged. The only way to put a beast like him down is by finishing the Petrovs once and for all. And I will keep Alora under my protection until that day comes. Because despite the fact that the club surveillance will all be wiped clean, and there won't be a speck of evidence that she was ever here, Ilya still saw her face and requested her company. His family owns the business and property, so there's a chance the knowledge of her existence extends beyond him and to his brother and father. And even though Ilya's gone to meet his maker, I won't gamble with Alora's safety.

But she's taken off running, no doubt in horror of what she just witnessed. I need to handle this with care or I run the risk of her vanishing for good.

Pulling my phone from my pocket, I dial Sloane.

"Send a cleanup crew to the club."

A low whistle comes from the other end of the phone. "Get a little carried away, big guy?"

I groan, my patience wearing dangerously thin. "Just send them over and keep it quiet."

She pops her gum. "That bad, huh?"

I hang up and leave the private room, checking the hall for any onlookers before shutting the door behind me. I need to find Alora right the fuck now. It occurs to me that she's going to see me like this. And I fucking hate myself for it. But she's in danger, and her safety is all that matters to me right now.

I follow my instincts and run toward the emergency exit at the end of the corridor, bursting through it and out into the dark, empty alleyway and searching the street. I call Sloane again as I haul ass to my motorcycle.

"Hey, buddy," she chirps.

I skip past her pleasantries and get straight down to business.

"Alora took off running. Pull up the street cams and find her," I snarl.

"You got it, boss." I hear her fingers hammering away on her keyboard as she locates Alora with expert efficiency.

"Looks like she's headed to her apartment," Sloane tells me, clearing her throat and adding a little more softly, "She looks terrified, Liam."

My chest tightens at the thought of Alora running helplessly down the street, fear powering her strides and causing her distress.

I mutter a quick thanks then hang up and kick my Harley into gear, taking off down the street toward Alora's apartment. An apartment Sloane informed me is registered to a Jessica something or other. It's the same name she uses when she's hustling. The same phony name she gave me when I asked her in the Champagne Room the other night.

I pull up to the old, run-down yellow brick building, glaring at the busted front entrance. It's clear the glass door was shattered by vandals and the secured access no longer functions. So anyone can come in or out of the building at any time. It's a thought that royally pisses me the fuck off, but also works to my advantage at the moment. I also know she's on the third floor and which apartment is hers.

Parking my bike around the side so it's out of direct view of passersby, I storm straight through the front door and take the stairs in multiples up to the third floor. The corridor smells of cooked food and stale cigarettes, as well as a few other familiar scents that don't blend well together. I stand in the hall outside her door, staring at the flaking paint and shoddy doorknob that could easily be busted off with one swift kick.

Releasing a held breath, I reach for the handle and turn it slowly, surprised when the door swings open, its hinges creaking as the slab parts way.

Unlocked. Silly girl.

I take a step over the threshold and close the door quietly behind me, my eyes darting all over the small space. Vibrant oil paintings of every landscape you can imagine are propped up against every wall, stacks upon stacks of them. They're all the same style, the brushstrokes all wild and chaotic. All the same artist. I recall one small detail from Alora's file—that she attended art school but dropped out before graduation. Did she paint all of these?

The place is otherwise tidy. And it smells faintly like Alora, sweet and citrusy.

The creaking of floorboards snags my attention, and I whip my gaze to the left to find myself staring straight down the barrel of a handgun.

Well, fuck me sideways. If this isn't the hottest goddamn thing I've ever seen …

"If you don't leave on the count of three, I'll put a hole between your eyes," Alora threatens, her voice shaky but her grip on the gun firm and confident.

If she's nervous, she's not showing it in the least. Splatters of crimson dot her face, chest, and arms. Drying blood is smeared around her mouth from when she nearly severed Petrov's thumb with her teeth, but it's obvious she's tried to swipe it away. Pride mixed with something else swells inside my chest as my dick lengthens in my jeans.

When I don't respond, she cocks the hammer and angles her head, testing me.

"One," she rasps, her voice cracking under the pressure. Christ, now I'm leaking precum. "Two."

She inhales a calming breath and makes the mistake of blinking. I reach out and snatch the gun from her, twisting her around and shoving her against the wall. Her breath hitches when I mold my body to hers, her ass pressing against the rock-hard bulge at the front of my jeans. I snake my free arm around her waist and hold her close, my chest to her back.

"Do you feel that, sweetheart?" I snarl in her ear, inhaling her addictive lemon scent. She struggles against my restraint, but I tighten my grip and hold her still, ensuring I'm not hurting her but that she can't wiggle out of my arms. "Standing there in a dress that barely covers your ass and tits, coated in blood and aiming a gun at my fucking head … It makes my heart skip a beat, Alora."

Her green eyes blow wide at the use of her real name, her mouth parting briefly before her jaw clicks shut. I can practically feel the rage coursing through her veins as if we share a lifeline.

With one hand, I engage the safety on the gun and tuck it into the back of my jeans. I use my now free hand to cup her jaw and tilt her head to the side so she's staring up at me. Her lips are begging to be tasted, her long lashes fluttering as her nostrils flare in defiance. But she's struggling to not break, and something in my chest cracks wide open. I swipe my thumb over her bottom lip, lewdly smearing what's left of Ilya Petrov's blood across her cheek, reminding her of the power she holds. Of how capable she is.

I nuzzle into her hair and skim the tip of my nose up her neck to the shell of her ear, filling my lungs with her scent.

"No more running, little thief. I've got you now."

Eleven

Alora

I've NEVER BEEN MORE afraid in all my twenty-six years of existence.

But here I am, slipping into costume and refusing to cry, even as the man I just witnessed violently stab another human being to death rips the only form of defense I have right out of my hand and throws me against the wall like some sort of rag doll.

I should have called the police. I should have taken off some-where else and waited out the storm. I should have found a dark corner to hide in and cowered until the chaos subsided and it was safe to crawl back out and face the weight of the situation. But all my brain cells crystalized from shock and the only thing I could think to do was run. And somehow, I knew in my bones that Liam would hunt me down, and it would be a waste of energy to even try running from him. So I made the bold decision to face him instead. To show him I'm not afraid of him.

Except now my plan has backfired, and I'm at his mercy.

"You don't *have me*," I sneer, wetting my lips and tasting the coppery tang of the blood around my mouth.

Liam tracks the movement the way he does, his gaze darkening to that of thick molten lava, desire flowing through them at a deadly pace, searing straight through my resolve.

"You've been mine from the moment I watched you lift the watch off that prick in the casino, Alora."

I flinch at my real name again. But then I remember he said he had a friend hack into the auto parts store database, and that he somehow knew where I lived, so I shouldn't be so shocked to find he knows my true identity.

He presses his big, solid body into mine, reminding me who has the upper hand here, asserting his dominance like the predator he is.

My head moves side to side in denial, and I glare up at him over my shoulder. He's so imposing and tall that I'm going to need a neck brace pretty soon or my head is going to roll clean off my body. Except that won't matter because when Liam's finished killing me, he'll probably decapitate me anyways. Smaller parts are easier to move, after all.

"Women like me can't be owned. You're wasting your time trying."

"Hmm," he growls hotly in my ear, his breath warm and minty and clinging to my skin. "I have plenty of time to waste, little thief."

His expression softens slightly before his hand drifts from my stomach, skating slowly over my thigh and bunching the fabric of my dress up. I close my eyes and breathe through the anxiety threatening to explode from my chest.

"Have you been hurt by a man before, sweetheart? Is that why you're so bitter?"

He asked this same question out at Jimmy's earlier, but it still catches me off guard. What does it matter to him if I've been hurt before? Why would he care?

Despite my best efforts to remain cool, a small whimper bubbles from my throat as Liam's hand flattens against my bare stomach.

"No," I breathe out. "I already told you I haven't."

"Good," he acknowledges, his tone low and sending a wave of heat to my center. "Because if someone touched you, *hurt* you, I'd kill them too and not even think twice about it." A deep, satisfied rumble vibrates against my back as he makes some sort of primal sound that sends a flurry of bumps scattering over my sweaty body. "Covered in blood and pinned against the wall by a killer. If I were to touch your pussy right now, Alora, would I find it wet?"

I swallow. Hard. Because yeah, I'm soaked.

"No. You're a cold-blooded murderer," I remind him, refraining from admitting a truth I'm not ready to reveal. That I'm confused. That every part of me wants to trust him. That he makes me feel things I've never felt. "You're a psychopath."

He pauses in thought. "A psychopath."

I nod. "Yes. I think that's how the judge will see it."

A large, rough finger dips beneath the thin layer of fabric separating my throbbing pussy from him, and my breathing stalls as my heart lodges itself into my throat. It's been so long since I've been touched that I'm overly sensitive, my body practically humming with adrenaline. My legs threaten to give out on me, but Liam coils an arm around my middle and holds me upright. I rest my cheek on the cool drywall, my palms splayed flat on either side of my head, but the cold surface does nothing to settle the raging inferno tearing through me.

I gasp when that same finger slides up my seam, gathering my juices and circling my clit. I scrunch my nose at the thought of the blood on Liam's hands mixing with my arousal, mentally bitch-slapping myself for allowing this to happen but welcoming the twisted sense of security Liam provides me.

"Call me a cold-blooded murderer again, little thief, and I won't be so gentle with you."

"You said you're not a threat to me. That you won't hurt me," I rush out, reminding him of his promise when he followed me out to Jimmy's.

His hand stills as his nose grazes the soft flesh beneath my ear before his tongue darts out. I shiver as he licks from my collarbone up the length of my throat, tasting me. Savoring me. A shudder racks my body, and the air in my cozy apartment turns stiflingly hot.

"I won't hurt you, Alora. But I will devour you."

"You can't have me."

His fingers start working again, circling and rubbing at a painfully slow pace, teasing me until my hips are rocking against my own volition.

"Yeah, I could. Right here if I wanted." His threat feels empty, and I pray to a god I'm not sure exists that I survive this. "But it's what *you* want that interests me," he whispers in my ear.

My eyes flash open. *What I want.* I pounce on the opportunity.

"I want to know who you are and why you've been following me."

His fingers stall again. "Is that all?"

I shake my head and bite my bottom lip to stop from moaning. "No. I have questions. Many. And I want answers before the cops show up and haul you away."

"The cops aren't coming for me, sweetheart."

"How do you know that?"

His fingers move and he picks up the pace and applies more pressure. My legs become jelly, and there's a whole orchestra of sex noises lodged in the back of my throat.

"Because there's no evidence left for them to find. Next question."

I exhale a shaky breath. He must notice me relaxing into him, because he dips his finger lower and slowly pushes it inside of me. The intrusion causes every muscle in my body to tense.

"I said next question."

"Wha-what's your last name?"

"Davis," he tells me without hesitation, sliding his finger almost all the way out before pushing back in. I can feel myself growing wetter with each agonizing second that passes.

"You've killed before." It's more of a statement than a question, but he responds anyway.

"Many times."

"Why?"

"Because it's my job, Alora. It's what I've been trained to do."

He keeps his finger plunged deep inside my pussy as his thumb begins its torturous ministrations against my clit.

"Ah," I breathe out, earning me a deep growl against my neck that drives me wild. "You're an assassin," I guess, rocking my hips in tune with Liam's hand.

"I'm a mercenary," he clarifies. "Part of a specialized team who take out organized crime groups." He slides out of me then adds a second finger, stretching me out and making my legs tremble with need. "Anything else you'd like to know before I let you come?"

A team who takes out organized crime groups. He could easily be lying, a ploy to earn my trust.

"Do ... Oh god ... Do you know who the man you killed was?"

He pauses again. Gah! This stop and go is going to kill me before Liam ever has a chance to.

"Ilya Petrov," he says, his tone thick with disgust. "A human trafficker."

"Ilya," I repeat quietly, his name somewhat familiar. But just as the last syllable drips from my lips, a rough hand comes around my throat, squeezing enough that no air can pass through.

I react, bucking back and grappling at a strong forearm, digging my nails in until they're carving half-moons into his skin.

"Don't ever say another man's name again while I have my fingers buried in your tight, little cunt. Do you hear me?"

I nod quickly, desperately.

"Good," he growls, his grip loosening so I can breathe, but he doesn't remove his hand from my throat.

Instead, he slips his fingers out of me and spins me around, shoving me roughly against the wall and pinning me in place with one solid thigh between my legs. His hand comes around my throat again, his thumb sliding beneath my jaw and tipping my head back so I'm staring up at him. His scar is pinched tight, his brows furrowed, and danger dances in his eyes.

He brings his lips to within an inch of mine, and my heart pounds so hard I'm certain it's going to burst from my body.

I work to slow my breathing as Liam brings his blood-stained fingers—now glistening with my arousal—to my mouth. He smears the mixture lewdly over my bottom lip then pops his wet fingers into his mouth, casually licking them clean.

Definitely a psychopath.

The act is so primal and disturbing. But it causes something dark and depraved to unfurl inside me. I shouldn't enjoy the sight of him licking another man's blood and my juices off his fingers. But I do.

Sick, sick, sick.

He backs away, taking his skilled fingers and hot mouth with him while I remain plastered to the wall, panting like I just ran the Boston fucking Marathon.

He makes quick work of flipping all six of my dead bolts, so my door is securely locked, then returns to me. I try to speak, to say something—*anything*—but all that comes out is ragged breaths from deep within my lungs.

"Anymore questions, little thief? Or are you satisfied?"

I'm tempted to tell him I'm far from satisfied since he's neglected to finish what he started. But I think better of it and snap my jaw shut.

"Do you trust that I won't hurt you?"

My mouth pops open.

Don't do it, Al. Don't admit you trust the unhinged psycho.

"Yes."

It's official. You're an idiot.

"Alright then. Go take a shower and pack what you need. You're coming with me."

***

Liam's out there somewhere, patiently waiting for me. Oddly, I feel safe with him lurking around my apartment like a ghost, his fists balled and footfalls heavy while I wash the remnants of tonight's nightmare from my body. Closing my eyes, I repeat the name in my head like some sort of mantra.

Ilya Petrov.

Why can't I pinpoint where I've heard that name before? After he told me I stole from him, I recognized him as one of my marks but remembered that he was also one of the few men I've hustled that never actually gave me a name. So I had to have heard it somewhere else.

The entire situation weighs heavy on my chest, and I can feel myself cracking beneath the pressure. I suck in a breath and stiffen my chin.

Crying is for babies. Not grown-ass women.

But the tears escape anyway. And while Liam's out there and I'm locked in here, I allow myself one quick moment of weakness to let it all out. It's something I've mastered over the last couple years. But after pretending to be strong when all I really wanted to do is crumble to dust, I finally open the floodgates and let the emotions I've bottled up run rampant. Better to get it over with in the privacy of my own bathroom than make myself vulnerable in front of a man. Nobody needs to see this shit. And I certainly don't want the pity that comes with being a sad, broken woman.

I realize this must be what my mother felt all those years. This is why she'd drink herself to sleep every night. But as much as I've tried to defy the laws of nature ever since she died, I've been walking in her very footsteps. The only difference ... she was soft and sweet and allowed it to break her. She was fragile.

You're not her.

Stiffening my quivering lip, I decide my moment of weakness is up and squirt a glob of shampoo on my hand. I lather my hair and use the soapy bubbles to scrub away the dried blood on my body and face, watching as the pink-tinged water swirls down the drain at my feet, disappearing as if it never existed.

Splatters of red flash behind my eyelids, and I blink the memory away. The blood Liam shed for me—his white-hot rage that was so raw and palpable that I could feel it even through the haze of the knock I took to the back of my skull. And the way he touched me like I was the most delicate thing in the world. Until I muttered another man's name, and it was like the flip of a switch. He became so overly possessive and jealous. And it was ... satisfying.

I've always been a bit of a tough nut, rebellious and bold in a way. And although I wake up and slather my face in makeup, wear skimpy clothing and heels so high I could star in a circus, I'm not exactly a girly girl. It's all a costume—one carefully crafted to ensure men let their guards down around me. Because if there's something I've learned over the years, it's that men often avoid women like me. The kind of women who can fix their own cars and repair their own leaky sinks. The kind to not really need a man for anything except a few of his best swimmers.

But that feminine side of me that's always been missing seems to crop up when I'm around Liam. He's all male. And in the short time I've know him, he's allowed me to be who I am, raw and unfiltered and a little bit tough, yet somehow makes me feel so dainty. As if his masculine energy brings out my feminine energy. It's unnerving. Concerning, really. But it feels natural in the strangest way.

When the water runs clear, I step out of the shower, shivering when my bare feet meet the cold floor. I grab a clean towel from the shelf and dry myself off, then wrap my hair up in it on the top of my head. When my eyes go to the cracked mirror above the vanity, I freeze and stare back at myself.

My cheekbone is bruised and swollen from the backhanded slap I took. My face is ghostly pale and my eyes hollow looking. It's not that I've lost weight. It's that I look … haunted. I suppose in a way I am.

I allow my gaze to roam freely over my body, pausing when I see the fingerprint-shaped bruises on my thigh. A reminder. Wonderful. But bruises heal. And other than a few bumps and some aching muscles, I'm perfectly intact.

Thanks to Liam.

There's a soft knock on the door, and I call out, "Just a minute," as I scramble to get dressed, slipping into a pair of sweatpants and removing the towel from my hair to pull my tank top over my head. I don't need a bra because gravity has not yet robbed my tits of their perkiness. And it's not like they're big anyways. The only time I bother strapping these babies down is when I'm going out in public. Otherwise, they're free agents and can do as they please.

I rewrap my hair in the towel and open the door to find Liam leaning against the jam, his arms folded and a stern expression on his face. The scar running through his eyebrow stares back at me, and it occurs to me that I know absolutely nothing about this man beyond the fact that he's a part of a team of mercenaries who fight organized crime. If that's not all a big, fat lie, of course.

"My boss called a meeting. We're heading into HQ."

I hook my mouth into a smirk and pop a hip. "HQ. Wow. Sounds official. Think he's pissed about your Michael Meyers impersonation?"

His jaw ticks in irritation as his wolf eyes roam over my body, engulfing me in their heat. I've certainly had better days, but the way his irises flare makes me feel like a pageant queen about to take the crown.

He skips past my comment. "You need to eat something. When we're done at HQ, you can rest."

My brows shoot to my hairline. "I'm not doing anything until you answer more of my questions. This time, without touching me."

His scowl intensifies. "Fine," he agrees reluctantly, then steps back so I can walk past him and into my living room.

I flop down on the couch and drop my head back, peering at him standing ramrod straight on the other side of the room.

"Would you like a shower first?" I ask, finally mustering up some hospitality even though I truly have no energy for it.

"So you can take off running again?"

I roll my eyes. "I won't take off running. You've already proven it would be pointless."

"Ask your questions, Alora. But make it quick." He folds his giant, blood-spattered arms over his chest and widens his stance while I fire off a thousand burning questions and he answers every one of them with the seriousness of a full body rash.

By the time we're done, my head feels like it's about to explode.

"I was going to be trafficked," I repeat for the fourth time, still not quite sure how I managed to choose one of the world's most vile criminals to steal from. Clearly, Ilya Petrov didn't take too kindly to being duped by a woman and decided to hunt me down and get his revenge. Fortunately for me, Liam's team—Sweetwater Security—had been tracking him.

"Yes," Liam responds with the same short answer he's given me each time.

My cheeks expand as I blow out a breath. "And you thought I was involved with the Petrov family because I kept popping up in the same places you were tracking Ilya to."

"That's right."

I ball my fists and press them into the couch on either side of my hips. "That's a lot to process."

Liam appears in front of me, bringing with him the metallic scent of the blood he's still covered in. I release another ragged breath and stare up at him. I can tell he wants to touch me based on the way his hands are flexing at his sides. But he makes no move to do so, and a pang of disappointment hits me square in the solar plexus.

I remind myself that I asked him not to, and he's just doing as I requested.

"Everything will be alright," he tells me plainly.

I gnaw on the inside of my cheek and nod. Even though I have every desire to argue that things will, in fact, *not* be alright.

Mentally, I'm drained and need a break from this conversation. So, instead of continuing on, I blink up at him and ask the first thing that comes to my mind.

"Are we taking your motorcycle?"

Twelve

Liam

I snatch Alora's small hand in mine, lacing our fingers as I lead her around the side of her apartment building to my bike. I half expected it to be vandalized parked on this side of the city, but it sits just as how I left it—shiny, black, and completely untouched. Alora pauses and stares at my Harley with trepidation and something resembling excitement entering her expression. I hop on without releasing her hand and tug her toward me so her knees are grazing my thigh.

"No helmet?" she asks, quirking a brow.

"I have one at my cabin for you."

"Cabin?"

"That's right. Now get on."

She stares at me for another beat, probably planning her next escape attempt. But to my surprise, she adjusts the straps of her backpack filled with whatever items she tossed in there and slides on behind me without protest.

"Arms around my waist," I instruct, kicking my motorcycle to life and gripping the handlebars. "Now, Alora."

She complies, coiling her arms around my torso and resting her cheek against my back. I've never had a woman on the back of my bike. And fuck if I'm not happy that she's the first. And if I have it my way, she'll be the last too.

"Hold on tight," I tell her, then take off down the street to headquarters.

The rest of the team will already be there, tossing ideas around and shooting the shit. And while Alora was getting changed into a pair of jeans and a sweater and stuffing a change of clothes and some toiletries into a backpack, I put in a quick call to Rachel to make sure she could keep Alora company while Sweetwater goes wheels up whenever Sloane tracks Ivan and Viktor Petrov down. She agreed, practically squealing at the prospect of her older brother bringing a girl around for the first time. I grumbled about it, but her excitement is a sign she's in a good headspace.

With each mile, I feel Alora's body melt against mine. I have no doubt she's considered jumping off and running every time I have to slow or stop, but all that would do is put us right back where we started.

When we come to a stoplight, I peer over my shoulder to see her letting her natural hair fall free of the high ponytail she had it tied up in. She avoids eye contact with me as she runs her fingers through her locks, shaking them loose before returning to her position as the light turns green.

I log a mental note to take her out on my bike again, next time purely out of enjoyment and not necessity.

A large, windowless concrete building comes into view, and I pull into the parking lot of Sweetwater's headquarters. I park my bike and Alora hops off, looking entirely too fucking good standing next to my Harley with her wind-tossled hair. I snatch her by the wrist, feeling something cold and metallic slip out from beneath her sleeve and bump my fingers. I peer down at where our skin meets, confirming my suspicion.

She's wearing my watch again.

Possessiveness courses through me, and I haul her across the asphalt toward the secured entrance. Alora's on edge, once again looking like a cornered animal. She checks her surroundings as we pass through two sets of steel doors, both secured and requiring fingerprints and eye scans to admit access.

Within minutes, we're standing in the doorway of the war room, a large, round wooden table the focal point. There are computer monitors and leather chairs and the kind of overhead lights you see in interrogation rooms in the movies.

Alora's gaze darts around the open space, cataloging any threats and searching for alternative exits. I suppose when you've spent two years breaking the law, you learn to prepare yourself for making a break for it.

"Alora," Sloane says excitedly, approaching and holding her hand out for her to shake. "I'm Sloane."

Alora slips her hand into Sloane's but is swiftly pulled in for a hug. Sloane whispers something in her ear that causes Alora's eyes to blow wide and a pink hue to dust her cheeks. Pulling back, Alora blinks animatedly as the team huntress smiles brightly back at her.

I seal myself to Alora's side and lean into her while Sloane takes a seat in front of her computer.

"What did she say to you?" I ask lowly.

She peers up at me through her lashes, her expression giving nothing away. "She said that if I hurt you, she'll gut me like a fish. Then she said we should grab a drink sometime."

I'd laugh if I thought Sloane was joking. But I know she's protective of us in her own way. Like a feisty younger sister watching out for her brothers.

Mac, Joel, and Zak filter in moments later, and Sloane takes it upon herself to make the introductions. We all take a seat around the table, and I post up beside Alora and pull my switchblade out, flipping it open and closed as Mac and Sloane give us the rundown of what transpired after I requested the cleanup crew for Ilya.

In a nutshell, there's no trace of evidence that Ilya Petrov was ever there and is now feeding the fish at the bottom of the Pacific. But there's still one small issue that hasn't been resolved: the Petrovs own The Afterlife.

"We've done some recon on the club employees. There's nothing out of the ordinary to report. The women are all innocent civilians. The club manager, Stanley Burns, knows nothing about the illegal dealings taking place behind the scenes. From all appearances, the Petrovs purchased the business for the sole purpose of laundering money. So for now, we'll fly below the radar in case Ivan or Viktor decide to visit the club."

Silence stretches on as we all mull this intel over in our heads. When Mac's confident he has our full cooperation, he continues on.

"Miss Berkley," he says, earning Alora's dutiful attention. "Is there anything you'd like to add that might help us? Anything Ilya said to you before ..."

Right now, every set of eyes in the room are on the little thief sitting next to me. I can tell in the subtle way she shifts in her chair that she's uncomfortable, but otherwise, she shows no other signs. No emotion.

"No, sir. I've got nothing," she responds with her chin held high.

I narrow my eyes on her as I fiddle with my knife. She glances in my direction, and that's when I notice her pupils dilating as she clears her throat and quickly averts her eyes.

She's lying.

I watch her closely as Mac rambles through the logistics of where Sloane tracked the remaining two Petrovs to. It seems while Ilya's been gambling and frequenting clubs here in California, his father and brother have been busy running the trafficking business.

"There's a twelve-year-old girl named Tanya Richardson that went missing several days ago. She was nabbed up walking home from school. Sloane's been able to locate her on the dark web, but we're not sure if she's still alive."

Alora's shoulders snap into a tight line. "They took a little girl?"

Mac nods once, and Alora slumps down into her chair, a defeated look washing over her as she begins gnawing anxiously on her thumbnail, her eyes darting all around the room. She pauses several times to mouth *Ilya Petrov* to herself, as if saying the name might ignite something in her brain.

"Do we know if she's been sold yet?" Joel asks. He has his own kids now—a four-year-old daughter, Lainey, and a baby boy, Finnegan. And every time we're tracking a child, that fatherly instinct to protect them grows stronger, and his anger becomes palpable. Whereas Zak is the cool, collected medic, Joel is hotheaded with a short fuse. And I fall somewhere between the two.

"No," Mac responds. "But she was used as ..." He clears his throat. "Entertainment."

A thousand disturbing images roll through my mind at what using a child as entertainment might entail. My monster wakes from his slumber, and I close my eyes to silence the voices urging me to snap. A small, warm hand touches mine beneath the table, and I peer down at Alora's tiny fingers wrapped around my much larger ones, squeezing reassuringly. I lift my gaze to hers and find her green eyes filled with something resembling sadness.

"A live stream of her torture was auctioned off to the highest bidder. We managed to hack in long enough to pin down a location. But there's a very real chance we won't find her alive."

"The location?" I ask, my chest tight with anxiety.

Mac hits me with an empathetic look. "The Kolyma Mountains."

White-hot rage spreads like wildfire through my system, burning my remaining self-control so all that's left is black ash and soot. The Kolyma Mountains are the same part of Russia we found Rachel in several years ago. But the region is vast and rugged, and there's no way of pinpointing exactly where the Petrovs will dump their victims next. It's like playing a game of Whac-A-Mole, and I'm growing tired of losing.

"On the off chance Tanya is still alive, the Petrovs may be nearby. But I'm afraid it's unlikely."

I glance down at Alora again who's now perched anxiously on the edge of her seat.

"So, now what?" she asks, directing her question at boss man, who's pacing the head of the table and raking his hand through his salt-and-pepper hair.

He stops and props his hands on his hips.

"Now we go find her."

"We're going to Russia?" Alora asks, her tone slightly elevated.

"Not you," I grumble. "You're staying with my sister at my cabin while I'm gone."

She scoffs. "I don't fucking think so."

I groan but don't respond as Mac finishes detailing our departure and plans for the mission. The team files out, Zak slapping me on the back as he saunters away, his hands tucked in his pockets as he shakes his head and chuckles softly to himself.

We're the last to leave, and I pull Alora along behind me as she struggles against my grip on her hand and fires off a line of questions.

"Where's your cabin? How long will you be gone? What am I supposed to do with this, Liam?"

We exit the building and storm across the parking lot.

"My cabin is just north of the city. I'll be gone at least a few days. But you'll be safe there. And I'm sure you'll keep yourself busy. Rachel will keep you company."

When we reach my Harley, I stop and spin her to face me. Her palms fly to my chest, her tiny hand splayed flat over my heart. I reach out, hesitating as my fingers hover over her forehead before I tuck her silky hair behind her ear.

Her shoulders lower as she stares up at me. "The little girl ... What are the chances you'll find her alive?"

Another crevice forms in my chest, splitting me open and flooding me with something I refuse to label.

"Slim."

Water pools in her eyes, the sunlight bouncing off the glistening tears and making her irises appear a shade lighter than their usual deep emerald.

"And if she's dead? Then what?"

"We'll bring her body home to her family. And any other victims we find there. And then we'll keep looking for the Petrovs."

She blinks away the tears and stiffens her bottom lip. "I want to help, Liam."

"There's nothing you can do," I tell her truthfully. "If there's anything you think of while we're gone ... anything Ilya might have said to you ..."

She jerks away from me and begins to pace, dragging her hands through her hair and tugging at the strands. "No. There's nothing he said that would help. But his name is familiar, and I can't place where I've heard it before."

This surprises me. It's a unique name—not one most people would have heard in their lifetime. I want to press on. I want to shake whatever memory is rattling around in her brain loose. But there's nothing I can say or do that will make that happen.

When she's practically worn a hole through the asphalt, I snatch her elbow and drag her back to me.

"You're still in danger, Alora. You're staying put at my cabin. My sister's already on her way up there. And when I'm back, you'll remain under my protection until it's safe to let you go."

Let her go.

The words leave my mouth, but I'm not sure I mean them.

Thirteen

Alora

L IAM'S CABIN IS NOT at all what I expected. Part of me assumed it would be a shack in the side of a mountain with limited electricity and running water. Maybe a woodstove for heat and cooking and an outhouse instead of a proper bathroom. You know … considering his caveman tendencies, gruff demeanor, and unquenched thirst for blood. But here I am, completely stupefied and in awe.

I stroll through the large open concept living area of the two-story log home, taking in the high vaulted ceilings and solid wood beams running throughout. The floors are black birch wood, which I can tell are heated based on the warmth radiating up through my soles. The kitchen cabinets are dark and ominous and stretch far higher than I can reach. The countertops are polished concrete and free of clutter. The walls that aren't exposed logs are all painted a matte black, except for the deep rusty-orange one where the flagstone fireplace stretches from floor to ceiling. But there are no pillows or blankets on the caramel-colored leather couch. There are no paintings or family photos on the walls. There's nothing to indicate a human being lives here.

It's dark, moody, and beautiful. Much like the man himself.

I drag a lazy finger across the fireplace mantel and peek over at Liam leaning against the island with his arms crossed and one ankle hooked over the other. He looks so broody and intimidating with his dark hair and the angry scar on his face. But the way his whiskey-colored eyes track my every move, almost predatory ...

"When will your sister be here?" I ask, curious how much time I have before I'm forced to endure several long days of awkward conversation with a woman I've never met.

Girl talk is not my thing, so I'm dreading this.

"Shortly."

"I still don't understand why I can't just stay at my apartment. Nobody of any importance knows I live there. I'd be perfectly safe. And I promise not to run."

"You wouldn't be safe," he argues.

I know I'm not going to convince him otherwise. But that won't stop me from trying. I roll my eyes and stroll over to him.

"I'm capable of taking care of myself. I don't need a babysitter."

But he doesn't budge. There's no winning with this guy.

A soft knock on the side door of the house has my spine straightening, my nerves suddenly a little frayed. I've never met a man's family before. Not that Liam and I are in a relationship. But still

... this is a first for me. And I'm not oblivious to the fact that most people will assume we're romantically involved.

"Hey, bro," a soft female voice calls out from around the corner. I hear the clanking of a chain and glance over at Liam who's standing in the same place I left him. There's a slight tick in his jaw as he shifts his wolf eyes from me to the doorway, seemingly assessing whether this was a wise idea.

On his part ... yes, it was. Because there's not a doubt in my mind that if he left me alone here in his cabin in the woods, almost an hour drive outside of the city, that I'd take off on foot the second his back was turned.

But instead, I'm being babysat by his younger sister.

"Incoming," Rachel hollers. Then, to my surprise, a goofy-looking Belgian Malinois comes flying around the corner. Its tongue lolls out the side of its mouth as it gallops across the house and shoots straight toward Liam, leaping into his outstretched arms. The dog licks and slobbers all over him, and I'm left watching in awe as Liam returns the affection, roughing up the dog's ears and jowls and kissing him on the head.

So he *does* have a soft side. Interesting.

The dog comes to me next, its tail wagging and cold nose nudging at my hand in demand of attention. I reach down and pat its head, not really sure how to react.

"And what's your name, cutie?"

Rachel appears from around the corner, her eyes the same warm amber color as Liam's but hair a lighter shade of brown and pulled back into a loose braid that hangs over one shoulder. She's beautiful in a soft, demure sort of way. And she's wearing a pair of black leggings and an oversized blue sweater that says "Touch my dog and I'll fuck you up" across the front.

"That's Onyx," she tells me, then thrusts a hand out. "And you must be Alora. I'm Rachel. It's so nice to meet you." She beams at me, her smile reaching all the way to her sparkling eyes.

"Nice to meet you too."

Rachel smiles a little more, her eyes shifting to her older brother before returning to me.

"I hear you've been sentenced to lockdown," she says earnestly.

I chuckle softly at that. Because yeah, it does feel a little like a sentencing. But also a little nice. My mother and grandpa both cared about my safety, but they're gone now. And it's been a hot minute since I've felt like anyone gave a shit.

"Well, either way." She hooks a thumb over her shoulder at Liam. "I promise I'm not nearly as overbearing as this guy. Plus …" Her hand disappears into her duffel bag before withdrawing a bottle of vodka and waving it in front of me. "I hear you like lemon drop martinis."

"Vodka. Life's lubricant."

Rachel laughs and walks toward the kitchen, playfully bumping her shoulder against Liam on her way past.

Maybe this won't be so bad after all.

Liam departs a few hours later, shooting me a pained look before pulling the door shut behind him and securing the alarm system.

I'm left to my devices in his house with Rachel who's been incredibly friendly and has a similar dark sense of humor as I do.

I sit with my legs crossed in front of me on Liam's leather couch, gnawing on my thumbnails until they're bleeding as I stare numbly at a spot on the wall. The blender turns on full blast behind me in the kitchen then shuts off a moment later.

"Do you like a little vodka or a lot of vodka?" Rachels calls out, glasses clanking as she rummages around in the cupboards.

"A lot, please," I respond with a smile, glancing over my shoulder at her.

My favorite drink appears in front of me a moment later, a curly slice of lemon slung over the rim of the glass. I accept it with thanks and suck back a good half of the beverage in one gulp.

"You're right," I say to Rachel as she seats herself on the other side of the couch and folds her legs up under her, slurping on her drink. "I needed this."

"Right?" She giggles when Onyx hops up on the couch between us and flops down, his doggy eyebrows twitching as he glances between his mama and me.

"So, Alora," Rachel begins. "I have to ask because Liam doesn't tell me a whole lot. How'd you and my brother meet?"

I take another sip, this one smaller, contemplating how to answer that for a moment. "You sure you want the truth?" I ask, only half joking.

She gets a little more comfortable, shifting on her bottom and clasping her ankle in her hand. "Let me guess ... You guys locked eyes from across a crowded room and instantly fell in love."

I burst out laughing. "We're not in love. We barely know each other. But I guess in a weird way, yeah, that's how we met."

She eyes me skeptically and hooks her lips into a mischievous grin. "Liam's always been a man of action. Words don't mean a whole lot to him. I'm sure you've figured that out by now."

I nod in understanding. "I get that. But in all seriousness, we're just ... friends?"

Is friends the right term for it? Fuck no. But what else am I supposed to tell his sister? That he started stalking me after witnessing me steal a watch off a man's wrist at a casino? That he paid me more than a month's rent for a lap dance in a private room of a club I don't work at? That he followed me out to Jimmy's and helped me work on my car? That he violently stabbed a man to death in front of me then hunted me down and forced me into this entire situation?

"Mhm. Well, I for one am happy he found you. He needs a little excitement in his life beyond torturing and killing people." My mouth pops open, but words escape me. I know Liam has to kill for his job at times, but torture? Rachel continues on as if this isn't a massive revelation. "I mean, they're all rotten to the core and deserve it. But still. His job is scary as fuck and nobody, not even my closed-off, broody brother should be forced to stew in that much darkness every minute of every day."

"He tortures people?" I'm still a little dumbfounded.

She swats the air. "Duh. He's like … kind of the best at it." She takes a sip of her drink. "I mean he takes it a little next level at times, but he's all heart, I promise. God," she says wistfully, "he's the reason I'm still breathing."

"I don't mean to pry or anything. But …"

She smiles at me, but this time it looks forced. She tucks a few loose strands of hair behind her ear and sniffs. "I was trafficked a few years back by the Petrovs. So this mission is more than just business for Liam."

My hand flies to my mouth in shock and horror. "Oh my god, Rachel. What happened?"

"I took a cab home from my shift at a bar one night. The driver was one of the Petrov's men and took me. I belonged to them for nine months. They forced drugs into my veins. Had me so hooked that I'd do anything for my next hit. Liam never gave up looking for me. I was almost dead when he found me in a bunker in Russia, discarded like old trash and nearly frozen solid and starving to death."

I sit still as a statue, my heart aching at the thought of what Rachel must have endured for nine months. Of what so many others must endure. But then my mind slips to Liam again, remembering how irritated he was at Jimmy's when I insisted on taking a cab home instead of accepting a ride from him. And it all becomes a little clearer.

Rachel twists her mouth before continuing on, her tone softer and a little strained. "He brought me home and got me the help I needed. It was a long struggle for several years. I'd get clean, then every few months end up relapsing. It was a vicious cycle. And Liam just ..." Her eyes fill with water, and she stares down at the glass in her hand. But she swallows her emotions and forges on. "He refused to give up on me. He's not just my big brother. He's the best guy I know. He's my fucking hero." Her eyes droop downward, a haunted look marring her pretty features. "But he's different now, you know? It changed him."

I lean in, captivated by what she's telling me, in awe of the man that not even twenty-four hours ago I was certain was a certified psychopath. "What do you mean?"

Rachel begins fidgeting, picking at a stray thread on the hem of her shirt.

"He wasn't always like this. He was a SEAL for I don't even know how many years. He loved being in the Navy. Loved serving his country. But he was gone on missions more than he was home. And every time he came back, it was like another piece of him was missing, and in its place was darkness. But then when I disappeared, he fell apart completely. Physically, I recognized him when I first saw him coming toward me in that bunker. But mentally and emotionally, he wasn't the same person anymore."

Rachel pauses to take another sip of her martini, then begins slowly stroking Onyx's tail. The dog lets out a long sigh as he stares up at Rachel with love in his beady black orbs.

Tears sting the corners of my eyes and rocks lodge themselves into my throat. "What was he like before all of that?"

Rachel tips her head back and forth in thought, a small smile gracing her lips. "He was practically a genius. Still is. But in a different way, I guess. He really liked working with his hands, fixing up old motorcycles and rebuilding engines. And he liked to read, always spouting random facts about things most people don't care about. There isn't much that Liam takes on without giving it his all. I suppose in a way, he's still like that, but instead of hobbies, he's buried himself in the art of torture. I'm afraid if he doesn't take the Petrovs down soon ..."

Her throat works as she swallows. She doesn't need to finish that sentence. She's afraid if Liam doesn't get the revenge he's seeking—the justice he needs—that he'll drown in his own pit of darkness.

My heart breaks for him and Rachel, my breathing ragged as a flood of emotions go barreling through me.

Clearing my throat, I croak out, "Do you think he'll ever go back to the way he was?"

She lifts her gaze to mine and presses her lips into a firm line. "I'm not sure. But one thing I know for certain is that he won't rest peacefully until the Petrovs are dead."

Fourteen

Liam

THE PLANE RIDE TO Russia is long and turbulent. Mac orders us to get some rest and fuel up in case the mission takes longer than expected. We all obey, catching a few hours of rack time and hydrating, then suiting up for a potentially lengthy stay in the desolate northeastern parts of the frigidly cold country. We transfer to a helo once we're there and drop into the Kolyma Mountains where Sloane last tracked the little girl to. The cold here is bitter and deadly, and even dressed head to toe in arctic gear, it penetrates my exterior and settles deep into the marrow of my bones.

We locate the building and move boots through the underground bunker. My eyes flick over decomposing body parts that litter every dark corner, snagging on the ass end of a rat as it scurries down another empty hall.

Sloane comes in over my comm. "I have thermal registering in a room west of you, Davis."

I scan the corridor through the scope of my rifle, keeping my footfalls light as I round the corner and follow Sloane's direction west. Rough strokes of white air paint the space in front of my face as I exhale slow, steady breaths, my stomach roiling from the stench of death and decay. But with every step forward, my heart beats faster and the satisfaction of bringing a victim home swells inside me.

The girl has been down here without food or water, and every second that ticks on is a second too long that she's resided in this hell.

If she's even still alive.

The steady drip of a leaking pipe slices through the silence, its pitch scaling nearer as I approach the next doorway, the concrete walls yawning around its shadowy emptiness. I raise a fist in the air to signal for my teammates to pause, and cup my hand to my ear to strain against the deafening silence. The only sound is the constant drip and the hushed chanting of the demons that lurk in the dark corners of my mind.

There's a faint shuffling sound, like someone scurrying across the floor, followed by a small, suppressed cough. I keep my rifle aimed, finger on the trigger, and slip into the room, my eyes immediately locking on the source of the disturbance. The voices in my head grow silent as the whoosh of the blood in my ears intensifies. My eyes dart over the child huddled in the corner, her twiggy legs curled into her chest as she grips her knees with trembling fingers.

She's dressed in nothing more than a white cotton nightgown. Her thin body racks uncontrollably, trying and failing at creating its own source of heat.

She whimpers in fear, and my blackened heart splits wide open.

I lower my rifle and take a cautious step toward her.

"I'm not going to hurt you, little one."

She lifts her head, her long dark hair a curtain around her pale features as she sits paralyzed in fear. My gaze fixates on the deep gashes across her knees, puss oozing from the blistering holes. Closing my eyes briefly, I rein in the urge to put my fist through a wall. Memories filter back of the day we found Rachel in a bunker nearly identical to this one, her body sickly thin and littered in track marks.

I forced myself to watch the live stream of what they did to this girl, and I'll be damned if I don't use the image to fuel the rage burning inside me. The innocence they ripped from her sweet little soul, only to fill the gaping holes with sheer horror. And even now, two days later, her terrified screams still haunt my every waking moment.

I already know there's no way the Petrovs are down here with her. This is what they do to their victims when they're no longer of use. They don't even spare these poor souls a bullet to end their suffering. Instead, they dump them in a hole and leave them to starve to death and rot for eternity—a fate I wish nothing more than to gift them in return.

Joel appears at my side a moment later, an angry groan rising from beneath his gear.

"Tanya. That's your name, right?" he asks as unthreateningly as possible.

But we're large men dressed head to toe in camo, our faces concealed behind masks and our bodies weighed down with weapons and ammunition. The girl has ample reason to not trust us. Christ. She has reason to never trust anyone ever again.

I remove my mask and night vision goggles from my head and her large, round eyes meet mine briefly before fixating on the scar slashing through my eyebrow.

She curls in on herself, tightening her grip on her legs and flinching when Joel drops to his haunches in front of her.

"You're alright, Tanya. We're here to take you home," he tells her gently.

I lay my rifle on the floor and shuck off my jacket and hold it out for her, refraining from making any sudden movements in case she tries to bolt.

"It's still warm," I tell her, keeping my tone low and as soft as I can.

Tanya's chin wobbles as she reaches out with trembling hands and grips my jacket in her tiny fingers.

"Good girl," Joel tells her. "Now snuggle into it."

Panic sweeps over her expression as she drops the jacket to the floor, her head whipping side to side in refusal. Normally, it would be smart of her to refuse. But today's not that day. Her eyes dart from me to Joel then back to me.

An image of Rachel's hollowed face flickers behind my eyelids. I blink it away before it has a chance to consume me.

It would be easy to scoop Tanya up and haul her out of here without her consent. But there's a chance she'll attempt to break free and run, and that would do more harm to her already-fragile state. So, we patiently wait for her to warm up to us. She's been forced to endure unwanted touch enough as it is. And I can't bring myself to scare her beyond what's absolutely necessary.

"My name's Joel. And this is Liam. And there's one more of us out in the hall. His name is Zak. We need to get you out of here before anyone finds out we've come for you, okay?"

She opens her mouth to speak but instead is thrown into a violent coughing fit, her chest rattling from the fluid in her lungs and body shivering from the fever she's no doubt fighting. I glance over my shoulder at Zak who's hovering in the doorway, his medic-trained brain already working out a plan for treating the girl's injuries on the flight home.

When Tanya comes down from coughing, I creep forward and pick my jacket back up, gently draping it over her meek frame and praying the warmth she hasn't felt in weeks will sway her decision to come easily.

"Let's go, little one." I sling my rifle back over my shoulder and move toward her. "I'm going to pick you up," I tell her, carefully scooping one arm beneath her knees and the other around her back, stilling when she tries to shove me away. Her pained cry forms a crevice in the hollow space behind my sternum, and I lift her featherlight body to my chest, keeping her fully cocooned in my jacket. It takes her a minute to realize I'm not hurting her and that she's safe with me, but she eventually nestles into me and sobs quietly.

"Close your eyes, Tanya. We'll have you home in no time."

Fifteen

Alora

MY LIDS CRACK OPEN, and I blink into the darkness, allowing my pupils a moment to adjust. I haven't slept properly in three days—ever since Liam left for Russia. Rachel's been here with me, reassuring me he'll be home soon, but she has no way of knowing if he's dead or alive. If he's injured or safe. And after everything she shared with me, my heart aches for him. I don't know him well enough to say he's deserving of my empathy, but I feel it regardless.

I've tried to numb the feelings with as many lemon drop cocktails as my stomach can handle, but it's been a pointless feat. He's already begun embedding himself into my thoughts.

I roll onto my side and bury my face into the satin-covered pillow, inhaling Liam's lingering scent. Although it's only been a little over a week since we met, I can't help but find comfort in his presence, even if it does contradict everything I believe to be true about men and their motives.

Liam's dangerous and overflowing with unresolved trauma. But he's also loyal to a fault. Protective and honest and literally capable of taking the life of any man who dares cross what he believes to be his to protect. And as it appears, I'm on that list. I just can't understand why.

I relax my mind and begin counting backward from one hundred, visualizing myself painting each number, my brush strokes steady and slow as I let go of the thoughts plaguing my mind. Just as I'm drifting off again, a crashing sound startles me awake and I sit bolt upright, clutching the sheets to my chest as I scan every dark corner of the room for any signs of movement. That's when I spot the soft glow of light escaping from the crack beneath the ensuite door.

My ears strain against the silence. Seconds tick by where my heart beats like a kick drum in my chest. When another loud bang echoes through the walls, I whip the covers off my body and stand on shaky legs, creeping on tippy-toes to the bathroom door.

I listen for a moment longer before gripping the doorknob and slowly turning it. The door parts way and I stand there in stunned silence, my jaw unhinged as I stare at the scene before me.

Liam stands naked in the shower, the hot spray misting off his broad, tattooed back. His spine is arched, and one hand is propped against the glass shower wall, his head bowed and wet hair hanging in front of his face, small drops of water clinging to the strands. I track a lone droplet as it cascades down his wide, muscular chest, zigzagging through the valleys of his abs before reaching the deep V carved between his hips.

My gaze lands on his cock, hard and thick with a large vein running down the bottom of it as he wraps his free hand around the base and strokes himself.

A deep, agonized groan, like that of a pained animal, echoes through the empty room, and my breathing stalls, my heart failing completely and feet weighing me down like lead anchors.

When Liam lifts his lashes and peers at me with those haunted amber eyes, my face heats with embarrassment. His hand stalls briefly, his grip tightening as a bead of precum leaks from the swollen tip. I clench my thighs against the desire pooling in my panties.

But he doesn't make a move to cower away or hide what he's doing. Instead, he swipes his thumb over his tip and strokes himself harder, his wolf eyes locked on mine as he wets his lips and breathes through his mouth. The act is primal and animalistic. He's the hunter and I'm the prey. God, how I want him to eat me alive.

My body sways like there's a rope lassoed around my waist, dragging me into the depths of Liam's depravity. I take a step over the threshold, my bare soles meeting the heated tile of the bathroom floor.

"Liam," I rasp, his name barely a whisper through the pelt of the shower. "Are you okay?"

His eyes flutter shut and his hips rock forward. I've never seen a man masturbate before. And I certainly never imagined it would be so fucking hot. Or maybe it's just this particular man that has me enthralled. The sheer power of his muscles, the light smattering of hair that dusts his heavily tattooed chest, the rise and fall of his big body as he breathes through the pleasure. The clench of his jaw when he cracks his lids and stares at me again.

My feet carry me across the room so I'm standing mere inches from him, nothing but a slab of steamed-up glass and the thin fabric of my sleep shorts and tank top separating us. His breath fogs the pane in front of his face, and my tongue darts out to wet my dry lips. He tracks the movement, and his gaze darkens.

I'm on autopilot as I reach for the shower door, watching Liam's reaction as I step fully clothed inside and let the door swing shut behind me. A confused look enters his expression. But he doesn't stop me.

My fingers skim over his tense back, the silkiness of his skin a stark contrast to the hard planes of his body.

When I dust my fingertips over a jagged scar on his ribs, his hand flies out and catches me around the throat, shoving me back against the shower wall. My breath hitches and my hands fly to his forearm, gripping at him as he pins me in my place. My heart slams over and over, beating wildly as something terrifying possesses him.

"Liam," I choke out, and his expression softens a fraction, his grip loosening just enough that he's not hurting me and I can breathe.

His other hand strokes his cock, fast and hard and angry, as if he's furious with himself for allowing me to see him in such a vulnerable state.

What the hell happened in Russia?

My pajamas absorb the shower spray, but my panties are soaked for an entirely different reason. His touch is rough, then gentle, then rough again. I can't keep up with his sudden mood swings, and I tell him so.

"What do you want, Liam?"

He groans and takes a step into me, my head tipping back and skull pressing against the wall as I stare up at him. His height and size dwarf mine, his strength and power undeniable. Even if I wanted to fight him off, I couldn't. He could snap my neck with one hand if he wanted to.

"You know what I want, Alora," he grates out, his tone laced with desire and just a pinch of anguish.

I swallow against his palm. "Then take it."

He shakes his head, his wet strands sticking to his forehead as his mouth hovers over mine, his hand still pumping his cock.

"No," he tells me. "Not like this."

"Why not?" I whisper, releasing my grip on his forearm and sliding my palms over his broad shoulders and up his neck. I cup his jaw with both hands, feeling his beard, springy and rough, beneath my fingertips.

He drops his forehead to mine, his eyes closing as he jacks himself off. Our breaths mingle between us, and we inhale each other's air. It's not enough to fill my lungs with him. I want to be consumed by him completely.

"Because I'm not in a good place. I'll hurt you." His admission hits me square in the chest, and a piece of my heart breaks off and shrivels up to die.

"You won't." I stretch up onto my toes and brush my lips over his in the softest of kisses. The contact causes every nerve in my body to tingle, and that dull ache in my core intensifies to the point that my hips rock forward. The hand around my throat tightens again, pushing me away as he takes a step back. His eyes flick over my face as if committing this moment to memory. Committing me to memory.

"I'm a monster, Alora."

My head whips side to side as a wave of sadness crashes over me. "No. No, you're not."

I flatten my palms to the wall beside my hips and stare back at him, watching in rapture as he takes his frustrations out on his cock while holding me roughly against the wall by my throat.

He squeezes his eyes shut and fucks his fist like it's somehow wronged him. A whimper escapes me as I stamp my desires down and refuse to beg him to use me instead. Because I *do* want him to use me in the worst way. I want him to unleash whatever torment he's facing and give me everything he has.

My nipples harden with every rise and fall of my chest as I breathe erratically, the wet fabric of my tank top brushing against them, teasing until it's almost painful. I slip my hands beneath the hem of my shirt and brush my thumbs over the hard ridges, moaning as the sensation travels straight to my clit.

Liam's eyes fly open, and he watches my fingers move beneath my shirt. His lips curl into a snarl, as if touching myself is some sort of crime. A crime he wants wholeheartedly to commit himself.

"I want to feel you," I tell him, arching my back and teasing him with another soft moan.

Once again, he shakes his head in refusal, but there's a glimpse of remorse filtering into his eyes, dampening the flames burning behind his irises.

"Touch me, Liam," I whine, praying to god his rough hand slides south of my throat and down into my shorts, touching me where I crave him most.

As if reading my mind, his fingers unwrap from my windpipe and dust featherlight over my collarbone, down my torso, and drift beneath the hem of my top. When I go to lower my hands so he has full access to my body, he halts me.

"No," he growls. "Keep touching yourself like that."

I oblige, drawing circles over my puckered nipples while Liam's fingers splay over my bare ribs. He pushes me back, my spine flattening to the wall behind me.

"Don't move," he instructs, wetting his lips as his hand travels north. He cups the back of my hand with his as I continue to toy with my aching breasts.

I open my mouth to speak, to tell him I want to feel more of him, but he stops me before I have a chance to say a word.

"Don't speak," he adds, his demand leaving no room for protest.

My jaw clicks shut. I can tell he's close to coming, his face shrouded in arousal and hips rocking forward at a quickening pace as he fucks his fist. He drops his forehead to mine again, his eyes pinched tight as he grunts out his release, his warm cum jetting from his body and painting my bare stomach.

"Liam," I moan, my voice thick with desperation. Because that's what Liam does to me. He makes me feel desperate and vulnerable in all the best ways. And fuck if I don't love feeling safe enough to be unfiltered and raw around him.

He releases his cock and guides my arms over my head, pinning my wrists against the wall in one of his hands. He closes the small space between us, his cum smearing between us as he seals his naked body to my clothed one. He holds me there, stretched out in front of him, and dips his face to mine and takes my mouth in a hungry, desperate kiss, his tongue greedy and possessive as it sweeps in and tangles with mine.

Bursts of color explode behind my eyelids as he deepens the kiss, devouring me. Owning me. His mouth is hot and wet and skilled, and I want him to brand every inch of my body the way he's branding my lips.

I whimper in response, my body humming with arousal and every blood cell heating and expanding until I think they might burst like overfilled water balloons.

His other hand roams hungrily over my curves, his fingers digging into the soft swell of my hips and gripping me tight, tugging me roughly against him. I moan into his kiss as he sweeps his thumb over my cum-smeared stomach and lifts it in front of my face before pressing it to my bottom lip.

"Suck," he demands.

I stare wide eyed at him as I wrap my lips around his thumb, sucking it clean and tasting his salty arousal on my tongue for the first time.

He removes his thumb with a pop and grabs the hem of my top and slowly drags it up my body, inch by agonizing inch, exposing my breasts. He slips the soaked fabric over my head, and a renewed hunger flashes across his face as his eyes dart between my hard nipples. He hooks his fingers into my shorts and slowly lowers them down my thighs, along with my panties, the wet cotton clinging to my skin before landing on the floor of the shower with a sopping splat.

Liam's eyes roam all over my body, and he huffs out a shaky breath.

"Fuck, sweetheart," he growls, then wraps me up in his arms, holding me tight as his mouth explores mine.

"I want you," I murmur into the kiss.

He groans, his big, hard body closing in and sandwiching me against the wall. "You shouldn't."

"I know. But I—"

He crushes his mouth to mine and quiets my protest.

When he finally breaks the kiss, he grates out, "I'm not good, Alora," his voice strained and teeth clenched. "People who get close to me only end up hurt."

My heart sinks like a rock in the lake. He truly believes this about himself. I search for the words to say, to tell him he's so much better than he gives himself credit for. To tell him I know what he's capable of. And why he does the things he does.

But all I come up with is, "Then hurt me."

His jaw ticks. Once. Twice. He studies my face. Just when I think he's going to retreat and remove his hands from my body, he spins me around and shoves me against the tile wall, my nipples puckering against the cold, wet surface. My cheek rests against the wall, my wrists bound behind my back in one of Liam's hands.

He kicks my feet apart and brings his lips to my ear, his scruff scraping against my jaw and sending a shiver rolling down my spine.

"You want me to touch you, Alora?"

I nod eagerly. "Yes."

"Fine. I'll touch you, sweetheart. I'm going to finish what I started the other day. I'm going to let you come. But I'm not going to hurt you. And I'm not going to fuck you right now, either. Because once I do, you're mine. And claiming you—possessing you the way I plan to—that's something I'd rather do when I'm fully in control of myself. Because I'm going to make you scream, Alora. Over and over again. And I'm not going to hold back. You'll bleed for me, little thief. And you'll pay for teasing me the way you have. You'll get the pain you're asking for ..." He nips at my earlobe. "But not tonight."

I squeeze my eyes shut and inhale a sharp breath when his fingers delve between my folds. He gathers my wetness and circles my clit with one finger, and my knees buckle from the sensation. I'm panting now, and Liam's hot breath is on my neck, his lips searing my flesh with gentle kisses and nips.

"Liam," I moan when he pushes one long, skilled finger inside of me. He adds a second shortly after, stretching me and crooking his fingers and stroking a deliciously sensitive spot inside of me I hadn't known existed until now.

He uses his thumb to apply pressure to my clit, teasing and rubbing and flicking it until I'm writhing, desperately rocking against his hand. I can feel my juices dripping out of me, coating the insides of my thighs and Liam's fingers. Heat coils around the base of my spine, a pressure building low in my belly.

He bites down on my shoulder and I cry out, my orgasm barreling through me unexpectedly, the lines between pleasure and pain blurring until I'm not sure which is which anymore. Wave after wave, my pussy throbs around his fingers, gripping him and aching for more. Every nerve in my body sizzles and zaps, the heat around my spine dissipating through my core and consuming me whole.

"Christ, Alora," he groans, and I feel his hard cock pressed against my backside.

My body trembles before it goes slack, my orgasm subsiding and breathing ragged as Liam licks and sucks and kisses my neck and shoulders and back, showing me a tenderness I don't deserve.

When he releases my wrists and steps away, I turn around and prop myself up against the wall. He stares down at me, frustration painted all over his handsome face. He leaves the shower without a word, snatching a clean towel off the rack before disappearing out of the bathroom completely.

And I crumple to the floor and wonder what the fuck I've just gotten myself into.

Sixteen

Liam

I've spent every second since our moment in the shower wishing I could go back in time, wrap Alora's legs around my hips, and drive my cock deep inside her the way her emerald eyes were begging me to do. But instead of taking what she offered, I've been avoiding her like the fucking plague while she traipses around my cabin wearing her ripped jeans, cropped T-shirts, and skimpy little sleep outfits while she paces anxiously and gnaws on her fingernails. She's bored out of her mind and probably itching to get back to her life. But her days of stealing and conning men are up.

I warned her that once I'm inside of her, she'd be mine. But that was a fucking lie. Because Alora already belongs to me. It's just a matter of time before I cave and officially stake my claim.

Exhaling a frustrated breath, I flick the signal light and round the final corner to Alora's apartment building and park my truck on the street. After a long night of tossing and turning in my guest room while Alora slept in my bed—*on my fucking pillow*—I agreed to bring her back to her apartment to pick up a few more things so she's more comfortable.

Alora unbuckles her seat belt and turns to the door to hop out. But I halt her with my hand around her bicep, my gut swirling with unease and something else I can't nail down. Something ... palpable.

She stills, her face angled so just her profile is visible. The same angle I first saw her from across the crowded casino. And it still stops my heart the way it did that day.

"I go in first," I tell her.

She tucks her bottom lip between her teeth and rolls her eyes. "Fine."

She climbs out of the truck, hopping down onto both feet and swinging the door shut. She's a shortstop, and my truck isn't small. But the way she maneuvers herself with such ease—like climbing out of big vehicles is something she's a pro at—is sexy as hell. I've never been much for the ditzy, girly type who pretend to be incapable of taking care of themselves. And Alora's exactly the opposite of that. It makes me hard as hell for her. Although she's incredible in a skimpy dress and her face painted in bold makeup, too.

I snatch her hand in mine, lacing our fingers and hauling her across the street to the busted front entrance of the building. The shattered glass that's still not repaired sends home the fact that she's better off staying with me. I swing the broken door open and tuck her behind me as we take the stairs up to the third floor. Holding her hand feels right, so I do it without shame. And she lets me.

"Liam," she whisper-shouts. But I don't stop moving. I'm on edge, my instincts firing on all cylinders. "Liam," she repeats a little louder, but we keep climbing. I reach for my handgun tucked into the waistband of my jeans. "Liam," she yells this time, jerking me to a stop.

She stands a step below me, her wide eyes staring up at me in confusion.

"Why are you being weird right now? And why the hell are you pulling your gun out?"

I glower down at her, unsure of what to say. That I'm feeling a little off? That my gut is telling me something's up?

I grit my teeth and give her hand a reassuring squeeze, then continue climbing without responding to her questions. She mumbles a string of colorful curse words, all of which are directed at me and my strange behavior. But she does as I instruct, keeping her front glued to my back.

When we hit the third floor and pad down the carpeted hall to her door, I discover the source of my unease.

"What the hell?" Alora screeches, trying and failing to bolt around me and to her busted-in door.

"Keep quiet," I tell her, shoving her back behind me as we scale the wall and I peer around the corner into her living space.

Her fingers grip my shirt tighter, and she releases a small whimper as we step into her ransacked apartment. Her hands tremble, her breathing ragged with hurt and anger.

I drag her along behind me, broken glass crunching beneath our shoes as we move through each room to clear the place. When I'm satisfied whoever broke in is long gone, I release her. She pushes past me, stepping over shredded and slashed paintings and the contents of her kitchen drawers and little cabinet her small television sat on across from her couch.

I drag a hand through my hair and blow out a breath, following her through her upheaved home. She races into her bedroom and drops to her knees in front of her closet. Tears leak down her face, staining her flushed cheeks as she stares down at the hole in the floor.

Her shoulders slump in defeat and she sobs into her hands, her cries slicing into my heart like daggers and ripping my soul from my body.

My feet move on their own accord, and I find myself squatting behind her, my hand hovering over her back as I fight to find the words to say. Before I have a chance to speak, she turns and throws herself into my arms, her cries muffled by my chest, her tears soaking into the fabric of my T-shirt. I topple back onto my ass and haul her onto my lap, cradling her like a child, stroking her hair and shushing her.

I stare at the empty hole, wondering what the hell was in there that has her so devastated. It occurs to me that I know very little about Alora Berkley beyond the factual stuff Sloane dug up for me.

I replay her life in my head and try to piece it together as I rock her in my arms.

Her father was a deadbeat and abandoned her and her mother when she was a child. Her mother raised her alone until she was fifteen. Looks like she also spent a lot of time with her maternal grandfather—deceased. Then her stepfather, a defense lawyer, came into the picture and took Alora and her mother into his home. Gave them somewhat of a lavish life. Alora went off to college and studied art and, by all appearances, is incredibly talented and hasn't really put her skills and passion to work. She dropped out right before graduation and worked a bunch of odd jobs, never really settling down into a career. Then two years ago, she came home from her shift at a drive-through oil change shop and found her mother dead, an empty bottle of pills lying in bed beside her. An autopsy confirmed it was a suicide by overdose.

There's always the chance she's running from her past. But beyond using a fake name for her apartment and when she's hustling, she hasn't bothered to hide her identity. She owns a cell phone and bank account in her name. Has a valid driver's license that she renewed last year. There's no evidence she's on the run. No criminal record. So it's far more likely she's just unsettled and is afraid of commitment of any sort.

A free-spirited drifter who believes stealing from rich men will somehow balance the scales. Like a modern-day Robin Hood.

Alora's sobs fade to sniffles and hiccups, and she finally lifts her face and peers up at me with bloodshot eyes. I sweep her hair behind her ear and brush my lips over her forehead.

"What was in there, Alora?" I ask cautiously, a little concerned she's going to try to take off running again.

She sniffs and shakes her head.

"Alora." I hook her chin with my forefinger and force her to look at me. "Tell me what was in there. What were you hiding?"

She shrugs her shoulders and stares at my tear-soaked chest. "It was nothing. Just some stupid things of my mother's that I kept." She gazes back up at me with watery doe eyes and clamps down on her bottom lip to keep it from wobbling.

"Tell me."

She hesitates, her glassy eyes darting between mine, searching for evidence she can trust me with whatever secret she's harboring behind her elaborately constructed walls.

"Cash, mostly. And my mother's journal and a couple old flight tickets." When her jaw clamps shut and she shakes her head again, I know I'm not getting anything more from her right now.

◆○◆

I pace the width of my garage at my cabin, my boots heavy on the concrete and fingers tugging at my hair. After Alora had her meltdown on her bedroom floor, I hauled her back out to my truck and brought her back here. She paced for a little while then disappeared into the bathroom. When she reemerged with her eyes red and puffy and tired, she asked if she could get some fresh air. I lead her out onto the back deck so she could watch the sun set, and she's been out there ever since, staring off at the horizon and hugging her knees to her chest.

My mind flips back and forth from the Petrovs to the break and enter at Alora's apartment, wondering briefly if they're connected. If perhaps Ivan and Viktor Petrov are on the hunt for her after all. Sloane hacked into The Afterlife's surveillance and wiped it all clean, so if they've seen her face and know who she is, it's because of an entirely different reason.

My phone buzzes in my pocket and I nearly snap. Forcing myself to calm down, I retrieve my phone from my pocket and answer the call with a clipped out, "What?"

Sloane's words slam into me. "I've got a hit on Viktor."

I freeze and stare numbly at Alora's faded old Corvette. She doesn't know it's here yet, and I'm struggling to find the right time to tell her. It's risky, giving her a means to drive straight out of here. But I also get the sense this car holds some sentimental value. And I can't bring myself to keep it from her.

"Where?"

"Take a wild guess."

"Sloane," I say with warning.

She sighs and pops her gum. "Always so serious." More incessant chewing. "The Afterlife."

Ice-cold fury injects itself straight into my veins, and I ball my free hand at my side. This was exactly what we hoped for—that we'd watch the club from a safe distance and that one of the Petrovs would eventually pay it a visit. It feels as if the chips are falling into place.

"Have you bounced this off anyone else yet?"

"No. Thought you'd like to be the first to know."

I nod, even though Sloane can't see me. "So, what's the plan?"

"I'm glad you asked." She taps away on her keyboard. "Let's surprise this motherfucker."

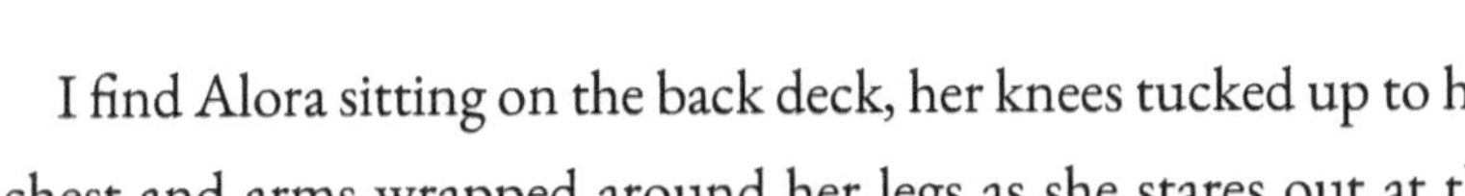

I find Alora sitting on the back deck, her knees tucked up to her chest and arms wrapped around her legs as she stares out at the setting sun. I pause in the doorway to take in the view. Not of the vast yard or thick tree line at the back of my property. But of her.

Full, pouty lips. Face free of makeup. Long black hair tied up in a messy bun on the top of her head. She's wearing a black tank top that clings to her lean body and a pair of cutoff jean shorts that show off her long, toned legs. My watch has crept halfway up her forearm, light bouncing off the face of it and winking at me. And that little butterfly tattoo on her ankle that pops into my head every so often is staring at me like I've lost my goddamn mind.

I think maybe I have.

I clear my throat, and Alora angles her head to peer back at me.

"Hey," she says softly, her voice strained. She looks exhausted.

"I have something for you," I tell her before gesturing for her to follow me through the house.

When I lead her into the garage and flip the lights on, she stands with her feet planted firmly on the concrete as she stares unblinking at her car. I fold my arms over my chest and lean against the wall, watching in rapture as she circles the antique Corvette and drags a finger over the curves of its classic body. The slow, seductive way she does it causes my dick to twitch in my jeans.

Everything she does has that effect on me.

"Why'd you do this?" she asks, knowing damn well that I did it for her.

"Because you need something to keep you busy while you're here."

She nods slowly, but I can see her contemplating something. "And how long exactly will I be here?"

"Until you're no longer in danger."

She nails me to the wall with a flat look. "You mean until you hack the last two Petrovs up into bits and pieces."

"I don't hack people up, Alora."

She rolls her eyes and blows out a dramatic puff of air so long it could give flight to a blimp. "Potato potahto."

"You're frustrated."

She laughs then begins pacing, stealing the odd glance at the car. "Any sane person would be frustrated with this situation."

"Any sane person would be huddled in a corner, clutching their knees and rocking," I correct her. "But not you."

She skids to a stop and points a finger at me. "Are you calling me crazy?"

I close the space between us, backing her into the side of her car and bracing both of my hands on the roof.

"You're off your goddamn rocker, sweetheart." She glowers up at me in stunned silence, her eyes flicking all over my face, studying me. Probably trying to decide if she'd prefer to stab me with a screwdriver or shove my hand into the garbage disposal.

I'd let her do both if it meant seeing her smile again.

She folds her arms over her chest, forcing a few inches of space between us that I don't fucking like. We're standing almost toe-to-toe, but my size and skillset are no match for her ability to weaken my resolve with just a look. She holds the key to my monster's cage, and right now, she's dangling it right in front of my eyes, testing my patience and willpower.

"Well, crazy or not, I have some questions."

I grunt. "Imagine my surprise."

Her brows furrow low at my brute response. I don't particularly care for chitchat and the like. But for her? I'll tell her anything she wants to know. I'd slash my own wrists if she asked to see the color of my blood. I'd split my chest wide open if she wanted to know what it felt like to hold my cold, dead heart in the palm of her hand.

"How old are you?" she asks, surprising me a little.

"Thirty-four."

"Ooooh. Old man." She smirks. "Ever been married?"

"Not even close."

"Girlfriend?"

"I don't keep women, Alora."

"You don't *keep* them," she echoes, cocking a brow. "As if they're objects you can possess."

"That's not what I meant."

"But it's what you said."

I release a ragged breath and drag a hand through my hair. "Christ, woman. You know damn well I don't have a girlfriend. I wouldn't be touching you if I did."

She smiles sweetly at me, and my world rights itself. "Now look who's frustrated."

Our eyes are locked, and it takes every fiber of my being to not spin her around and fuck her against her car. She angles her head at me, sensing the shift in the atmosphere.

"You look like you have something to tell me," she says with skepticism.

I decide there's no sense in beating around the bush. Alora's strong and can handle the truth. And I'll never lie to her.

"Something came up and we need to head into the city tonight."

"Some*thing*? Or some*one*?"

"Viktor Petrov's in town. Probably searching for his missing brother. But there's a chance he's here in search of you as well."

She blinks. "Me?"

I nod curtly. "You're a target, Alora. You were with his brother before he took a nice long dirt nap. You lifted a watch off his wrist at a casino. And someone broke into your apartment."

"That—" She pauses, her brows sinking low over her eyes, the color of her irises darkening to a rich forest green as she falls deep into thought. "Viktor thinks I had something to do with Ilya's death." It's a statement, not a question. So I don't respond. "And now he wants revenge."

"It's a possibility. But we'll get to him first."

She nods in understanding, not an ounce of doubt in her expression. "And what exactly am I supposed to do while you're in the city?"

"You're coming with me. You'll stay in a surveillance truck with Sloane while we go in for Viktor."

"You're not locking me up with your sister again?"

"Not this time."

She blows out a breath. "Okay," is all she says. But I can see her clever little mind working overtime. "When do we leave?"

"In an hour."

"And where exactly in the city are we going?"

I clench my molars, less than happy about bringing her anywhere near the building she witnessed me murder a man in.

"The Afterlife."

Seventeen

Alora

"So, Alora," Sloane drawls, her eyes reflecting the blue light of the mounted screens in the back of the armored surveillance truck we're seated in. "Have you and Liam had sex yet?"

If I had a drink, I'd be spitting it out all over the side of Sloane's face.

"No," I tell her plainly, trying and failing at not sounding like a cranky bitch. But the truth is, I'm all strung out and this whole situation is giving me a case of the jitters.

Sloane chews thoughtfully on her gum as she taps away on her keyboard. "You plan on it anytime soon?"

Jesus. This woman is as subtle as a sledgehammer.

"I don't think so."

"Huh." She snaps her gum between her teeth. "I was kind of hoping you would. The big guy could use a little lovin'." She angles her head and peers over at me, a bright smile on her face, her white teeth practically glowing in the dark. I hate her for being so badass and beautiful.

I laugh awkwardly and swat the air. "Don't be ridiculous."

She nods, blows a giant pink bubble, and inhales it back into her mouth. The only way to describe Sloane is like if G.I. Joe and Barbie banged it out and had a baby. She's gorgeous, all harsh features and tanned skin. Her hair is dyed fire-engine red and pulled back into a sleek ponytail today. Her eyes are always a different color from the contacts she wears. I'm not sure if they serve a purpose replacing glasses or if it's just one of her many admirable quirks. But despite her beauty and petite frame and sweet tone of voice, she's fucking terrifying. Especially when she's dressed in her camo fatigues and a tank top that leaves little to the imagination.

She doesn't hide who she is, and I respect her for it. Maybe even like her a little more because of it.

She beams at me again, and I relax just a fraction. Except now my brain is swimming with thoughts of her and Liam. She seems more protective of him than she is of the rest of the guys. And the way he looks at her ... It's like they share a special bond. A secret, perhaps.

"Did you and Liam ever ... you know."

Fuck, Al. Spit the damn words out.

"You're asking if Liam and I ever hooked up?" I nod, and she bursts out laughing. "Oh, honey no." She laughs some more, and I feel my cheeks heat with embarrassment. "Liam's like my brother," she reassures me. "Besides, I don't have time for men. They're all just a bunch of cry babies with overinflated egos."

A laugh bubbles out of me, and I swallow the jealousy that was threatening to rear its ugly head.

When I come down from the humor of her statement, Sloane's eyes narrow suspiciously on me, the wheels in her head turning over. But she doesn't say anything further. Just turns back around and stares at the screen.

She speaks into the little device hooked onto her collar. "Target acquired. Back left corner of the lounge." She's back in full-blown operator mode now.

My eyes slam to the image of Viktor Petrov sitting at a booth in The Afterlife with a blonde woman, and all the blood leaves my head in a whoosh. Rose—pretty, naive Rose—is seated beside him in one of her tiny pink getups, her head tipped back laughing as her long, wavy hair tumbles around her shoulders.

"Rose," I blurt out, clambering to my feet and joining Sloane directly in front of the monitors.

It's not that I forgot Rose works here. In fact, it's been weighing heavy on my mind ever since Liam told me the Petrovs own the club. It's that I didn't expect her to be cozied up next to one of the world's most infamous human traffickers.

"That's my friend." Friend may not be the right word, but that doesn't matter right now.

Sloane's eyes slide to mine briefly before she nods once in ac-knowledgement, a silent reassurance that nothing bad will happen to the sweet woman who lives across the hall from me and occasionally sells the watches I steal.

Liam's voice comes in over the speaker, his deep baritone soothing the worry creeping in around my heart and squeezing. "I want him alone."

Sloane taps away on her keyboard. "I'm on it."

Seconds tick by where I watch Rose fiddle with a button on Viktor's dress shirt. He leans into her and murmurs something in her ear, but I can't make out what he's saying.

He stands. Rose stands. They start walking. And now my palms are sweating profusely while my heart slams in my chest.

"No, no, no," I chant over and over, pleading with Sloane to hurry the fuck up and somehow get Rose the hell away from Viktor. "He'll hurt her. You need to do something."

"I've got this, girl. Sit down," Sloane instructs softly. But I can't just sit down and watch this unfold. Instead, I hover, breathing down Sloane's neck as she does whatever the fuck she does.

The screen flickers and another image appears, this one of the hall leading to the Champagne Room. Viktor's following Rose, his face dipped low and eyes glued to her ass as she walks confidently in front of him, completely unaware of the monster she's about to vanish behind closed doors with.

There are no cameras in the Champagne Room. I know this firsthand because Rose told me the club doesn't record private dances out of respect for the patrons. They disappear behind the door.

I slam my hand down on the table and spit out, "Get her out of there. Now!"

Sloane shoos me away like a pesky fly, her cool demeanor grating on my last nerve. Panic seeps into my pores, poisoning every one of my cells.

I'm going to sell your used-up pussy to the lowest fucking bidder. Because if there's one thing I've learned, it's that the ones willing to pay the least are the cruelest.

Fuck this. I'm not waiting around. The last Petrov to sit in that room tried to rape me. And I refuse to let Rose, the nicest person I've ever fucking met, fall victim to them the way I nearly did.

I turn on a heel and bolt for the back door, pushing the lever and bursting out of the rear of the armored truck. The cool evening air slaps against my heated skin as I pump my legs toward the front entrance of the club. I hear Sloane shouting at me from the truck, but I'm fast and I know she can't leave her post on surveillance.

I shove through the steel doors and into the stifling club. Swarms of suits and boisterous laughter assault my eyes and ears. The DJ's animated voice bellows over the speakers. Strobe lights splice through the crowd.

The memory of leaving the Champagne Room after Liam stabbed Ilya to death causes a wave of nausea to roll through me. But I tuck my head down and shoulder my way through the lounge, not caring that I'm completely out of place in here with my ripped jeans, worn-out sneakers and cropped eighties band T-shirt. I feel the gazes of strange men and a few curious strippers on me as

I beeline it for the hall leading to the room Rose is locked in with a fucking monster.

A flash of movement—of something big and angry—catches in my peripherals. And I know without looking that it's Liam. And he's pissed off and charging straight for me. No doubt Sloane tattled on me and told him I'm in here and about to throw a wrench in their plan.

My feet move faster. My strides grow longer. I'm running now, desperate to get to Rose.

But just as I break through the crowd and into the dimly lit hallway, the Champagne Room door cracks open, and soft, feminine laughter drifts through the air. I freeze, my feet planted in the plush burgundy carpet as my pulse beats loudly in my temples.

Rose steps out from behind the steel, flipping her hair and giggling innocently. "I'll be right back with your drink, honey," she says sweetly before she closes the door.

Her blue eyes find mine from down the hall, and she falters for the briefest of moments. She struts toward me, all blonde hair and sparkly pink bikini and long legs.

"Rose," I rush out breathlessly. "You can't be in there with that man. He's—"

Her lips hook into a smirk as she closes the space between us and pulls me in for a quick hug. "I know," she whispers in my ear. "But it's fine. I promise. It's all part of a plan."

I rear back and stare at her, blinking a few times. "What—"

Her eyes dart over my shoulder. I feel Liam approaching me from behind. Solid heat presses against my backside, a wall of muscle and rage.

"He's all yours," Rose says sweetly to Liam before playfully bumping my hip with hers and sauntering out to the lounge as if this is all fucking normal.

I spin around to find Liam towering over me. All dark hair, blazing wolf eyes, and palpable waves of tension radiating off him.

"What the fuck is going on?" I blurt out, confusion and irritation slashing through me like a hot knife through butter.

He wraps his big hand around my bicep and hauls me down the hall, past the Champagne Room, and out the back exit. I jerk away from him the second I step out into the dark alleyway.

"What the hell, Liam?"

"I told you to stay in the truck with Sloane," he growls.

"Yeah, you did. And I would have. But Rose…" I shake my head and close my eyes.

Inhale. Exhale. Don't kick him in the shin for being a giant asshole.

My eyes flash open to find his.

In a calmer tone, I demand, "Explain."

He opens his mouth to speak, but the back door flies open, effectively ending our conversation.

Out steps Joel and Zak with an unconscious Viktor Petrov in tow. Zak shoots me a wry smile while Joel tips his head at me.

"Take your time, brother. He'll be out for a while," Zak says, shooting me one last smirk before him and Joel disappear out the end of the alley and into the dark.

I return my attention to Liam, whose anger is simmering on low behind his amber eyes. He backs me against the wall, his hand curling around my throat—gently but warningly—and brings his face within an inch of mine. I glare up at him, daring him to test me right now. Sweetwater put Rose at risk. And I'm furious.

"You could have blown it for us," he snarls. "Do something stupid like that again, and I'll take you over my knee and spank you into next fucking week. Got it?"

"Put my friend in danger again, and I'll kick you in the dick and run."

His lip twitches, his grip tightening around my throat. I bring my hands to his thick, corded forearm, the Rolex around my wrist sliding up to my elbow and calming the storm brewing inside me. But with Liam's lips mere inches from mine and his whiskey eyes darting over my face before fixating on my mouth, I find myself clenching my thighs together as heat settles low in my core.

His lips brush over mine, dusting them with a soft kiss. I release a strangled whimper and dig my fingertips into his flesh, eliciting a low groan from him.

"You can run, Alora, but I'll always find you. And when it comes to Rose, we hired her to lure Viktor into the Champagne Room so we could take him out quietly without anyone seeing. She was never in any real danger. You have my word."

I swallow, my throat working against the palm of Liam's hand.

"So, now what?"

He releases me and backs away, the air between us thick and hot.

"Now I have work to do."

Eighteen

Liam

JOEL AND I WASTE no time hauling Viktor Petrov's limp, waste-of-flesh body down into the basement of headquarters. Alora's upstairs, her bare feet wearing a groove in the floors as she paces anxiously while Sloane keeps an eye on her. I hate that she's here for this. That she's privy to what's happening down here. But I can't trust her to be alone at this point. So she's remaining under the watchful eye of the team huntress while I do something I've been yearning to do for years.

I lock the soundproof door and flick on the single bulb dangling over the stainless table in the center of the room. The place is familiar and comfortable, and I have ample room to do my best work. I drop Viktor's body onto the steel slab and strap him down. Joel watches me closely, his piercing blue eyes shifting from me to Petrov to the wall of torture devices I've mostly handcrafted myself. But those devices will all remain untouched tonight. Because I made a promise to myself when Rachel went missing: the Petrovs will all die beneath the cold steel of the knife she gifted me when I moved up the ranks in the Navy.

I know what my teammate is thinking. That I'm twisted and enjoy this shit. But the truth is, I fucking hate every second of it. The screaming. The stench of piss when their bladders release. The nightmares that often visit me afterward.

But despite the fact I don't want it, I *need* it. I was built for it. Trained to hunt, maim, and kill. And it's become a source of stability in my life. A feeling I can rely on.

I glance over my shoulder at Joel.

"Go home to Stella and the kids. I've got this," I tell him.

He sweeps a hand through his hair and blows out a breath. "I'm not leaving you alone with him, brother." He takes a seat in a chair against the wall and settles in for what's to come as I loom over Viktor and watch in fascination as his eyes flutter open and realization settles in.

"Good morning," I greet him sardonically, my fingertips pulsing with adrenaline and heartbeat picking up speed.

"Wh-who are you?" he stammers, his voice raspy and Russian accent thick. His instant fear scratches an itch nothing else can quite reach. I think of Rachel. Of little Tanya Richardson. Of all the other women and children we've saved and lost.

Make him scream.

Closing my eyes and exhaling a calming breath, I regain my focus and tell him truthfully, "I'm your worst fucking nightmare."

Make him bleed.

I drag the tip of my blade down the side of Viktor's face. Blood bubbles from the deep gash and a sick thrill moves through me like an undertow, violently swirling beneath my cool, calm surface.

He garbles out a string of nonsensical words, pleading to me for mercy on his cold, black soul. I'll show him no such thing.

Make him pay.

I don't hold back, flaying his skin from his body, slicing and dicing and dumping ice water over his head every time he threatens to pass out. I inject him with adrenaline to keep his body humming and nerves sensitive. His warm, thick blood coats my hands, tiny splatters of it decorating my bare chest and stomach as I rein in the urge to drive my blade deep into his heart and end his miserable existence.

Every scream, every fucking cry for help, acts as a sedative to the monster inside me. Every inch of skin I remove from his body a satisfying stroke to my rage. Soothing. Calming. Fucking *everything*.

"Did you show Tanya any mercy when you robbed her of her innocence in front of a camera?" I tap the photo of the girl we pulled out of Russia that's tucked into the frame of the mirror looming directly over Viktor's horizontal body. "What about this girl?" I tap another photo and bring my face within inches of his, sneering when his rancid breath reaches my nose. "Or what about my baby sister? Surely you remember her." I point to a photo of Rachel, and my monster roars to life inside me, my demons chanting and egging him on.

Pure depraved destruction is what's about to unfold.

His snake eyes blow wide as he puts the pieces together. "Th-that wasn't me."

I hear Joel grunt in the background then shift in his seat. But he remains quiet otherwise, having seen me at work countless times before.

Angling my head, I drag the point of my blade down Viktor's narrow chest, the hair smattering his torso now tinged a shade of brown from blood that's been exposed to air. We've been at this a little while now, and I'm still nowhere near finished with him. I slice lengthwise down his sternum, not deep enough to cause any real damage. Only deep enough to inflict pain and induce an incredible amount of fear.

Viktor's pleas escalate to wails and an attempt at bargaining with the rage-filled man hovering over him.

"I-I have resources. I can get you an-anything you want."

I don't respond, and my silence causes him to grow more anxious as terror rips through him the way I desperately want to.

"Money. I have money. Lots of it. I can make you a rich man. J-just let me go."

With a flick of my wrist, I split Viktor's flesh open between his thumb and forefinger. His screams are absorbed by the thick concrete walls surrounding us. It's music to my fucking ears.

"I have money. *Lots of it.*" I match his arrogant tone. "What I want cannot be purchased."

Leaning down, I snarl in his face, "I want justice for every woman and child you've ever fucking touched. But since the system we rely on is broken, I've decided to seek it out another way.

I want you to scream the way they did. I want to hear the sounds of every one of your bones snapping like twigs. I want to watch you bleed slowly until your organs shut down, one at a time, and you take your final breath. And then I'm going to hunt down your sick fuck of a father and do the same to him." I slice another web of flesh between his fingers and he screams. "And only when the fish are feeding off all three of your filthy, rotting corpses will I feel that justice has been served."

Four and a half more hours pass where I carve Viktor's body up into a bloody, glorified version of Swiss cheese, his cries and agonized moans a lullaby soothing the roaring chaos inside me. By the time I'm done, his intestines are spilling out around him, dangling from the stainless table he's sprawled on. His genitals are in a bowl beside his head, along with all twenty of his fingers and toes.

And just as I knew it would, the moment he takes his final breath, the chanting in my head subsides, the monster raging within me quieted by the euphoria of revenge.

Two Petrovs down. One to go.

Joel calls for a cleanup crew while I use the shower in the basement of headquarters to wash Viktor's blood from my body, then change into a spare set of clothes I keep here for times like this.

When I head back up to the main floor, I follow the sweet sound of Alora's laughter to the kitchen, surprised to find her completely relaxed and gabbing away with Sloane as they sit on opposite ends of the small dining table. The space between them is littered with empty beer bottles, and I feel a strange pull in the pit of my stomach.

Seeing Alora here, joking with Sloane and seemingly completely in her element, does something to me.

Sloane's eyes move to me as I hover in the doorway. "Hey, big guy. All finished up down there?"

I nod once, fixing my gaze on Alora as she turns around in her chair and smiles crookedly at me.

Christ. She's drunk.

"Liam," she chirps. "Come have a drink with us." She pats the chair beside her. "Sloane was just telling me how she met you guys."

I glower at the only female member of Sweetwater. "Was she, now."

"Yeah." Alora hiccups. "She wanted to know if you still have the lucky underwear you used to wear around base camp when you were training." Sloane snorts, then takes another swig of beer. Her words are a little slurred, but not terrible. "You know … the ones with the little yellow smiley faces on them."

Sloane quirks a brow at me, her lips hooked into a cocky grin.

I stomp over to Alora, pluck the beer bottle from her hand, and finish the rest of the drink in one long pull.

"Let's go."

Emerald orbs stare up at me, her brows knitted and eyes glassy. It's nearly two in the morning, and it's time for her to get some rest after an eventful night. She folds her arms across her chest and draws her face into a pout.

"I'd rather stay with my new bestie, Sloane."

I glance at Sloane, who's smiling now. She shrugs. "What can I say? We bonded."

Groaning, I scoop Alora up into my arms. She lets out a little yelp then flings her arms around my neck and kicks her feet playfully.

"Guess we're leaving. Bye, Sloanie bologna," she hollers over her shoulder as I shoot my teammate one final glare before storming out of headquarters.

I slide her into the passenger seat of my truck, reaching across her body to buckle her in. Her fingers delve into my damp hair, tugging at my scalp. I freeze and lift my gaze to hers, our faces inches apart.

She wets her lips, her eyelids heavy with exhaustion.

"Alora," I grate out.

"Liam," she mimics, her eyes fixating on my mouth. "Kiss me."

I swallow, wanting to do just that. But she's intoxicated, and I've had a long fucking night. My head isn't straight, and I still have far too much adrenaline coursing through my system from the hours I just spent torturing Viktor.

I pull back, Alora's hands dropping into her lap as she rests her head on the seat and peers at me with hooded eyes, disappointment leeching into her inebriated expression.

I check to make sure every part of her is tucked away before gently closing her door and rounding the hood to the driver's side. I slide in behind the wheel and glance over at her again.

It's a matter of seconds before her lips are parted, small puffs of air leaving her mouth as she falls into a deep alcohol-induced sleep.

I make the hour drive out of the city and up to my cabin, carrying Alora inside and setting the alarm system before laying her down in my bed. I gently remove her shoes and pull a blanket over her body, then I sit in the chair in the corner of the room and watch her. Only when I'm certain she's not going to vomit do I make my way to the opposite end of my cabin and fall into my guest bed, sleep coming for me almost immediately.

Along with every routine nightmare that visits me after a kill.

Nineteen

Alora

*I*STARE DOWN INTO *the rectangular hole carved into the earth as my hand hovers in the air before me. I pry my fingers open and drop a loose clump of soil on top of the cherry casket. The priest rambles on at my side, but I don't hear a word of it because none of this feels real. It's as if I'm suspended in time, all sounds and feelings drowned by a numbness that only the death of my mother can bring.*

"Goodbye, Mama. I'll be seeing you." It's barely a whisper, a cool autumn breeze sweeping in and carrying my words away.

I lift my tear-filled eyes from the wooden box my beloved mother is resting peacefully in and stare at my stepfather, Charles, across from me. Unlike me, his eyes are dry and his expression is stern and unforgiving. His cold demeanor solidifies that he never really loved her. Their marriage was one of convenience. She was a woman in need who would go to immense lengths to have someone financially stable at her side. Someone she could rely on to take care of her and her daughter. So, when he came along with his fat wallet and polished good looks and chose her as his wife, her fate was sealed.

It should be him in that box. Not her.

I wonder why he even bothered to come, but then remember that he has an image to uphold.

I blame him for her death. If he hadn't drowned her in his sexual indiscretions and threatened to take everything from her if she left him, then she wouldn't have sunken into such a deep depression.

I spare the casket one final glance then turn and walk away. I don't bother with goodbyes because I'm tired of feigning a care in the world of what people think of me.

"Alora. Where are you going?" Charles calls out to me.

Without looking back, I flip him the bird and keep moving, dead leaves crunching beneath my shoes as I saunter through the cemetery. I hear the whispers from the people at my back as I put distance between myself and my mother's corpse as it's lowered into the ground. I don't care that I'm being rude or disrespectful. Me witnessing it won't serve her in the afterlife, and it certainly won't aid in the grieving process.

And I don't need any more fuel to feed my rage. I have plenty of that already. So much, in fact, that I need to disappear before I do something irrational. Not that I could commit to taking action. Sticking with things has always been something I struggle with. And now that my mother is gone, I have nothing tethering me to this place. It's time for me to move on from here.

I approach the waiting cab and a shiver rolls down my spine. I fucking hate cemeteries. They're loaded with ghosts and ominous energy.

Ignoring the tingling sensation creeping across my skull, I slide into the back seat of the car and instruct the driver to take me home.

Resting my head against the cool, tinted window, I watch the trees whip by, one after the other. I don't know what my future holds, but one thing's for certain: my life has been flipped upside down and inside out. Charles is the only family I have left, and he's nothing more than a violent storm of chaos and ruin. It's time I disappear and take cover before he sucks me under the way he did my mother. I'm a coward for the decision I've made, but I'm also smart enough to know that there's no winning. There's no coming out on top.

There's no justice because the system is corrupt and broken. He's the reason she chose to end her life. And that makes him just as guilty as the vile criminals he defends.

The car rolls up to the front of my stepfather's home, and I clamber out of the back seat to make my way inside. I close the door behind me and press my spine into the solid wood at my back, taking a few calming breaths and blinking away the tears that threaten to fall.

It's been three days since I found my mother's cold, stiff body lying still in bed with an empty bottle of pills next to her. And I haven't had dry eyes since. But that ends now. Because crying won't solve a fucking thing.

Kicking my heels off at the door, I pad barefoot to the bar and drag a lazy finger over the mahogany countertop. Browsing through the collection of bottles, I uncork a bottle of Mama's favorite tequila and pour a generous glass. Bringing it to my nose, I inhale the earthy scent. Normally, she'd mix this with lime and ice and whatever else goes into margaritas. But right now, I need something strong and undiluted.

I bring the glass to my lips and taste the alcohol. Deciding I'd thoroughly enjoy getting shit-faced off it, I take my glass, the bottle, and grab a blanket from the linen closet and make my way outside to the backyard, dropping into a lounge chair and stretching out like a cat beneath the thick, warm flannel fabric. On weekends and holidays when I'd return from university, this is where my mother and I would gather, talking about things that don't really matter. Like how my classes are going, what paintings I'm working on, and all the places I'd like to travel someday.

But whenever I'd ask her about her life and how she's doing, she'd hem and haw before redirecting the conversation back to me again. For years, I watched the light in her eyes slowly dim out until there was nothing left but emptiness and pain. He was unfaithful to her and she knew it. But that wasn't the worst part. The worst parts were his business decisions and who he was getting wrapped up with. The criminal cases he was accepting were growing more and more dangerous. She often wrote about them in her journal. Along with the threats he'd utter when she confronted him about it.

And as much as she raised me to be strong willed and independent, she was neither of those things. She was soft and weak and tired of fighting for measly scraps from a man who had promised her the world on a silver platter.

Tears prick at the corner of my eyes, and I gulp down half the glass of tequila, the alcohol burning my nose on the way down.

I stuff my hand into my pocket and retrieve the two crumpled pieces of paper I've been carrying around with me ever since I found her body—the flight tickets she surprised me with. My fingers brush over the fine print of the seat numbers and the date of departure—tomorrow.

But she chose to leave this earth. To leave me. And as much as the desire for revenge burns through my veins, I'll never have it. So instead, I'll pack up and run the way she should have the first time he wronged her.

I know Charles will attempt to buy my affection as his stepdaughter. I know he'll claw to preserve his reputation. But fuck him. I won't accept a single penny from that monster because every dollar he possesses is tainted with the blood of the victims of his clients.

Charles Gregory is dead to me. And so are any ties we once had.

I wake in a startle, my body slick with sweat and heart pounding in my chest. I blink my vision into focus, recognizing my surroundings instantly. I'm sitting behind the wheel of my Corvette in Liam's garage, the engine rumbling lowly beneath me as my fingers grip the wheel.

It's clear I was just sleepwalking—something I haven't done in years. But stress brings it all back, and my somnambulism has returned with a vengeance.

The garage door begins sliding up. Slowly. So slowly that my bare foot is hovering over the gas pedal, vibrating in anticipation.

I blink. Once. Twice. Ten fucking times.

What the hell am I doing?

The door flattens to the ceiling, and I find myself shifting into gear. Tires crunch on gravel as I creep down the long dirt path away from the cabin. Away from Liam. Away from ... I don't really know. I'm on autopilot, my nightmare fueling my every stupid move. The warm glow of the outside lights slowly fades behind trees and into the darkness as I pick up speed down the road and put as much distance between myself and Liam's cabin as possible. I'm unfamiliar with the area, and it's pitch black out here in the sticks. But when I spot a sign for the highway, I veer left and punch the gas pedal, swerving and weaving recklessly through the thin traffic of the early morning. The only vehicles on the road at this hour are transport trucks and early commuters.

And cops.

I let off the throttle and slow the car to a reasonable speed, my fingers gripping the steering wheel tight as adrenaline courses through my body.

I shake the intruding thoughts from my head.

This is wrong. It's all wrong. I'm still in danger. Still a potential target for Ivan Petrov.

I make a sudden U-turn, rubber screeching on asphalt as I head back in the direction I came from. I'll just sneak back into the cabin and crawl into bed. Pretend like this never happened. It was a moment of weakness where the sleepwalking disorder I was diagnosed with in college came creeping back from the pressure I'm under.

Six dead bolts.

It took me years to discover that's what it takes to keep me within the confines of my apartment when I'm sleepwalking. That's what it takes to give me a feeling of control over my disorder.

A single bright headlight appears ahead of me, its rays glaring and causing me to squint against the assault. It whips past me, and I check my rearview mirror and almost shit a brick when it turns around and eats up the space behind me. I'd recognize that shiny, black Harley anywhere. And the big, angry caveman it belongs to.

Without thinking, I roll my window down and let the wind rip through my hair as I lay my lead foot down and internally squeal as the speedometer rises. For reasons unknown, I'm feeling especially reckless right now. And I know I should seek therapy for my destructive, self-sabotaging behaviors. But with every inch the speed hand moves, my heart beats that much harder.

Faster. Faster. Faster.

But that lone headlight behind me grows brighter, picking up speed and closing in on me. Liam rides my ass, taunting me, before falling back. He speeds up again, his engine humming in tune with mine.

A fresh wave of adrenaline seeps into my veins, this time blending with excitement instead of cold, hard fear.

I've never felt so free in my life, even with a pissed-off mercenary gaining on me as I tear down the open highway.

The floorboard grows hot, the pedal beneath my bare foot heating with every second that ticks by. But then smoke begins rolling from beneath the hood of my car and my heart plummets into my stomach like a rock in the lake.

"Fucking cracked radiator." I smack the steering wheel, angry at myself for forgetting that I still haven't replaced the leaking rad.

I don't know what possesses me to do it, but I slam on the brakes and pull over, gravel and dirt flying up and pinging off the side of my overheated car. I whip the door open and scramble out, my soles smarting as I take off down the ditch and into the inky darkness of the forest that creeps along the highway.

I can sleepwalk my way out of a cabin and open a garage door and turn a car on. Why couldn't I stop to put on some fucking shoes?

Sticks and rocks stab into the bottoms of my feet, but I forge on, using my arms as a shield to shove stray branches away from my face as my legs pump as fast and hard as they'll carry me.

I'm not sure why I'm running from Liam. I guess it's a natural reflex for me at this point, like when the doctor taps your kneecap with a rubber mallet and your leg jumps. That reflex is natural to me. And Liam's that fucking rubber mallet causing me to jump.

I hear his motorcycle engine cut out, but I'm already deep into the woods with nothing but the moonlight and stars to guide the way. My breathing is labored, my lungs burning from the cold night air I'm forcing into them.

When my foot snags on a stump and I land face first in the dirt and dead leaves, I hiss out a string of curse words and roll onto my back to catch my breath. I stare up at the black sky, the silhouettes of the trees looming above me reminding me of one of the paintings I made for my mother when I was in college. A blend of navy and black and a million specks of twinkling white stars with a lowly hung moon peeking through the thick clouds passing over it.

Tears fill my eyes and I snap my mouth shut, forcing myself to calm down and think things through. I could get up and keep running, but there's a good chance I'll get lost. At least from here, I can still hear the faint roar of the highway. But I know I'm at least a few hundred feet deep into the woods now. There are animals and snakes and all sorts of nasties out here that I'd really rather not face.

A twig snaps from somewhere nearby, and I crawl onto my hands and knees and search around the darkness for the source of the sound.

Just as I get my feet under me, a large, lethal shadow appears from behind a tree.

Liam.

With disheveled hair and dark eyes, he looks wild—feral—out here in the woods with nothing but the moonlight and stars illuminating his deep scowl and the tattoos on his flexing forearms.

I shriek, scrambling to get my bearings and take off running. But I'm violently jerked back as a familiar arm galvanizes around my waist, hauling me against a wall of pure muscle. The smell of spearmint, something woodsy, and a hint of leather fills my lungs, and I relax a fraction at the comfort of his familiar scent.

"Why are you running, little thief?" he snarls in my ear as he drags me backward, shoving me against a nearby tree. The rough bark scrapes my cheek as Liam sandwiches me between him and the unforgiving surface.

"Because ..." I pant. "Because you're chasing me," I answer honestly, my voice raspy and throat dry.

"Is that your solution to everything, Alora? To run? Even when you have no reason to?"

"Yes," I rush out. "It's worked this long."

A dark chuckle vibrates against my back. It's such a deep, beautiful sound, I can't help but want more of it. But now's not the time for laughter. Because this, right here, is no fucking joke.

"I don't think it has." He grinds his hips against my backside, and I feel his cock pressing into me. God, he's big. Everywhere. Imposing and all-consuming in the most dangerous of ways. "In fact," he says lowly in my ear, "I think all that running has worked against you."

"Oh yeah?" I pant out. "How so?"

He sweeps my hair over my shoulder and brings his lips to the sensitive spot beneath my ear. His teeth graze the flesh, causing a flurry of bumps to scatter over my arms.

"Because now you're forced to face what I've been denying myself."

A familiar switchblade appears before my eyes, and my heart skids to a stop. My eyes widen in fear as moonlight glints off its silver edge before it vanishes again. Something cold and metallic skims lightly across my bare shoulder and all the oxygen in my lungs leaves in a whoosh. One quick flick of his wrist and the strap of my tank top breaks free, the cotton covering my breast hanging limply over one side of my heaving chest.

He won't hurt me. Liam won't hurt me.

"Wha-what are you doing?" I rush out, suddenly very aware of the predicament I'm in. I'm alone in the woods, in the middle of the night, with a man who I'm pretty sure is going to make me regret every stupid decision that got me to this place.

And I'm turned on.

Stupid, traitorous vagina.

"I warned you, Alora. Promised that if you continued to tease, I'd make you pay. And that's exactly what I'm going to do."

Twenty

Liam

EVERY FLUTTER OF ALORA'S long eyelashes, every ragged breath exhaled from her pretty, pink lips, every insignificant sound she makes has me folding like a used napkin.

She hasn't said no. She hasn't asked me to stop. The line I'm towing may be considered dubious, but her body is primed and willing. Even with nothing but the warm glow of the full moon casting long shadows through the thick trees, I can see her eyes lighting with excitement. The thrill of the chase has my little thief turned on. And as much as I've been fighting the urge to fuck her—refraining from allowing myself inside her—I'm only a man. And she's my guilty pleasure.

It's time I indulge myself.

I drag the tip of my switchblade across her bare shoulder, flicking my wrist and popping the other strap of her tank top open. The fabric falls loose but her body is pressed flush to the tree, so her tits remain covered.

"Are you afraid of me, little thief?" I ask lowly, my beard grazing her jaw. I plant a soft kiss where my stubble has rubbed at her skin.

"No," she responds, her fingers curling in on themselves against the bark.

I inhale her scent, blending so beautifully with the fear she refuses to admit she feels.

"Are you sure?"

Her eyes squeeze shut briefly, but when I coil her long hair around my fist and tug her head back so I can gaze down at her beautiful face, her answer comes out in a whoosh.

"Fine. Yes, I'm afraid. Terrified."

"Good. You should be." I nip at her pouty bottom lip. "But I won't hurt you. Not beyond the pain your body begs me for. Do you want to know why?"

Her emerald orbs flare, her throat working as she swallows. "Why?"

"Because as much as I want to mark you with my knife—carve my name into your soft, supple flesh—inflicting unwanted pain on you would kill me."

She releases a small mewl when I back off just enough to lazily drag my knife down the curve of her spine, careful to not break skin. The sound of fabric shredding slices through Alora's ragged breathing as I cut her shirt from her body so she's left in nothing more than her shorts.

"Just say no, little thief, and I'll stop."

She whimpers in response and arches her back to grind against me, testing my willpower once again.

A satisfied groan comes from within me, and I spin her around and shove her back against the tree, slipping my hand around her throat as her top falls away, exposing her gorgeous little tits that fit perfectly in my palms. I begin salivating at the thought of tugging her pert nipples between my teeth, sucking and tugging until she's dripping wet.

I shred her shorts from her body with my knife and drop the blade to the ground with her clothing. She stands pressed against the tree, her delicate form bathed in soft moonlight and her midnight hair falling around her shoulders as her chest rises and falls with uneven breaths.

I lower to my knees, worshipping her, running my hands down the length of her torso to her hips. I dig my fingers into her soft curves, relishing the way her pale skin bleaches white from my grip. My dick strains against the inside of my jeans, aching to be freed, only to be plunged deep inside of her tight cunt.

"Liam," she rasps, her breath hitching when I run the tip of my tongue up her glistening seam, tasting her in the most primal of ways. And fuck if she isn't the sweetest delicacy I've ever had.

A shiver racks her body, her skin peppering with bumps as I part her pussy lips with my thumbs, exposing her engorged clit to the cool evening air. I blow gently on it, staring up at her as she gazes down at me. I keep my eyes on her face as I lap at her again, sucking her sensitive bundle of nerves into my mouth, gently grazing it with my teeth. She hisses and her hands fly to my head, my scalp tingling as she drags her short black fingernails over my skull.

"Christ, sweetheart. Desperate little thing, aren't you?"

I coax her legs over my shoulders and seat her so the tree has her propped upright, her thighs wrapped around my neck and ankles hooked at my back. I take my time, licking and sucking as I devour her, eating her like she's the most delectable meal ever. Because she fucking is.

Everything about her fits me perfectly. Her small, firm tits. Her round little ass. Her smart, defiant mouth that I want nothing more than to stuff full of my cock just to see how beautifully her plump lips would stretch around it.

Her legs tremble with every lick and bite, and I grip her ass, squeezing hard as my fingertips dig into her flesh to mark her with this memory.

"You're so fucking sweet, Alora," I murmur. "I could die happy like this. With your tight pussy smothering me, robbing me of air."

Her head falls back, baring the long, slender column of her throat to me. I squeeze her ass tighter and eat her until she's moaning, her hands delved into my hair as she writhes and bucks against my face.

"Oh, fuck," she cries out, her legs shaking and back arching. Moonlight bounces off her pearly skin, highlighting every soft swell of her flesh.

Her body breaks out in a cold sweat, her pussy dripping and soaking my beard as she comes hard on my face. I lick every drop from her center, dragging the flat of my tongue over the inside of her thighs to clean her up.

When her grip loosens on my hair and her body goes slack, I slide her legs down my arms and coax them around my hips and rise to my feet. Her arousal smears across the front of my T-shirt as I crush my lips to hers, tasting her mouth and forcing her to sample herself.

I hold her up with one arm, her hands gripping my shoulders as I unbuckle my belt and unzip my fly.

I drop my forehead to hers, lining the tip of my cock up with her pussy, dragging it through her wetness and teasing her clit with it. Her lungs expand and contract, her pulse flying in her throat as she gazes back at me, her eyes hooded and a sleepy look softening her features.

This feeling, this overwhelming possessiveness I feel toward her, is new for me. It's something raw and unfiltered that I've never felt before. Something that's making me physically ill, causing my stomach to churn and blood to pulse violently through my body.

I line the tip of my cock up with her entrance. "You good, sweetheart?"

She nods, and with a groan, I push gently inside of her, shuddering as her tight pussy stretches to accommodate me.

Her head slams back and her eyes squeeze shut as her fingernails bite into my shoulders, grappling at my shirt.

"Oh god," she cries out, her body tensing from the intrusion.

"That's right." I pull back just a fraction before rocking my hips forward, pushing further inside her hot, wet cunt until the tip of my cock nudges her cervix. "Be a good girl and take every inch of me."

A tear forms at the corner of her pinched eyes, glittering like the most precious diamond in the world. I kiss it away, sampling her pain on my tongue.

Her ass cheeks tremble in my hand, her smooth skin now slick with sweat as I remain seated deeply inside of her, palming her breasts with my free hand and teasing her nipples until she's moaning. I seal my mouth over hers in a long, sultry kiss, silencing her cries as I abandon her tits and drag my hand down the front of her body to circle her clit with my thumb and coax her to relax around me.

"Fuck, Alora. You're so tight. So fucking perfect."

She releases a pained whimper. "It hurts, Liam," she admits, her voice shaky and weak. But her hips roll slightly, accepting another inch of me.

"I know, sweetheart. Relax for me." I gather wetness from where our bodies are connected and swipe it over her clit, drawing slow, calculated circles, massaging the tension in her body away. I feel her muscles soften, and her pussy takes the last inch.

I glance down at where I'm invading her, shivering at the way she's stretched so tightly around my thick cock.

A relieved sigh escapes me. Having her like this, owning her, douses the flames of my rage, sedating the roaring monster inside me. I've never felt more at peace than I do in this very moment.

"Fuck," I hiss, sliding slowly out, feeling her pussy grip me tight. "So greedy."

I push back in gently. Pain, in the most horrific sense of the word, is something I take pleasure in doling out, but I can't bring myself to hurt her. I can't rip her open and make her bleed the way I threatened I would. The way I want to when she's teasing me, irritating me. Making me question everything about myself.

I take my time, easing in and out of her, relishing the way her delicate limbs are coiled around me, clinging to me as if I'm her lifeline. The way her heart hammers against her ribs, clashing with mine. The way she moans and whimpers, every little sound that escapes her like a lullaby soothing my demons and righting my world.

"Liam," she breathes out, my name dripping from her lips like the sweetest fucking honey.

I bury my nose in her neck and thrust harder, pushing her just beyond the brink of pleasure and into the realm of pain, groaning as she reacts to my every touch. I inhale deeply, filling my lungs with her scent. *Fucking lemons.* I lick her neck to taste the salty tang of her sweat. Fuck her slow and deep to feel every bit of her, bare and wet and hot around my cock.

I commit this moment to memory.

"Liam. I'm going to …" she rushes out, her voice high pitched and strained. She tries so fucking hard to hold back, to slow this down. "Oh god."

"You don't need to wait for me, little thief. Come for me. Let me feel your greedy little pussy sucking me in, squeezing me so fucking tight that it hurts. Christ, Alora. You're fucking ruining me."

She arches her back, her pussy convulsing and legs tightening around my hips. She screams my name, her harsh cries echoing through the trees and slamming into my chest like a wrecking ball, shattering my hardened exterior and exposing every raw part of me.

I clench my jaw and hiss through my teeth as my balls draw upward, my cock hardening to steel inside of her. Every muscle in my body stiffens as I fuck her through her orgasm until warm cum jets from my cock, painting her insides and filling her up.

She pants heavily, dropping her forehead to my shoulder and releasing a sob. Her humid breath skitters across my throat, and I can feel her tears slipping down my chest. Her body shakes violently as she falls to pieces in my arms.

I don't withdraw from her because the loss would do me in. So I simply spin us around and slide to the ground, my back to the tree and her arms and legs wrapped snuggly around me, my cock still throbbing deep inside of her.

Just like the moment she broke on her bedroom floor, I sit quietly, soothing her, stroking her back and hair, kissing and licking away her tears as they tumble down her flushed cheeks.

"I—" She hiccups. "I don't know what the hell is wrong with me. I never cry like this."

"Shh." I cup her head in my hands and tip her face so she's staring back at me. I brush my lips over hers, tasting her tears on her lips. "You've been strong for so long. You don't need to be with me."

She sniffles, trying and failing to stiffen her chin and blink away the tears.

"Breaking down is good. Breaking down is necessary to rebuild and grow."

Her brows furrow, her eyes shining so bright against the dark forest surrounding us.

"Pretty deep words for a feral mountain man."

My mouth hooks into a small smile. Fuck, this woman. I can already feel my dick hardening inside her again, forcing my cum to seep out of her and coat both of us.

"Feral mountain man?"

She shrugs. "If it walks like a duck and talks like a duck ..."

My smile stretches further and I lift her ass off my hips, freeing my heavy cock. I shove her down onto her hands and knees between my legs and grip the top of her head.

"Clean me up, little thief. Then let's go home."

She doesn't fight me on it. Just positions herself between my thighs, her bare knees and hands planted firmly in the soil and dead leaves as she laps at my cock, licking my cum and her arousal up like a kitten. Her tongue swirls around my tip, dipping into the small seam. I twist her hair in my fist and lift her face.

"Keep that up and I'm going to fuck you again. This time with your ass in the air and face buried in the dirt."

Her eyes meet mine, flaring as she finishes cleaning me up, a playful smirk tugging at her swollen lips.

When there's not a drop of cum left, I stuff myself back into my jeans and buckle my belt, then help Alora to her feet, snatching my switchblade off the ground and tucking it into my pocket. Alora stands awkwardly in the dark, her arms coiled around her naked body and hands rubbing her arms to create heat.

I pull my shirt over my head with one hand and slip it over her body, then scoop her up into my arms.

"Silly girl, running without shoes," I growl into her hair as I move boots back to the road.

She buries her face into my bare chest and lets me take care of her. It occurs to me that even though Alora is tough and independent, more determined to take care of herself than most women, she secretly enjoys being cared for. She appreciates the small things like being held when she's hurting. Being carried when her feet are bare. Being eaten out like she's a fucking meal.

Alora Berkley's a simple girl with simple needs. And I find myself wondering if maybe I could be enough for her after all.

Twenty-One

Liam

I SEAT ALORA ON the back of my bike and retrieve the keys from her Corvette, locking it up before returning to her. I'll deal with her abandoned vehicle later.

She slides back slightly, allowing me room to settle in front of her. Her arms instinctively wrap around my waist, and I kick my bike into gear and take off down the highway. My left hand settles on her calf, my fingers drifting lazily over her smooth skin.

When I pull into the driveway of my cabin, she pulls back from me and asks, "What about my car?"

"I'll call a tow truck in the morning."

I park my bike in the garage and lift Alora into my arms and carry her inside, setting the alarm on my way in.

I toe out of my boots at the door and saunter straight back to my bedroom and into the ensuite bathroom, flicking the light on before setting Alora on the black marble vanity.

"Don't move," I tell her.

She shifts back and folds her hands in her lap, her legs swinging as she watches me rummage around in the medicine cabinet for my first aid kit. I lay it down beside the bathtub and turn the faucet on and adjust the temperature then return to her, my eyes fixating on her bare thighs pressed tightly together.

She cocks a brow and stares at me like I've lost the plot. It's becoming increasingly obvious that I have.

When I reach for the hem of my shirt at her thighs, she goes rigid.

"What are you doing?" she asks, and I almost swear I hear a hint of trepidation in her tone.

I lift my lashes and meet her curious gaze. "I'm taking care of you."

Her shoulders snap into a tight line. But her uncertainty is swiftly replaced by a plastic veneer of confidence. She's not used to being cared for, of this I'm sure.

"Alora."

She rolls her eyes and lifts her arms, allowing me to remove the shirt and toss it into the laundry hamper. Her ebony hair cascades in loose waves around her shoulders, the ends brushing over her dusty pink nipples. I pluck a stray twig out of her hair and a slight pink hue rises in her cheeks.

A sick flare of possessiveness lights inside me as I take inventory of the bruises and scrapes on her knees, the small bite mark I left on the valley between her neck and shoulder. My eyes flutter shut, and I breathe in a lungful of air to ward off the erection threatening to bust from my jeans.

Seeing her marked like this—marked as *mine*—is something I wasn't mentally prepared for, despite it being everything I've wanted since I first laid eyes on her in that casino.

It takes me a moment, but once my shit's in check, I scoop her off the counter and set her in the tub, keeping my eyes cast downward and away from her naked body as I roll a towel up and prop it behind her neck for comfort.

She sits in stunned silence, watching me with a slightly confused look etched onto her face as I gently rinse her injured feet, washing the filth from the forest floor down the drain. I use the showerhead attached to the side of the tub to rinse her knees and hands as well before pushing the plug and letting the tub fill. I reach for the jar of Epsom salts I keep on hand—for days I'm sore and drained—and dump a scoop beneath the running water.

"How's the temperature?" I ask, keeping my tone low and eyes averted.

She sighs and sinks lower, the rising water creeping up over her hip bones. "It's perfect."

I lower to my knees beside the tub and lay another fresh towel down on the ledge and pat it.

"Feet up," I instruct, and she obliges, carefully placing her heels on the plush terry cloth in front of me.

I pop the first aid kit open and begin cleaning her cuts, gently dabbing the scrapes with alcohol-soaked cotton. She hisses at the sting, but when my thumb brushes soothingly over the butterfly tattoo on her ankle, she seems to relax. I stare at the small patch of blue ink, wondering what it means to her, if anything at all.

"It's symbolic," she offers lowly, answering the question I never voiced. "Butterflies represent a fresh start. New beginnings. Growth."

I peek up at her, noting the hesitation seeping into her expression as silence stretches on between us. What I said to her earlier about breaking being necessary to rebuild plays over in my mind. A clean slate. Fresh start. But that requires destroying what was previously there.

When I narrow my eyes on her, trying and failing at figuring out what's going on in her head, she shifts in the tub and attempts to pull her feet away, but I wrap my hands around her ankles and stop her.

"You want a new beginning, little thief ... Why don't you start with answering a few of my questions?"

She frowns at me, obviously displeased with my request. I ignore it and continue on what I set out to do, carefully applying an antibiotic ointment to her wounds to soothe and prevent infection. I wrap her dainty feet up in gauze, feeling her gaze on me the entire time. My thumb brushes over her tattoo again.

"Why'd you take off running tonight?"

She lies stock-still beneath the clear bath water, nothing but the steady drip of the faucet cutting through the silence.

She clears her throat before telling me, "I was diagnosed with somnambulism when I was in college." I angle my head at her, unfamiliar with that term. "I sleepwalk," she explains. "It's been a couple years since I had a problem with it. But it gets worse when I'm stressed out. And, well … hello stress."

"Ever seek treatment for it?"

"Several times. But medication doesn't cut it for me. So I just cope with it." She shrugs a shoulder. "It's not a big deal."

"You took off in the middle of the night. You could've gotten hurt."

"Six dead bolts," she blurts, and I stare at her in confusion. "It takes me unlocking five before I wake up and realize what I'm doing. So I've always had a sixth as a precaution. It took me a while to figure that out, but eventually I did. So everywhere I've ever lived, I've installed six dead bolts."

I mull her admission over in my head, recalling the six dead bolts on her apartment door. I had chalked it up to her being extra cautious living on the east side. But now I realize it's because she was afraid she'd walk straight out of her apartment and wander around half-asleep.

"After your mother died, you took off. Why?"

The girl is a vault of kept secrets. But the longer I stare back at her, the more her eyes gloss over, pooling with tears she refuses to let fall. And I know her biggest secret of all is that she's afraid to face her emotions and work through the pain of losing someone she loved.

She sniffs, stiffening her quivering lip and pressing her shoulders back. My gaze flicks over her chest before I regain my focus and look her in the eyes again. But all I find there is anguish and heartbreak. And it nearly splits me in two.

"My mother was severely depressed," she tells me quietly, her voice cracking with emotion. "By the time I realized how bad it had gotten, it was too late. After she died, I decided to read her journal. What I found there was more than a little disturbing. Charles, my stepfather, had been cheating on her for years. Countless affairs with younger women. Sometimes he'd even sleep with the wives of the criminals he was defending. Really fucked-up shit. But that wasn't all."

She pauses briefly to consider whether she should tell me more. She does.

"My mother went snooping through his desk one day and found some files. She never wrote about what was in them, but she confessed that Charles was getting involved with some people who were dangerous. He wasn't just defending criminals anymore. He was befriending them. When she confronted him about it, he threatened her. And since she was afraid of losing everything—of losing him—she kept her mouth shut. But I believe that's when she took a turn for the worst. He may not have been the one to force the pills down her throat. But he's responsible for her death nonetheless."

Alora's asleep in my bed, her glossy black hair fanned out across my pillow and pink lips slightly parted, small puffs of air leaving her mouth as she falls deep into her dreams.

After she told me more about her mother, her lips sealed shut and she refused to share anything further. I'd be frustrated if I weren't so familiar with what she's feeling. Sometimes turning away from the pain of your past and never looking back is all we can do to survive.

When I left her be in the bathroom while I went in search of one of my T-shirts for her to wear to bed, I returned to find the tub draining and her standing awkwardly with a towel slung around her shivering body. It took every ounce of restraint to not crawl beneath the sheets with her and pull her body against mine. To not wrap my arms around her and nuzzle into her hair. But somehow I found the strength to resist and tucked her into bed and waited patiently for her to fall asleep.

And now I sit quietly in a chair in the darkest corner of my room as I watch her rest peacefully, straight through eleven o'clock in the morning. She looks like some sort of dark, midnight angel with her shiny black hair and creamy skin. I've never met a woman who can tempt me to be a different man just by lying in my bed, her petite body swamped with blankets, one leg slung haphazardly over the comforter. Even with the blackout curtains drawn closed, I can see the faint outline of the butterfly on her ankle.

A new beginning. Could I give her that?

The blankets shift and her ankle disappears beneath the covers. The top of her head peeks out from under the comforter, a pair of striking green eyes glittering in the dark.

"Hi," she rasps, her voice sultry from sleep.

"Good morning."

She sits up slowly and shoves her long hair behind her shoulders and tugs the sheet up over her body. She glances around the dark room.

"Did you stay in here all night?"

"I did."

I stand and cross the room, watching as her fingers curl tightly around my dark satin sheets. I could so easily peel them from her grip and shred my T-shirt from her body.

"Oh ..." she whispers, clearing her throat as I approach.

The mattress dips with my weight as I take a seat beside her. I reach out and drag the back of my knuckles across her cheekbone, tucking her hair behind her ear before skimming the soft flesh of her neck and shoulder. She leans into my touch, and that small gesture warms the block of ice in my chest.

"Alora," I grate out, reveling in the way her hand settles on my forearm.

I watch the column of her slender throat work as she swallows again. Her hand lowers from my arm and she twists her fingers in her lap. She drops her gaze, and even in the dark, I can see her confidence melting away, seeping out of her cracked foundation and exposing all her vulnerability to me.

She lifts her lashes, and with the softest of whispers, she asks, "Have you ever been to Mexico, Liam?"

Her question surprises me, and I'm not sure where her head is at right now. But I answer, "I have."

"What was it like?"

"Hot."

Her cheeks round out as her lips curl upward. Fuck, her smile could bring an entire army to its knees.

"Were you there for work or pleasure?"

"Work. More times than I can count."

She nods thoughtfully. "Would you ever go back? I mean ... for pleasure."

I study her features, wondering what's possessing her to ask these questions. "Maybe someday," I respond honestly. "Why? You planning on taking off to Mexico, sweetheart?"

Her mouth twists as she gnaws on the inside of her cheek. She drops her gaze to her fingers again.

"My mother and I were supposed to go to Mexico. Lay on the beach until we were as red as lobsters. Drink margaritas until tequila seeped from our pores. She surprised me with tickets for Christmas right before she died." Alora glances around the dark room again. "What time is it?"

"I'm not sure. You stole my watch," I tell her with a smirk.

Her brows raise and she huffs out a soft, feminine laugh. That sound ...

"Oh my god. That's the first time I've heard you crack a joke. Was it painful?"

"Excruciating."

She laughs again, but it quickly diminishes as we sit silently in my bedroom, staring at each other. She shifts forward and rises to her knees, the hemline of my T-shirt falling mid-thigh as she moves toward me, crawling into my lap and straddling me. My fingers delve into her long black hair, sweeping it back and cupping her head with my hands.

"Kiss me," she whispers.

I do, sealing my lips over hers and sweeping my tongue into her hot mouth. She tastes like freedom and rebellion. *Trouble.* Fucking loads of it. And it satiates a part of me that's been starved for years.

It isn't long before she's mewling, her little noises traveling straight to my heavy, aching cock. I twist and lay back, guiding her legs on either side of my hips. Her bare calves lay flush against my sides, and I gently dust my fingers over her bandaged feet.

Her thick hair falls around us like a dark veil, closing us off from the outside world. All tenderness fades as her lips meet mine in a frenzy, her body rocking and bare pussy grinding against my jeans and causing her to moan into my mouth. Her hands dive into my hair, tugging as I let her take control of the moment, something I sense she needs right now.

She gasps when I roll my hips, giving her the friction she craves.

My hands roam freely from her feet, caressing the butterfly on her ankle before sliding over her calves. When they round over her knees, I press my palms into her thighs, coaxing her to shift back, her body bowing as she rolls her hips. My hands travel north to the small crease where her legs meet her hips, and I press my thumbs into the soft flesh, gripping her tight.

"Liam," she breathes out.

I hum in response, unable to form words. Not when she's teasing me like this.

"I have a question."

I groan and flip us, shoving my hips between her legs and shutting her up with my mouth on hers as my hands roam over her delicate curves.

"Liam," she murmurs against my lips again. And I know she needs to get whatever's on her mind out.

I lean back and stare down at her, her chest rising and falling with heavy breaths, a look of worry clouding her sparkly, green eyes.

"I, uhm ..." She fidgets nervously, then lifts her hand to her mouth and begins gnawing on her thumbnail the way she often does.

"Spit it out, little thief. Before I fuck it out of you."

She swallows and nods. "Okay. Just ... I ..."

"Christ, woman. What is it?"

"If I asked for your help with something kind of horrible, would you do it?"

"I think you already know the answer, sweetheart."

Her teeth work over her bottom lip as she nods. But that nod fades and soon she's shaking her head, her eyes pinched shut as she banishes whatever thought she had from her mind.

I grip her hair in my fist and angle her head back so she's staring up at me.

"Tell me."

"No. It was stupid and crazy. Don't worry about it."

I release her hair and stand. She pops up on her elbows and blinks at me, her eyes tracking me as I pace the foot of the bed and drag a hand through my hair.

I already know she's not going to willingly tell me what it was she was hoping I'd do for her. But I've mastered the art of persuasion in the deadliest form. And I refuse to let this go. If there's something plaguing her, I need to know about it.

When I stop and stare down at her, something in me snaps.

I lunge for her, snatching her by the wrist and pulling her to her knees.

"Liam," she screeches. But I'm not fucking listening. If I have to drag it out of her forcefully, then so be it.

I press my shoulder into her stomach and carry her fireman style out of my room. Her fists beat against my back as she kicks and screams and attempts to wiggle free. My hand splays wide over the backs of her thighs, pinning her down as I swat her ass with my free hand.

She gasps. "You did *not* just spank me, you fucking caveman."

I move through my cabin and down the stairs to the basement, flicking on the lights as I go. I snatch ropes from the corner where I keep my gym equipment and set Alora onto the pool table parked in the center of my den.

She kicks and claws at me, but I have her pinned down, my fingers coiled around her throat and pressing her into the table. The billiard chandelier dangles low over us, casting a warm glow over her wriggling body as I lay the ropes beside her head and bring my face within inches of hers.

She glares up at me, her short, gnawed-on fingernails biting into my forearm and smoke practically billowing from her flared nostrils.

"I've been more than patient with you, little thief. But that time has come to an end."

Twenty-Two

Alora

MY LUNGS EXPAND AND contract as I suck in impossibly large gulps of air. My chest is so tight with anxiety that it feels like it's going to explode. All the blood has left my head, and I'm dizzy, the world around me tilting off its axis.

I focus on Liam looming over me, his big fucking shadow swallowing me whole. When he leans back, I'm blinded by the bright pool table lights hanging directly above me.

I open my mouth to scream, but his hand seals over my mouth.

"Be quiet, Alora. Or I'll gag you."

My eyes blow wide at his threat. He wouldn't gag me. Would he?

I nod in understanding, desperate for him to remove his hand so I can lash out at him again. But when he slowly peels his fingers away from my face, I think wiser of it.

A wad of ropes appear before my eyes, and a new wave of panic sets in.

"Wha-what are you doing?"

He doesn't respond, and that only heightens my fear. The rope makes a soft hissing sound as he loops it strategically through the netted pockets on each corner of the table by my head. He doesn't remove his hand from my throat, and I don't remove my fingers from their death grip on his forearm.

When he's done looping the rope through the holes, he snatches my right wrist with his free hand.

"Let go, Alora. Or I'll pry your fingers back myself."

A whimper lodges itself in my throat, and I do as instructed. My right arm forms an L beside my head, and I stretch my eyeballs to watch him tactically wrap the rope around my wrist. Not once. Not twice. Three times. He cranks it tight and knots it with expert efficiency.

"Does it hurt?" he asks.

"Yes."

My arm jerks as he gives the rope one more tug, tightening it further. "Good."

He snatches my other wrist and repeats the process. It's torturously slow, and I wish he'd just hurry the hell up and get whatever this is over with.

When both of my wrists are secured, my arms framing my head, he releases my throat.

I test the restraints as Liam hovers over me again, eclipsing the blinding lights.

"You can struggle all you want, little thief. But you're not going anywhere."

When I sneer at him, he tsks and disappears out of sight, rounding the table above my head. He circles me slowly, stopping at the bottom of the table. I lift my head to peer down at him. Right now, he's darkness personified, an apparition I swear I've conjured up in my very wild imagination. His eyes are molten lava, his giant, tattooed fists balled at his sides as he glowers at me.

He's ... terrifying. But also hauntingly beautiful.

When his eyes dart to the space between my legs, I clench my thighs shut, blocking his view of my exposed center.

Big, strong hands close around both of my ankles, and I kick wildly.

"Don't you dare," I scream.

The smallest flicker of hesitation crosses his expression before he swiftly tugs me down the table, my bare ass burning against the assault of the rough fabric beneath me.

My heart picks up speed, my pulse flying a million miles a minute.

He makes quick work of parting my legs and securing both of my ankles to the netted pockets at the bottom of the table. My body is stretched and the T-shirt I'm wearing bunched up around my waist, baring everything to him.

"Liam. Don't do this."

He flattens his palms on the table between my feet, his head dipping low between his shoulders as he wets his lips and stares hungrily at the space between my legs.

I release the whimper I've been suppressing, and his lashes lift, his wolf eyes piercing mine.

"Do you trust me, Alora?"

"Liam, please," I whine. "Whatever I did ... I'm sorry."

His lip twitches. "Ready to tell me what it is you were going to ask of me?"

My head whips side to side. "No. It was crazy. It was irrational. You should untie me right now and check me into a mental institution."

Liam stands to his full height. A couple long strides bring him to my side, and I roll my head and stare at him, my breathing erratic and chest rising and falling with uneven breaths. Fear has quite literally paralyzed me.

He leans over me, dusting the lightest of kisses over my forehead. His warm, minty breath skitters across my sweat-soaked hair, his lips trailing down the side of my face to my jaw. He inhales deeply at my ear.

"Tell me you trust me, sweetheart."

"I trust you," I rush out.

A familiar blade appears before my eyes, and I begin backpedaling.

"Wait. Liam. God."

"God isn't here, Alora. It's just you and me now."

The cold press of metal against my cheek has me freezing, my breaths stalling, my heart plummeting. I should tell him. I should just spit the words out and pray he doesn't act on my request.

But he's unhinged, and I suspect that he'll bring my sick fantasy to life.

"Breathe, Alora. I'm not hurting you." There's an unspoken *yet* dangling on the end of that sentence.

I exhale a ragged breath as the pointy tip of the blade carves a gentle path down the side of my throat. It doesn't break skin, but the fear alone has me whimpering.

"The human body is capable of surviving immense amounts of pain. Mass losses of blood." His eyes flare wildly, as if the thought of watching me bleed out before him is something he's curious about. "But you know what it's also capable of?" He slips the knife beneath the collar of the T-shirt barely covering my tits. The sound of shredding fabric breaks through the sounds of my panicked breathing. "Blurring the lines between pain and pleasure." Cool conditioned air settles over my heaving chest as the fabric parts way.

"Liam," I plead again.

But Liam's not here right now. This man is someone else. Someone dangerous. Someone ...

He stops my downward spiral in its tracks. "I'm right here, sweetheart."

His eyes meet mine. And that's when I realize I'm crying, tears slipping free and plopping onto the table beside my head. Liam swipes a thumb over my cheekbone, gathering a lone droplet. He brings it to his mouth and sucks it clean before leaning over me. One hand lies flat on the table beside my face while his other grips the knife handle, dragging it slowly down my sternum. His eyes lock on mine, studying the fear lighting behind them as the blade moves south, so slowly that every inch of my skin peppers with bumps in its wake.

It stops just above my pubic bone as Liam nips at my trembling bottom lip.

"Don't move," he instructs lowly, sliding his tongue over where his teeth made contact. "I won't hurt you."

I nod slowly, every muscle in my body galvanizing as he presses the flat edge of the blade against my clit. A shiver racks my body, and I gasp, the cold steel chilling my overheated core. Liam's gaze darkens as his eyes sear a path of destruction all the way down my body, slicing and dicing and burning every inch of flesh they touch, branding me with his own personal stamp of ownership.

When his eyes reach the spot where his blade lies flat against my pussy, he wets his lips and groans.

"This knife has taken many lives, Alora. Including the man who dared lay his hands on you. And it will take many more."

The cold blade vanishes, replaced by his middle finger. I clamp down on my lip and suppress a moan as he circles my clit, massaging until all the tension in my body is concentrated in one spot.

"You're fucking perfect for me, little thief. Soft, creamy flesh. A smart fucking mouth I want to silence with my cock. It's third-degree torture. And I'm a glutton for it. I can't get enough of you."

He dips a finger inside and my back arches off the table. When he works a second finger in and crooks it up to that deliciously sensitive spot, my eyes roll back and a flood of warmth pools deep within me, wrapping around the base of my spine and coiling tight.

"God. Please, Liam. I can't—"

He withdraws suddenly, smearing my juices over my clit and leaving me achingly hollow and desperate for release.

"You can. And you will."

He pulls away completely this time, my trembling body sprawled out like a sacrificial offering.

He circles the table like a hawk, his eyes raking over my body as if appraising me, contemplating what I'm worth and how far he'll allow himself to take this.

"You're beautiful like this." His tattooed hands appear on either side of my face, his arms caging my head in as I stare up at his ruggedly handsome face. His scar pinches tight, warning me to cooperate. I squeeze my eyes shut and will away the tears that continue to fall.

My body feels like it's been hooked up to a generator, electricity coursing through me and lighting all my nerves on fire.

"Eyes on me, sweetheart."

My lids pop open. "You're scaring me."

The dark chuckle that leaves him is anything but reassuring. "I know. That's the whole point."

He kisses me where I lie, upside down to his right side up. His tongue delves into my mouth as one hand slinks around my throat. His touch is so fucking gentle that it's confusing. Hot and cold. Pain and pleasure. I can't keep up.

I writhe and sweat and moan, every bit of anxiety melting from my body as he drinks from me.

"I told you you'd be mine once I've been inside you. And I take care of what's mine, Alora. You're safe with me. But make no qualms about it … you're going to tell me what it is you want from me. One way or another."

He backs away and I'm once again wincing against the bright overhead lights. A lamp flicks on in the corner of the room. Then the lights above me dim out, relieving my retinas of the assault of the billiard chandelier.

Thank you lingers on the tip of my tongue, but the words fall to their peril.

Liam's back at my side, the whisper of his belt sliding through the loops of his jeans breaking the silence. Cool leather meets the heated flesh of my chest. It slips over my nipples, one at a time, causing them to pucker, before drifting lower. Over my belly button. Down between my hips. Over my wet center.

"Remember what I said, Alora. You're safe with me."

I nod fervently. "I remember." The words are barely a whisper, my throat clogged with thick emotion. Fear, mostly. But also something else I refuse to put a label on.

"Tell me you're mine."

My head moves side to side. "No. I'm not—"

Leather comes down on my pussy, the crack of Liam's belt snapping against my wet flesh. I yelp in shock, the sting of the contact sending a jolt of lightning through my body.

"Let's try that again, shall we? Tell me you're mine."

My eyes squeeze shut, my teeth clamping down on my lip until the taste of copper meets my tongue. Another swift crack, hard enough to make me flinch and moan, but not hard enough to hurt me in any real way. My walls clench, an orgasm building low in my belly as my juices coat the insides of my thighs.

"Open your eyes."

My lids crack open to peer down at Liam. He's standing between my feet, his belt folded in half and fisted in one hand, a wild look in his eyes.

"I'm not yours."

Crack.

"Fuck," I hiss out, my body lurching and back arching almost painfully. "Goddamn it, motherfucker. Okay, fine." I'm panting like a dog now. How embarrassing. "You win. I'm yours."

He hums in satisfaction, then saunters around to my side again and slides his middle finger up my seam, circling my clit.

"And what about this pussy? Is it mine too?"

The rebellious streak in me wants to spit flames at him, but every brain cell in my head is screaming *yes! More!*

"All yours," I rush out.

His smirk is wicked as he rewards me with a gentle massage where I need it most.

"Good girl," he growls hotly.

"Oh god," I moan as he brings me right to the edge, so close that every muscle in my body has stiffened, my nerves all coiled tight like springs and ready to pop.

"Not yet." He retreats, grazing his belt over my pussy once more, dragging the now slick leather back up my body. He teases each of my nipples with it before slipping it under the back of my neck. He loops it around my throat and secures it like a dog leash. It's not too tight for me to breathe, but it's snug enough that the fear of being deprived of oxygen is real. Palpable.

The cold steel tip of a blade scratches along the swell of flesh beneath my left nipple just as a warm, rough hand cups my pussy, one finger sliding inside with ease.

"Tell me what you want from me."

I blink up at him, darkness shadowing his features and giving him an eerily dangerous look. Because that's exactly what he is—dangerous. Asking Liam to do this is reckless and awful. I'd be no better than Charles if I do.

"No."

He works a second finger in, stretching me. My hips roll against his hand, his thumb rubbing my clit while he fucks me with his fingers. My cheeks heat with embarrassment at the wet sounds of him sliding in and out of me, crooking his fingers and torturing me.

He plunges into me until his palm meets flesh, picking up speed and pressure. My body writhes, that familiar heat coiling once again low in my stomach. The air in the room turns stiflingly hot, my skin slick with sweat and ears ringing. All I feel is Liam's touch. All I see is his face, everything around us blurring until it's only him and I and his big, rough hand working me over.

"Do you want to come, little thief?"

"Yes. Please."

"Then tell me," he growls.

"It's insane."

When the sharp point of his blade breaks the skin on the outside of my left breast, I squeeze my eyes shut and blurt out, "I want you to kill my stepfather."

Liam's hand stalls as hot tears tumble down my cheeks and I burst into a sob. His lips seal over mine, kissing me with a tenderness I can't comprehend right now. I feel a trickle of something warm trailing down my ribs from where his knife punctured me.

"Open your eyes, Alora."

I can't. Because I'm terrified that if I do, I'll realize that this isn't all just some horrific nightmare I've plunged into. That this is actually my life. That the words really did just leave my mouth and I can't take them back.

"Eyes, sweetheart."

The pointy tip of his blade threatens to break skin again, and I snap my eyes open to find Liam's. But what I see there isn't fury or disgust. It's empathy. Concern. Pity. And I hate him for it.

"You want revenge."

I swallow the mountain-sized rock in my throat and rasp out, "Yes."

"Eyes, open." His tone leaves no room for protest, so I oblige.

Liam doesn't grace me with a response. Instead, he kisses me, his fingers moving inside me and thumb working my clit over until the pressure is almost too much to bear. When his blade cuts into my flesh, nicking me right beside the last mark, my pussy constricts around his fingers and my orgasm rips through me, detonating every nerve in my body. Bursts of color splash against the dark insides of my eyelids as I arch my back and cry out.

Wave after wave of pure ecstasy crashes through me, the aftereffects of my orgasm lasting longer than my fragile mental state can handle.

"Mm," he growls, his fingers slowing inside me as my body falls limp, my legs shaking and mouth bone dry. "I knew you'd bleed beautifully, little thief."

I'm still blinking away the stars dotting my vision when I feel him moving around at my feet. My ankles are swiftly released, Liam's thumb caressing the raw skin from where the rope rubbed. He dusts a finger over my tattoo before untying my wrists. I'm jerked upright by the lead of the belt around my neck. The T-shirt still slung around my arms falls free, and I'm moved swiftly to the edge of the table, my ass perched on the ledge and body bowed as my arms fall limply at my sides.

Exhaustion takes over and I feel myself slipping into a daze where nothing really makes sense.

The sound of a zipper brings me to, and I snap to attention, gripping Liam's shoulders as he lines himself up with me and slams into me.

I cry out from the sudden and unexpected intrusion.

His thick cock is buried to the hilt, my pussy aching and stretched painfully. It feels like a punishment. Perhaps I deserve it for thinking such horrible thoughts. But as he rocks his hips and whispers words of adoration in my ear, I relax around him, hooking my ankles behind his back as he plows into me, hard and unforgiving.

"You're mine, Alora. Mine to eat. Mine to fuck. Mine to make bleed. But fuck if you're not also the most precious fucking thing in my life. And I'll protect you with my life, sweetheart. I won't kill your stepfather for threatening your mother, but I will make him pay. Do you understand me?"

His wet mouth drags over my jawline, peppering soft kisses all over my face and neck as he holds me against him with his belt around my throat while he drives into me, his other hand gripping my hip and bruising my flesh.

"Yes. I understand."

My head falls back when he lowers his mouth to my nipples, his skilled tongue swirling and teeth grazing the sensitive buds. He gathers a drop of my blood on his finger and licks it before bringing his lips back to mine and kissing me. The metallic tang of copper floods my mouth, his tongue delving in and tangling with mine.

I've never been fucked so thoroughly in my life. I've never been tortured with pain and pleasure because I never knew a man who could toe the line as expertly as Liam.

He thrusts into me hard, his hand moving from my hip and thumb finding my clit. He applies firm pressure, rubbing hard and fast, back and forth, my slick arousal ensuring his thumb glides smoothly over the sensitive bundle of nerves.

"Come for me, sweetheart. Let me feel that tight cunt flex. Let me feel you shatter in my arms. Show me you're mine, Alora."

And that's all the permission I need to break again. I cry out, my thighs quivering and nails clawing at his broad shoulders and back. He muffles my screams with his mouth, drinking thirstily from me. Fucking me through my orgasm until I'm begging him to stop. His thrusts become so forceful, the legs of the heavy billiard table scrape against the floor.

Liam's hard cock galvanizes to steel as warmth spills inside me. I feel him throbbing as he slows his pace, grunting out his release and dropping his forehead to mine.

"Fuck," he growls, his breathing ragged and heart pounding in his chest.

He plants a chaste kiss on the tip of my nose before making quick work of unbuckling his belt and slipping it off from around my throat.

"All mine." He nuzzles into my hair, his hot breath clinging to my neck as he licks the sensitive flesh below my ear. "Every broken piece of you."

Twenty-Three

Liam

P EACE CLOAKS ME LIKE a heavy fog, blurring my vision and calming the turbulence normally churning inside me. My monster sleeps, my demons silenced by the overwhelming satisfaction of having Alora coiled around me, her small limbs squeezing me tight as she clings to me like a koala bear. I'm not ready to let her go, so I keep my cock seated inside of her and carry her up the stairs and into my ensuite bathroom.

The motion sensor nightlight blinks on, casting us in a soft, warm glow as I step into the deep clawfoot tub and sit down. I reach forward and turn on the faucet, checking the temperature before pushing the plug and settling back against the cool porcelain. It was only hours ago that I had her in the bathtub while I cleaned her cuts and probed for information. But here we are again. And I'm not mad about it.

Alora's head lifts from my shoulder, green eyes hooded and her expression slack.

She's exhausted, and fuck if that doesn't cause a sliver of guilt to lodge itself into my gut.

"You cut me," she whispers, her emerald orbs darting over my face in search of any signs of remorse. She'll find plenty of it there because I hate myself for allowing my control to slip away. And there's a niggling sensation in my chest, the slight tug of a dangling string, that indicates I may also be a little sorry for scaring her so much.

"I did." I sweep her hair away from her face.

She wiggles back, my cock slipping free from her wet heat and bouncing against my bare stomach. She lifts her left arm and peeks down at the two small gashes that form a small L on the side of her pert little breast.

A smirk graces her lips, and she returns her attention to me.

"L for Liam?"

I exhale softly and shake my head, watching as she adjusts herself on my lap, one palm splaying over my throbbing heart. Her eyes roam over my tattoos as her fingers trace the outline of the eagle wings spanning the width of my chest.

Her thick, dark lashes lift, and she stares back at me with wonder etched into her features.

My lips press into a firm line as I recall what she asked of me.

"Do you still have your mother's journal?"

"No. Whoever broke into my apartment stole it."

She worries her bottom lip, and I give her a reassuring squeeze.

"It was a silly thing for me to ask of you. He's not worth it, Liam. Karma will come for him eventually."

My thumbs sweep over her cheekbones, and I tuck her hair behind her ears. "He might not be worth it. But you are."

She shakes her head. "No, I'm not. Really."

She's fishing for reassurance, and since she asks so little of the world around her, I'll give her what she's seeking without complaint.

"Listen to me. I'm saying you can trust me with your life, sweetheart. I'd move heaven and hell to keep you safe. Not because I have to. But because every fucking breath you take is worth more than the cold, black heart beating in my chest."

Her sadness evaporates before my eyes, replaced by something else. Hope, maybe?

"That's a lot of pressure."

I angle my head at her as she begins fidgeting anxiously, the bath water now rising up around her hips and causing her ass to glide easily over my thighs.

A long, pregnant pause stretches on before she finally rolls her eyes and blows out a frustrated breath. And now I'm smiling. And it feels a little less foreign than it used to.

"You're not allowed to do that," she huffs out.

"Do what?"

"Smile."

"And why is that?"

"Because my heart can't handle it."

I can't stop my lips from lifting further, and I feel it all the way to my eyes. Fuck, this woman has a way.

We stare at each other for a long, quiet moment, watching each other's facial expressions morph. I wonder what she's thinking. What haunts her nightmares. When her next attempt at running might be and how she feels about a real fresh start. Not the shitty kind she was scrounging and saving for. But a real, solid, promising fresh start.

With me.

When the water reaches her waist, I lean forward and turn the faucet off, snatching a clean washcloth from the shelf behind me and soaking it. I bring it to the cut from my knife and dab away at the drying blood. The gash isn't deep. Just a small flesh wound, no worse than a nick from a knife while chopping vegetables. But it'll leave a scar, and I can't help but feel possessive about it.

Alora sits quietly, watching me clean her up.

When the blood is wiped away and the cut has cauterized, I spin her around and pull her between my legs so her back is resting against my stomach and her head is on my chest. We lie in silence, soaking in the warmth of the bath, my arms coiled around her tiny waist, hugging her tight, her hands hooked over my forearms.

I stare down at our bodies sealed together like two perfect puzzle pieces.

And there's not a doubt in my mind that after years of fighting to keep my monster at bay, years of being focused solely on missions and hunting down the men who hurt Rachel, that I've found a peace I never knew I could have.

But that peace is short lived. Because just as I'm helping Alora out of the tub and draping a towel around her shivering body, my phone buzzes with a call from Sloane. And when I listen to what she has to say, my demons begin their chant, waking my monster from his slumber.

Twenty-Four

Liam

T HE HEELS OF MEN'S polished dress shoes click on the dusty concrete floor as the man we've been summoned by makes his way across the empty warehouse, the obnoxious sound echoing off the steel walls and slicing through the silence. His silver rings and white teeth glimmer in the limited sunlight filtering through the dirty windows. His black hair is slicked back with not a strand out of place. And his pinstripe suit is perfectly pressed and tailored to fit his large frame. If it weren't for the tattoos dusting his knuckles and creeping out of his shirt collar, I'd say he's a pretty boy. But I know better. This is a man who enjoys getting his hands dirty when the time is right. This is a man not to be fucked with.

Mikhail Osmanov. The leader of the Federov Bratva.

Four soldiers flank his sides, all strapped with weapons, just as we are. Their gazes shift to each of us, assessing the situation for what it is—incredibly volatile.

But if all goes well, we'll leave here in one piece and with a plan to take out Ivan Petrov.

"Gentlemen," Osmanov greets with a sly smile, his pale green eyes scanning all four of us, taking in our military fatigues and weapons. "It's nice to see you all in good health." His gaze slides to Zak, and he nods once at him. This motherfucker is the reason Zak's still breathing. He's the reason my teammate and best friend survived the Colombian cartel's attack two years ago. But that doesn't mean he's to be trusted. Because if there's one thing we all know, it's that a man as powerful as Mikhail Osmanov does nothing without ensuring his own personal gain.

Mac steps forward. "It's my understanding that one of our own took it upon herself to cut a deal with you." Mac's tone is calm and collected, but there's an underlying hint of displeasure there. And Osmanov doesn't miss it.

He smiles, the skin around his eyes crinkling.

"She did," he acknowledges coolly. "Is that going to be a problem for us?"

"Not if you don't abuse the privilege. Sloane's a highly valuable asset to our team and part of the family. We won't stand for her to be harmed."

The Russian's smile flattens. "Do you take me as a vile man, soldier?"

"You're the leader of the Federov Bratva. I'd be stupid to believe you're not capable of committing vile acts."

It's a bold observation, but Osmanov's head bobs in under-standing. He swipes a thumb over his bottom lip and glances around at each of us again. Sloane's pushing her luck, and I get the sense this prick is going to take advantage of that when the opportunity presents itself.

"I suppose you're right," he murmurs before returning his at-tention to boss man. "But you have my word. Your girl will see no harm. As I've mentioned in the past when we collaborated, her skills could be of use to me in the future."

Mac's shoulders lower just a fraction, and my mind darts to Alora who's sitting with Sloane in an armored truck a few clicks out. Sloane's running surveillance on this place, and after the last time I stuffed Alora into the surveillance truck with her and she busted out and walked straight toward the danger, we decided to put more distance between her and this situation. And the last time Sloane and Osmanov came face to face, she stood confidently in front of him, chewing her gum and beaming up at him as if he's no threat to her at all.

But he fucking is. And there's no way the tab she's racking up with him will go unpaid. So it's for the best that both women are nowhere near the building right now.

"Alright then," Mac cuts in. "Let's hear your proposal."

Osmanov stuffs his hands in his pockets and slowly paces the space in front of us.

"We combined forces to take out the cartel that's been causing problems for my business. Although there were a few bumps in the road ..." He glances at Zak again who's got his finger over the trigger of his rifle that's currently pointed to the floor. "I feel it went well and would like to form another alliance to handle the remaining Petrov."

"Why?" Mac asks, his gray brows lowering over his eyes.

Osmanov pauses and sighs. "Because those fuckers are like cockroaches and have been a nuisance to my family for decades."

I shift on my feet, my guts churning with the knowledge that Osmanov's family was ever involved with the Petrovs. But I remain silent, listening to what he has to say. Acting irrationally right now would only delay me getting my hands on Ivan and finishing this once and for all.

"And since I know this is somewhat personal for your team ..." He glances at me, his lip twitching. "I'd like to capitalize on the opportunity. It's not lost on me that Sweetwater is responsible for taking out both of Ivan's sons. As you all know, I'm a resourceful man and can find this information at the drop of a hat. But the leader, Ivan, the worst one of all, is still breathing. And I suspect at some point, he'll crawl out from whatever rock he's hiding under and ask for my help in solving his pesky little problem."

Us. We're his problem. Because we're the biggest threat to his life and trafficking business.

"We weren't aware your families were ever involved."

The Russian begins pacing again, the gears in his genius mind turning over.

"We don't deal in the flesh trade anymore, but there was a time that was a large part of the family business. The Petrovs were merely a source of skin. Our wholesale supplier, for lack of better words. And we were dealers, reselling the stock for a premium to those willing to pay. But that was prior to my father's leadership. He put an end to it years ago. And we have no intentions of ever returning to it." He pauses again and turns his attention to me, arrogance radiating off him in waves. "I hear Rachel is keeping well."

I step forward, fury ripping through me at the mention of my sister's name.

His lip twitches again, and I just know this fucker is trying to pull a reaction from me.

"Stand down, Davis," Mac orders.

My blood pumps violently through my veins like white water. I would love nothing more right now than to put a bullet between the Russian's eyes. But instead, I groan and fall back in line with Zak and Joel. But that long fuse I possess has been lit, and it's taking everything in me to slow the burn so it doesn't reach the end and blow.

Osmanov smirks and strokes his short manicured beard with his knuckles. He saunters toward me, his shoes glinting before stopping two feet in front of me. I feel every set of eyes in the warehouse on me, waiting for my reaction.

"Your girl," he says lowly. "Her name is Alora, am I right?" My finger itches to pull the trigger of the gun hanging at my side. But I refrain. "She must have made quite the impression on Ilya for him to want revenge the way he did."

"Alora has nothing to do with this."

He nods in agreement. "Of course not. And it will remain that way. But it seems Ivan is now out for blood because he believes Alora is responsible for not just Ilya's death, but Viktor's as well. Which means not only do you have beef with the Petrovs since they hurt your sister, but now your woman is at risk, too."

I exhale slowly and work to keep my monster at bay. Osmanov hasn't threatened Rachel or Alora, but his keen interest in them is enough to make me want to rip his head from his body and watch his blood spray the walls.

"Your point," Mac pipes up, redirecting Osmanov's attention.

Osmanov sighs. "My point, gentlemen, is that it appears you're in over your heads. And I'd like to help."

"How?"

"Ivan has something that I want. And I have every intention of getting my hands on it. So, when he reaches out to me for help, which I'm confident he will do, I'll set up a face-to-face meeting with him. And when I've legally acquired the asset I'm looking to purchase, I'll send you the details of his location, and he's all yours."

"You're looking to purchase a human life," I sneer accusingly. "What makes you think we should trust you?"

He levels me with a sober expression, his Russian accent thick when he says, "It's not a human life I'm after, soldier."

Mac speaks up. "And in return for giving us his location?"

The Russian smiles, his straight teeth white and fucking menacing looking. "Just the favor already agreed upon by Sloane." He claps his hands. "Now, do we have ourselves a deal?"

We all glance at each other, checking in to get a grasp on how we feel about this situation. But ultimately, our hands are tied, so we accept.

Mac and Osmanov work the details out, and we file out with the promise from the Russian that he'd give us the date, time, and location of his meeting with Ivan if and when he reaches out to him. Which poses another question ... Why is Osmanov so sure that Ivan will contact him?

Minutes later, I pull up to the surveillance truck and hop out of my pickup. The back door of the armored vehicle flies open and out hops Sloane, a smug grin on her face as she chews on a wad of bubble gum. Alora appears next, not sharing the same satisfied look as Sloane.

"Told you it would all be fine, big guy," Sloane chirps, patting me on the chest as she strolls past.

My feet carry me to Alora, who's currently leaning against the truck with her arms crossed and hip popped. Her emerald eyes are piercing and lit with frustration. Her right to make decisions for herself has been revoked after she fled the truck outside The Afterlife. And that means that despite her efforts to prove she can behave, I stuffed her in the truck with Sloane and warned her that if she tried to run or caused any grief, there'd be hell to pay.

"Time to go," I tell her.

She rolls her eyes. "More orders. Shocker."

Sloane snorts somewhere behind me, and I ball my fists at my sides and work to calm my breathing. After our moment in the bathtub yesterday, I switched back into my default mode of overbearing dick, and Alora switched back to grating on my last goddamn nerve.

And if she keeps it up …

"My patience is wearing thin, little thief. So, I suggest you move boots and get your ass in my truck before I put you there myself."

She unfolds her arms and scoffs, stomping past me and waving goodbye to Sloane. She climbs up into the passenger seat of my truck and flips me the middle finger before slamming the door and disappearing behind the tinted window.

I turn to Sloane and glower down at her. "You're getting yourself in some hot water, Sloane. I don't like this arrangement with the Russian."

She smiles up at me, all bright eyed and bushy tailed.

"You boys and your overprotectiveness." She plucks a piece of lint off my shirt. "That gangster is nothing but a big ole pussycat. You've got nothing to worry about." But as I stand here staring down at her, her smile fades and a serious expression takes form. "You carry the weight of the world on your shoulders, Liam. Don't you think it's time you stop worrying about everyone else and get some for yourself?" Her eyes, today magenta from her tinted contacts, dart to my truck then back to me. "You deserve to be happy, big guy. Lord knows you've earned it."

Alora sits quietly in the passenger seat, her fingers knotted in her lap and gaze lost somewhere beyond the trees lining the highway.

When I take an exit that doesn't lead toward my cabin, she perks up and glances over at me.

"You missed your turn," she points out.

"I know."

"Well, aren't you going to turn around?"

"No."

She folds her arms across her chest and narrows her eyes on me.

"And why not?"

"We need to make a stop at my house before heading back to the cabin."

Her brows inch up her forehead. "Your house? I thought the cabin was your house?"

"No."

There's a pregnant pause before Alora asks, "So, what do you need to stop at your house for?"

"A couple packages were delivered and I need to pick them up."

"Hmm," she hums, feigning thought. "More body bags perhaps? Pickling jars for fingers and toes?"

When I scowl at her, her cocky little grin vanishes before my eyes, and she returns to staring out the window.

When we roll into my driveway, her posture stiffens, and she peers around as if her eyes are deceiving her.

"Jesus," she hisses. "Murder pays well, huh?"

I suppress an eye roll and put the truck in Park.

"Stay here," I tell her, shooting her a warning look.

She smiles brightly and responds, "No place I'd rather be," in the most sarcastic tone I've ever fucking heard.

Grumbling, I hop out of my truck and head to the front door to scoop up the stack of varying sizes of brown shipping boxes. I slide them into the back and shut the door, then hop back behind the wheel. Alora peeks at the packages behind the front seats, but she doesn't ask what's in them.

When we turn back onto the highway to make the drive back to my cabin, I peer over at Alora. She's got her bottom lip tucked between her teeth as she gnaws away on it, her fingers once again knotted in her lap. And her shoulders are all the way up to her pretty little ears.

I reach over and snatch her hand in mine, lacing our fingers and propping our hands on the center console. It's a silent truce to whatever warpath we're on right now.

She clears her throat and shifts in her seat. "I uh ..." she starts. "I was wondering if it would be alright if I got a new cell phone since I lost mine at The Afterlife."

"A cell phone," I deadpan.

"Yeah. You know. The little boxes that people talk into and occasionally send or receive nudes to random people you meet online."

I shoot her a wry look and she smiles back at me.

"Why do you want one?"

She shrugs. "Because normal people have cell phones. And right now, I feel like I've completely lost my independence."

She's right. I've unintentionally robbed her of all her independence. And even though her car has been towed back to my cabin and is now collecting dust in my garage, I haven't had the chance to replace her radiator for her yet, so she can't drive it.

"I'll get Sloane to get you one under Sweetwater's name."

"So you can track me if I take off running," she deadpans.

"Precisely."

She huffs out a defeated sigh. "Fine."

When silence stretches on between us, my thoughts begin to wander back to Alora's past.

"Tell me more about your mother."

"She was a painter, just like me. She gave everyone the benefit of the doubt. Saw the good in people, even when there wasn't an ounce of it in them. She was sweet and caring and too soft to survive this world."

"She saw the good in your stepfather."

"Yeah." She adjusts in her seat, turning her body slightly toward me. "What about your parents?" she asks curiously.

I grip the wheel tight, the small space in the vehicle not near big enough for the amount of emotion that bubbles out of me at the mention of my parents.

"They're gone," is all I offer.

Her tiny hand squeezes mine, and all the tension seeps from my muscles.

"What happened to them?"

"My father died from cancer when I was nineteen. My mother couldn't handle the heartbreak, so she took off about a year later. Haven't seen or heard from her since then."

"Your mom bailed on you? How old was Rachel?"

"Fifteen. I had already enlisted in the military at that point. So she went to stay with our aunt until she went off to college."

"So you have no idea where your mom is now?"

I shake my head in a silent *no.*

"Well ..." she starts. "For what it's worth ... any parent who can bail on their children doesn't deserve to see how incredible they are as adults." When I don't respond, she continues on. "You're good, Liam. All good. And I hope you know that you have a lot of people who care about you. Who want to see you happy."

My jaw threatens to crack from how hard I'm clenching my teeth. But I force myself to not react. To not turn to her and grab her and kiss her and shake her for being so fucking frustrating and insightful and beautiful. I don't deserve an ounce of the praise she's giving me. Not when I've taken so many lives in such brutal manners, whether they deserved it or not. I'm going to hell for the life I've lived. And the thought of dragging Alora there with me is gnawing at my insides like a famished wolf.

I release Alora's hand and focus on the road in front of me. But I can feel her concerned gaze burning a hole through the side of my face.

"Karma comes for us all eventually, Alora. Mine will too."

Twenty-Five

Alora

WHEN WE GET BACK to Liam's cabin, exhaustion settles in, and I lay down for a short power nap with the hopes a snooze will help clear the fog from my overused brain. But when I wake and step outside onto the back deck to get some fresh air, all the confusion and uncertainty I thought I compartmentalized comes rushing back.

My feet bolt themselves to the deck, my heart swelling and chest flooding with warmth as I stare at the tall wooden easel set up with its back to the forest and a matching stool parked in front of it. Unopened containers of paint are lined up on the ledge, right beneath the big blank canvas resting against the frame. A glass mason jar filled with new brushes sits on the railing beside it.

I press my palm to my chest in an attempt to shove the emotion bubbling to the surface back down where it belongs. But I fail miserably, and my eyes well with tears.

Besides from when I volunteer at the nursing home, I haven't painted since my mother died. And after my apartment was ransacked and the remaining fragments of my past were ripped right out from under me, I forced myself to suppress the memories. Suppress the joy I once felt while sweeping a brush across a blank canvas. Suppress the hope I had of ever being able to do what I love most.

The sound of the patio door sliding open steals me from my teary-eyed thoughts, and I spin around to find Liam standing there, arms crossed, brows furrowed. Dark, moody, and grumpy.

"This is what was in the boxes you picked up from your house?"

He nods once but doesn't move. This man is unpredictable. I don't know whether I should scream at him for being a giant dick most of the time or throw myself at him for doing the nicest thing anyone has ever done for me.

I turn to face the canvas and easel again, feeling him creep up behind me. The heat of his body falls over me like a big, cozy blanket, and I turn around again, coming face to chest with him.

Lifting my chin, I stare up at him and croak out a sincere, "Thank you."

He nods again, his fingers combing through my hair and cupping the back of my head. He leans down and dusts a soft kiss on the top of my skull, inhaling deeply before he pulls away.

"Hungry?"

I grin up at him as he swipes my tears away as they fall. "Starving."

I sit perched in front of the canvas, watching the sun set. I've sat out here a few evenings now, so the scene is nothing new to me. But the way the sun dips low behind the thick line of trees at the back of Liam's property is still just as awe inspiring as the first night. I've decided I like it out here in the woods. The fresh mountain air. The space. The tall trees and starry skies.

The big, broody caveman who brought me here.

I could stand right here and scream at the top of my lungs, and only the birds and woodland creatures would hear me. Out here, I'm safe from everything and everyone.

I peek over at Liam, my fingers tightening around the crystal glass filled with my favorite lemony vodka drink as I watch him flip the steaks on the barbecue. His black T-shirt is stretched tightly over his broad shoulders and back, his muscles rolling and tensing as he cooks us dinner.

I've never met a soul with so many demons. A man with such dark, terrifying tendencies, who can put all my worries at ease with just a look. Even if that look is a scowl.

A warm breeze sweeps in and kicks up a few strands of my hair that have fallen loose from the messy bun I threw up on top of my head. The air is crisp and clean with just a hint of cedar. I realize now that's where Liam's woodsy scent comes from. I can picture him chopping wood out here, his faded jeans slung low on his hips—no T-shirt because I'd request he do it shirtless—all those big muscles rippling with every swing of the axe.

A small smile graces my lips at the thought of being barefooted in his kitchen, cooking him bacon and eggs and whatever else he likes for breakfast. He'd come in from outside, his body slick with sweat, and he'd kiss me. Then he'd probably bite me, maybe tease me some before shoving his giant ...

He turns around and I clear my throat, averting my eyes.

When I peek over at him again, he's leaning casually against the railing beside the barbecue, his arms folded and one ankle hooked over the other.

And as always, he's watching me closely. And scowling.

But this scowl is different. More like he's trying to solve a problem in his head. A very complex math problem. Or maybe he's envisioning all the ways he could torture me and make me come.

When I'm done undressing him with my eyes, I straighten my spine and select a brush from the jar. I dab the bristles into the blue oil paint and touch the tip to the canvas, releasing a sigh of contentment as I smear the white material with my favorite color. With each swoop, I fall deeper into a trance. I get lost in creating. Lost in the colors. Lost in the smell of the paint mixing with the mountain air.

And for the first time in what feels like forever, all my worries melt away.

Liam plates our dinner and we eat at the small bar-height table on his deck. The second my tongue meets the buttery-soft steak, I moan in pleasure.

"This is delicious," I mumble through another bite of food, feeling Liam's heated gaze on me as I practically inhale my meal. "Where'd you learn to cook?"

Peeking up at him, I notice a slight twitch in his cheek. When I swipe my lips with my napkin, his eyes fixate on my mouth and my cheeks warm from the heat of his stare.

"Taught myself between military stints after my mother took off," he tells me.

"Well, I've never met a man who can cook, so kudos to you for figuring it out." That earns me a slight smirk. "Better be careful, though," I add playfully. "A woman could get used to this. You keep treating me like this and I might end up sticking around."

The second the words are out, Liam's smirk vanishes and instant regret swoops in and bitch-slaps me. The last thing I want to do is make him think I'm clingy and intend on overstaying my welcome.

"Alora—"

I throw a palm in the air, halting him before he has a chance to say whatever it is he planned on saying. Because I'm almost certain it's going to be some sort of rejection and bum me out. And right here, eating this delicious food on the deck of Liam's beautiful cabin with a canvas and paints a few feet from me … I refuse to be saddened by being told I can't have something I never thought I'd want.

His frown deepens and he glances at my half-eaten steak before returning his eyes to mine. I adjust my posture and take a calming breath. When he looks at me like that—like he'd rather eat me than the hunk of meat on his plate—I lose all sense of clarity. He dissolves the certainty I had about my future and what I had planned for the rest of my time here on earth.

His utensils clank against his plate as he stands and pushes his stool back, rounding the table and snaking his giant hand around the back of my neck and sealing his lips to mine. My fork hits the ground, and I grip his T-shirt and hold on for dear life as he drinks from me, stealing every bit of oxygen from my lungs and destroying my thoughts with his hungry kiss.

My stool slides back, and I'm swiftly hoisted into a pair of solid arms, my legs instinctively wrapping around his hips as he carries me across the deck and perches me on the railing beside the easel. His hands roam my body, snaking beneath my shirt to find my breasts. I've always been a part of the itty-bitty titty committee, but Liam's never complained. And when he swipes his thumbs over my hardened nipples and releases a satisfied groan, I wonder if he's more than a little okay with my lack of endowment.

"You're sinfully beautiful, little thief," he murmurs against my mouth, squashing any self-consciousness I had about my body.

He slips my shirt over my head, the soft cotton brushing my nipples on the way past. The warm evening air cloaks my skin, the setting sun heating my back as Liam's searing gaze sends shivers down my spine.

He kisses me again, slowly this time. Deeply and with more tenderness than anyone would believe possible from a man like him. It's disarming and concerning. And I'm not sure if I should get to work fortifying my walls or let him tear them down with his bare hands the way he seems to enjoy doing.

He pulls away briefly and grabs the back of his shirt with one hand and removes it, exposing his muscular chest and all those dark, haunting tattoos. I trace a path with my fingertips, brushing over the soft swell of several scars littering his impressive body. He tenses when I touch the one on his ribs, just like he did when I stepped into the shower with him after he returned from Russia.

"What are these from?" I ask cautiously, fully prepared for him to retreat.

But he doesn't.

"Shrapnel."

"From an explosion?" I probe, blinking up at him.

He nods slowly, and I swallow the lump that forms in my throat at the thought of Liam putting himself in danger the way he's done for so many years. All in the name of making the world a better place, even if it means losing his life—his soul—in the process.

"When?"

He inhales a deep breath and grips the wooden railing on either side of me, his nose dragging up the side of my throat to my ear as he releases a pained groan.

"Nine years ago in the Middle East. My SEAL team was moving in on a group of terrorists. But they had a sniper and pegged one of my teammates in the stomach. He was still alive, so I moved to drag him to shelter before they could put more holes in him, but a bomb went off before I could make it to him. He was killed instantly, and I was sprayed with shrapnel."

The ache in my chest intensifies, and I find it hard to breathe properly.

"But it was a long time ago," he adds, as if that's any reassurance at all.

"Did you know him well?" I ask, dragging a finger over another one of the scars.

He rests his forehead on mine and nods.

"What was his name?"

"Tucker Bishop. It was his first mission. Had a wife and new-born baby back home. Too fucking young to die. And I wasn't quick enough. It should have been me. Not him."

Liam's eyes droop at the edges, sadness and guilt sweeping over his expression. I cup his face with my hands, feeling his coarse facial hair beneath my fingertips.

"You can't blame yourself for that, Liam. Yes, it's horrible. But it's obvious you live in a perpetual state of guilt for other people's misfortunes. You hold responsibility for things that aren't your burden to bear. You're the best man I've ever met. And anyone who has you in their life is incredibly fortunate. You're loyal to a fault. And protective beyond belief. You don't need to carry the weight of other people's decisions the way you do. And you certainly don't need to be riddled with the guilt of your teammate's death when there was nothing you could have done to save him."

We sit in silence for another moment. The only sounds around us are the light breeze and crickets singing in the background.

Liam shifts, and something cool and wet touches the side of my breast. His finger lazily wanders, smearing what I know is paint across my ribs, right beside where his knife nicked my skin. When I try to pull back from him and glance down, he stops me with his free hand and continues his ministrations. He dips his finger back into the blue paint and finishes his little art project. It feels like he's writing something, but I'm too distracted by the hungry look in his eyes to follow the lines with my imagination.

When he's finished, I lift my arm and peek down at my side, my heart launching into my throat when I realize exactly what it is he drew.

Liam, with the scar from his blade acting as the L, is painted across my rib cage. Just as I had joked about in the bathtub.

I blink up at him, feeling his possessiveness rolling off him in waves.

When I nod, a satisfied rumble comes from deep within his chest, and he lifts me off the railing, coaxing my legs around his hips as he buries his face into the crook of my neck and carries me inside.

My bare skin meets the cool satin sheets of his bed when he lays me down and lowers himself over me. His lips find mine in a deep, patient kiss that contrasts his usually rough demeanor. It's as if he's trying to tell me something without words. As if he's conveying a message with just his touch. And when I cup his jaw with my hands and stare up into his eyes, I find it there too.

But the words are never spoken. He seals his lips to mine again and we fall into a tender moment I never imagined a man like Liam could be capable of. His fingers skim over every inch of my body, a million goosebumps popping up in their wake.

Wolf eyes sear my flesh as he slips my shorts and panties down my legs and discards them on the floor. He sits up on his knees and takes me in, his tortured expression hardening further with every second that passes. So much anguish is etched into his beautiful face. It bleeds from him and into me, causing my heart to ache with something foreign. Something I can't bring myself to put a label on right now.

But when he removes his jeans and sinks slowly inside of me, filling me in one slow, deep thrust, relief washes over us and he releases a long sigh.

I rake my hands through his hair and wrap my legs around his hips, allowing him to take full control and to set the pace. When his thumb finds my clit and massages it with perfectly timed circles, all the tension in my body evaporates into thin air and I melt into the mattress. Heat pools low in my belly as Liam works me over so expertly that it's all I can do to simply keep breathing. To bury the emotions he makes me feel deep beneath the surface, even if for just a little while longer. Just until I'm out of here and can shatter to dust all alone.

The only problem with my plan is that I'm not sure I want to be alone anymore. Being here with Liam, surrounded by him completely, is confusing.

"Come for me, little thief," he growls against my mouth.

When he tilts his hips and his cock hits that deliciously sensitive spot inside me, I do just that. My nails bite into his bare back as I cry out his name, my legs trembling violently and any remaining tension and uncertainty dissipating.

"Good girl," he hums, stroking my hair as he buries himself deep and grunts out his own release.

His warm cum coats my insides, claiming me in a way I've only ever allowed Liam to do.

He collapses on top of me, and I accept all of his weight—despite the fact I can't fucking breathe—and soak it in. Liam flips us over, keeping himself buried inside of me. I lay my head on his chest and listen to his heartbeat. So steady and solid, much like the man himself. My eyes fall heavy as Liam's fingers skim up and down my spine and over my ribs. Over the scar on the side of my breast.

I'll miss this when I'm gone.

❖

I wake to a low whirring noise that bleeds through the thick slab of wood separating me from the rest of the house. I sit up and glance down at Liam's side of the bed, feeling the cool sheets with my hand.

Whipping the covers off my legs, I stand and slip into Liam's discarded T-shirt and pad barefooted through the cabin, following the sound. I find Liam at the front door, his back to me as he drills a hole in the frame. The power drill stops, and his arm falls to his side as he angles his head to glance over his shoulder at me.

"It's three in the morning," I rasp out, my voice groggy from sleep. "What are you doing?"

"Six locks," he says numbly.

My eyes slide to the locks he's installed on the door, unable to pinpoint the emotion that's lodged in my windpipe.

"Liam," I whisper, barely able to form words. "Those holes are permanent. You didn't need—"

He turns to me and snaps out, "I know they're permanent, Alora. That's the whole fucking point."

I shake my head and go to him, sliding my hand from his shoulder, all the way down his arm to take the drill from him.

"Come back to bed."

He frowns down at me, the darkness shadowing the skin beneath his eyes making him appear a decade older than he is. Between the unexpected tenderness of last evening and the gruffness of now, my head is spinning.

"You can add fifty more locks if you want. Just not tonight." I lace my fingers with his and lead him through the dimly lit cabin, noting the plastic wrappers and screws scattered haphazardly on the floor of the foyer.

As we pass through the kitchen, I spot more unopened packages of locks.

Was he planning on putting six locks on every damn door?

When we cross into the bedroom, he shucks out of his jeans and we crawl beneath the cool satin sheets. His arms instinctively come around my midsection, hauling me against him. He holds me tight, his nose nuzzled in my hair. We lay awake for a while with just the sounds of our breaths and steady beating of our hearts.

And when those intrusive thoughts of leaving this place, leaving Liam and never returning, filter back into my racing mind again, I swallow the boulder lodged in my throat and remind myself that nothing this good can ever last.

Twenty-Six

Alora

TWO MORE DAYS PASS in a blur. I spend most of my free time napping, eating the delicious food Liam cooks for me, and working on my car. Liam's been especially quiet, and I get the sense he needs some space to process whatever it is that's going on between us. So I've kept my distance and my mouth shut. For the most part. Besides, it's easier that way because every time I think I have something to say, all that wants to come out is a plea for him to not let me go.

I glance around the open backyard, my bottom lip clamped between my teeth. I told Liam I was going to sit on the deck and work on the painting I started the other night. But after staring at the tree line at the back of his property for what feels like hours, I finally give up the fight with myself and trudge across the lawn and duck into the forest.

A sliver of guilt niggles at me. I should have told him where I was going. But I also know he would have insisted on following me here. And I'm in dire need of some space to think for myself. To unknot my tangled-up emotions and tuck them back into their tidy, organized boxes. And I can't do that with him around, weaving himself into every fiber of my life and making it impossible to separate my feelings from reality.

I move slowly, sticking to the roughly stomped-down path that leads further into the bush. When I come to a clearing, I stop in my tracks, a smile tugging at my lips.

There's a man-made firepit in the center of the open space with three makeshift benches crafted from stripped and sanded logs surrounding it. Off to the side, there's a stack of firewood sheltered beneath a lean-to. The image of a shirtless Liam chopping wood springs back into mind.

And that image is exactly why I need space. Because even when he's not here, he's infiltrating my thoughts like some sort of emotional fucking terrorist.

Scowling now, I peer beyond the clearing at a rock wall that acts as a backdrop to the thick pines, green moss creeping up the gray stones and softening its otherwise jagged appearance. My feet carry me toward it, and as I approach, a deep crevice large enough for a human to squeeze through comes into view. A cave.

Curiosity gets the best of me, and I glance around, confirming I'm still alone, before deciding to explore further.

Someday, this untamed sense of curiosity is going to cost me. But for now, I'll relish in the freedom of being young and adventurous.

I turn sideways and shimmy through the cavernous hole. The air is cooler in here, and a shiver rolls down my spine, the dampness clinging to my skin and causing a chill.

Light seeps into the space from the opening on the other side, and excitement sizzles through me. I shoulder through, popping out of the crack and taking in my surroundings, breathing in deeply and finally feeling truly alone for the first time since I laid eyes on Liam.

A pool of crystal water serves as the focal point in the middle of the cave, a hole in the ceiling of the space allowing rays of light to stream in and bounce off the glass-like surface of the spring. The water is so clear, I can see every inch of colorful moss decorating the rocks beneath.

I peek down into the bottomless hole, my fingers and toes tingling with the desire to strip down and plunge in.

So that's exactly what I do, toeing out of my worn-out sneakers and peeling my jeans off my legs. My shirt flies off next, and I carefully unclasp Liam's Rolex from my wrist and set it on top of the pile.

I take a seat on the ledge and dip my feet into the water, gasping when I realize how cold it is. But I welcome the shock, and cold water's something I've never really been afraid of.

I turn onto my side and plant my palms on the slippery rock floor. Taking three calming breaths, I lower my body into the water, the iciness stealing my breath and nipping at my frazzled nerves.

With a sharp hitch of my lungs, I push onto my back and float on top of the water, my fingers skimming the surface lazily as I close my eyes and force my muscles to relax. To lean into the discomfort.

When I've breathed through the initial shock and my body has acclimated, I empty my lungs in one long exhale and sink beneath the surface. The steady whoosh of the water in my ears drowns out my thoughts, flooding my overactive mind with white noise. I open my eyes and drift further down. The water temperature plummets every inch, and my lungs strain against the desire to inhale.

I squeeze my lids shut, willing away the tears that sting the corners of my eyes. Small bubbles escape my mouth, the remaining oxygen being drained from my body. Darkness descends around me, and that loud whoosh and the steady beat of my heart intensifies.

Why I get a thrill out of doing silly things like this is something I'm not prepared to explore. Maybe I'm mentally ill, I don't know. But I've always been like this. A little bit curious. And a lot wild and free. Life's too short to be lived in fear, and I want to die with no regrets. I want to be able to say I didn't just survive, but that I was fully alive.

But just as I'm preparing to kick back up to the surface, I spot movement through the thin flesh of my eyelids. The calm water surrounding me stirs and tickles the tiny hairs on my body. I flash my eyes open in panic, catching a glimpse of something large and fast before a sudden warmth coils itself around my waist. I open my mouth to scream, but nothing comes out.

Up. Up. Up I go, rising at a speed unnatural to humans.

My head breaks through and I cough and sputter, struggling to clear my wet hair from my face as I kick away from whoever just dragged me up and out of my state of relaxation.

"What the fuck do you think you're doing?" I screech, spinning and locking eyes with a set of hot, anger-fueled coals. I glare at Liam, my body humming with adrenaline and teeth chattering audibly. The water's not cold enough to cause hypothermia, but the adrenaline of what just happened is enough to give me heart failure.

"Me?" he asks incredulously, his dark brows lowered over his molten eyes. His hair is near black and face shadowed in fury with only the small streams of sun casting light over his rugged features. "What the fuck are you doing letting yourself sink to the bottom of an ice-cold spring in a secluded cave at the back of my property, Alora?"

The way he says my name as he chastises me is infuriating.

I huff out a shaky breath and splash water at him. "I was perfectly fine, you ... you ... overbearing asshole!"

The scar on his forehead crinkles and he lunges at me, grabbing me by the wrist and hauling me effortlessly into him. I press my palms to his chest, my fingers practically numb from the cold. How he's still radiating heat like a fucking furnace is beyond me.

"You stupid, stupid girl," he grumbles, snaking his arm around my back and holding me close as he kicks us toward the ledge.

I wiggle out of his hold and push back from him, suddenly disappointed at the loss of his body heat. But fuck him.

"I'm not stupid. It's not like I was going to drown. I could have easily came back up for air."

He glares at me now, and that's when I realize he's in nothing more than a pair of black boxers. Jesus. The big, dumb idiot stripped down and jumped in after me, probably thinking I was trying to off myself. I'd roll my eyes if I didn't feel guilty about it.

He takes one stride toward me, his hair and face glistening with water droplets.

"Hold on." I raise a palm in the air. "I need some space." My voice rises an octave, and I hate how shrill it sounds echoing off the walls in here.

He doesn't respond, and with each passing second, I feel a little less frustrated and a lot more concerned for his mental state. And maybe mine too.

My mouth opens and closes, so many words lingering on the tip of my tongue.

A big, tattooed hand rakes through his soaked hair, and he releases some sort of strangled growl. Then he barrels toward me, water splashing as I shriek and try to swim away. But my limbs are aching from the cold now, and I'm fairly certain this guy is an Olympic swimmer or something because he catches me in no time and hauls me to the ledge. Strong hands wrap around my waist, and he lifts me onto the edge so I'm seated like I was before with just my feet in the water. How he managed to wrangle me without having anything to plant his feet on is beyond me.

I go to scramble away, but he snatches my ankles and holds me there.

"What are you doing?" I rush out, my lips trembling and teeth chattering violently. Every inch of my skin prickles with pins and needles as the air slaps against my icy skin. Cold water seeps from my sports bra and panties, pooling around my ass.

Liam props himself up onto an elbow and snatches his hoodie off the floor. He forces it over my head, and I pop my arms through. Without thinking, I bury my nose into the collar and fill my lungs with his scent, my body instinctively relaxing and my chill subsiding from the comfort of being wrapped up in him.

Oh, Al. You sick, sick bitch.

Cold hands meet my thighs, and he pries my knees apart. My hands fly to his shoulders.

"Hold on, pal. You can't just dive in after me, pull me out of the water, and expect me to spread my legs for you."

His lip twitches, and he grips the backs of my knees and tugs me forward so my bottom is perched on the very edge of the rocks, my panties wedged tightly between my folds and grinding against my clit. His broad shoulders brush the insides of my knees as he moves closer. His skin is icy, and yet he doesn't seem the slightest bit affected by the temperature. It dawns on me that it's probably because of his SEAL training.

"Liam."

He stares up at me, all hooded eyes and dark hair and big, rippling muscles covered in black ink.

"Alora," he parrots, his voice all gravel.

"You're freezing." I press my fingers into his shoulders, watching as the skin around them blanches. "Get out of the water."

His jaw slides as he skims his big, rough hands up my thighs, causing a fresh flurry of bumps to pepper my skin. His thumbs graze the hem of my panties, right at the juncture where my hips meet my legs.

"No," he says lowly, his hot breath skating over my bare skin and thawing my core. "But you ..." He trails off, his thumbs drifting back and forth as he stares up at me with a distinctly terrifying look in his eyes.

He pulls my panties to the side and my breathing stalls, my heart picking up speed as his eyes sear a burning path from my face all the way to my exposed center. One cold thumb moves inward, pushing between my folds and sliding up to my clit.

"You're wet," he growls accusingly.

"Yes," I rush out, my grip tightening on his shoulders.

"Fucking soaked." He circles my clit and I arch my back, pleasure rippling through me and heating my flesh. He smears my juices around lewdly, sending his point home.

He swipes the tip of his nose through my seam, inhaling deeply. A satisfied hum vibrates from his chest, and I shiver in response. It's such a primal, animalistic thing to do. And it drives me wild with need.

"You get off on danger, don't you, little thief? The adrenaline turns you on."

My teeth rake over my bottom lip, my body practically vibrating from the slow, calculated circles of his expert thumb.

"Say it, Alora. Tell me your pussy drips every time you do something dangerous. Like sneaking away from me to go swimming in a cave alone. Or speeding down the highway in the middle of the night. Or stealing watches from dangerous men."

"Yes," I hiss out. "I like the thrill."

He clicks his tongue and his gaze darkens. "Silly girl."

When his mouth latches onto my clit, my head drops back on a moan, my hips bucking as his tongue lashes at the sensitive bundle of nerves. He guides my legs over his shoulders, leveraging my thighs to keep himself afloat as he sucks.

My body tenses, my orgasm building so fast that my nails are already carving half-moons into his shoulders.

And just as I'm opening my mouth to tell him I'm about to come, he withdraws his hands and backs away from me. My eyes flash to his as the loss of the orgasm sends a shot of disappointment through me.

"You're kidding," I deadpan, frustration seeping into my tone.

He smirks arrogantly, then splays his hands on the rock ledge beside me and lifts himself up, water streaming down his powerful body and disappearing at his feet. His biceps and forearms flex as he maneuvers so effortlessly. And when he stands beside me, my eyes are drawn to the bulge in the front of his boxers, the black fabric clinging to it.

My mouth waters and I pinch my thighs together. I let my gaze travel south over the tattoos on his thighs. The man's body is a work of art. One I'd pay handsomely for the opportunity to paint. He snatches his discarded jeans off the ground and slips into them, buckling his brown leather belt before stuffing his feet into his socks and boots.

His hand appears in front of me in offering, and I blow out an exaggerated breath and drag myself away from the thought of stabbing him in the eye. Reluctantly, I drop my hand into his and he helps me to my feet.

"You're an ass," I tell him as he gathers up the rest of our clothing and my shoes and gestures for me to lead the way through the crevice in the wall.

When we pop out on the other side of the cliff, I turn toward him and cross my arms. His expression is pure granite, not an ounce of emotion flowing beneath it. Or maybe there's a whole ocean of feelings churning under the surface, and he just doesn't let the world see it. The more time I spend around him, the more I suspect it's the latter. Long strides bring him to me, and he towers over me, casting a big shadow and staring down at me with something hot and fiery raging behind his eyes.

His free hand hovers in the air between us for the briefest of moments before he sweeps the pad of his thumb across my cheekbone. I have to physically refrain from leaning into his touch and rubbing all over him like a cat. He tucks a stray strand of hair behind my ear then hooks my chin with his forefinger and steps into me. My arms fall limply at my sides as I stare up at his ruggedly handsome face. His head lowers a fraction, and his eyes fixate on my mouth as if he's considering kissing me.

My tongue sweeps across my bottom lip in anticipation, and he tracks the movement, his eyes flaring with desire.

Please, for the love of all things holy …

But as quickly as the moment comes, it passes. He swoops down and throws me over his shoulder in one swift motion.

I gasp, my fists pummeling his firm backside as I wiggle and kick.

"Put me down, you mammoth."

But his forearm pins the fronts of my thighs to his chest and the struggle is pointless. Before I know it, my head is bobbing as the forest floor flies beneath me. I peek around as we pass by the firepit, the air in my lungs pulsed out of me with each of Liam's giant footsteps.

"I can walk, you know."

"I'm aware," is his dry response.

"So then put me down."

"Not a chance." His boots crunch on small twigs, and I stare down at the ground again, reminded of the night he chased me through the woods and I gouged my feet all to hell.

The stomped forest path turns to lush, green grass. Then eventually a wooden deck. And finally black birch wood floors. He lowers me gently to my feet, and my head spins from the blood rush. He thrusts my clothing at my chest.

"Get dressed and pack a bag. You're going to Joel and Stella's."

"What? Why? Where are you going?"

He spins and stalks down the hall, but I'm hot on his tracks, following closely behind and firing off a line of questions as we head toward his bedroom.

"What's going on? Why do I have to stay somewhere else? What should I pack? How long will you be gone?"

We enter his room, and he crosses the floor, disappearing inside the walk-in closet.

I stand anxiously at the foot of the bed, waiting for him to reemerge with an explanation. When he pops back out of the closet, he's carrying a suitcase.

He instructs me to pack enough for a few days then leaves, slamming the door behind him.

And well ... I guess I'm not getting any answers right now.

Twenty-Seven

Liam

Leaving Alora with Stella isn't ideal. And it sure as fuck wasn't easy to walk out that door knowing she's on edge and probably itching to take off running. But she'll be safe in Joel's house, locked up within the confines of the best surveillance and alarm system money can buy. And I've hired an old acquaintance from the Navy to keep his eyes on the house and follow the girls if they decide to go out. I'd rather be there with her, but I don't have any other option but to leave since Osmanov called with the details of his meeting time and location with Ivan Petrov. And with the end of this mission within sight, we need all hands on deck. All of Sweetwater is here on the plane, getting their heads in the game and catching some rack time before we land in Russia and ambush Petrov.

But my head is swimming with incoherent thoughts. I'm unfocused and especially uneasy for some reason. The alarm bells in my head are blaring as my instincts fire on all cylinders. There's something off about the situation with Petrov, and no matter how hard I work to stamp down the feeling, it continues to creep back up like a bad weed.

I lift my eyes from the floor of the plane and stare at Mac at the head of the table.

He nods once at me, then begins detailing our plan of attack as I pull my switchblade out and begin flipping it opened and closed, the cold steel soothing and familiar.

"The plan remains the same as discussed," he begins. "Osmanov will cut his deal with Petrov, and once he's acquired whatever asset it is he's after and his men have all left the building, he'll give us the green light to move in."

"Remind us again why the fuck we're letting that Russian prick get what he wants?" Joel asks, his piercing blue eyes fixated on boss man.

Mac splays his palms on the table in the center of the plane and drops his head. "Because if we don't and things go awry, we won't be afforded another chance to use him to our advantage."

"What do you think it is he wants from Petrov?" Zak asks next, his gaze darting to mine before returning to Mac.

"Not a fucking clue. But he's reassured us it's not a life."

"I don't trust him," I voice. "There's something off about this."

Mac blows out a ragged breath and rakes his hand through his silvery hair. "I feel it too. But we don't have a choice right now.

Sloane will work surveillance during Osmanov's meeting with Ivan. If she spots anything out of the ordinary, we pull out."

I glance over at Sloane seated across from me, her combat boots casually propped up on the table and ankles hooked. She's staring back at me, her jaw working as she chews thoughtfully on her gum the way she does. She shoots me a wink and hooks her lips into a smirk. Her confidence is unwavering.

"When have I ever let you boys down?" she asks, folding her arms and rocking back in her chair. Her relaxed state chips away at the cement in my lungs, giving me just a little room to breathe. For reasons unknown, she seems to trust Osmanov. I only pray it doesn't come back to bite her. After the shit she's been through—the harsh blows she took while in the military—she doesn't need the trouble. Doesn't deserve to have a man like Osmanov breathing down her neck and taking advantage of her.

She lowers her feet and stands, her black boots squelching on the floor of the plane as she paces the length of the table.

"Osmanov isn't going to screw us," she says with certainty. "In fact, I get the sense he wants to make this little alliance something bigger." She stops and smiles, her bright white teeth nearly blinding. "I think he likes us. Wouldn't mind keeping us in his back pocket."

"For what, though? Our entire purpose in life is taking assholes like him down," Zak reminds her.

She blows a bubble and pops it. "I haven't quite figured that out yet. But I'll get back to you when I do." She beams at me again, and I groan.

Sloane's getting herself in too deep with this Russian prick, stacking up the IOUs, all in his favor. Eventually, he's going to cash in on them, and I suspect when he does, there will be interest charged on the debt we've accumulated.

"Alright," Mac speaks up, rapping his knuckles on the table. "Get some rest. Fuel up. When we land, we'll haul ass in and sit back and wait for the signal. You all know the drill. Nice and clean. In and out." His eyes snap to mine. "We'll take Petrov alive if we can. Get whatever information we can squeeze out of him. Then we'll finish the job. Got it?"

Everyone around the table nods in agreement. Except me.

"I want him," I snarl, staking my claim to Petrov's final hours.

"And you'll get him," Mac acknowledges. "But we keep this quiet. We don't need authorities or civilians getting involved."

My palms are sweating, my blood itchy, and every hair on the back of my neck standing on end. *Something. Is. Off.* And I refuse to relax and sink into the mission the way I normally do.

"Osmanov's in," Sloane chirps in my comm. "Six armed guards in tow. No sign of Petrov yet."

Mac, Joel, Zak, and I are stuffed into an armored truck, dressed head to toe in our Sunday best, strapped and weighted down with weapons and ammunition, waiting for Sloane's direction. Waiting for Osmanov to give the signal that he's done doing business with Ivan.

And I'm growing impatient. One wrong move could cause me to snap like a twig and send me into a downward spiral. But we can't fuck this up. *I* can't fuck this up. Because this is our best shot yet at finishing off the Petrov trafficking ring. And I have a girl back at home I want to sink back into and fucking put this entire mission behind me once and for all. If for nobody else, I'm doing this for Rachel and all the women and children this sick fuck ever terrorized.

"Petrov is officially late," Sloane chirps.

Which means Osmanov will be growing antsy as well. The comms go radio silent for a moment, and I know Sloane's muted herself. Seconds tick by, and the four of us glance around at each other.

Sloane comes back in. "Osmanov's calling it. He's bailing."

"Fuck," I snap, standing abruptly and gripping my rifle tight. "Where the fuck is Petrov?"

"Maybe he had a bad feeling, the same way we did, and decided to not show," Zak levels. Always cool. Always collected. Always fucking rational. But my instincts are gnawing at my insides like a famished animal. And I know without a shadow of doubt, that there's a bigger picture to be seen here.

"Put me on the line with Osmanov," I growl.

"On it," Sloane chirps, her gum popping in my ear.

The comm switches.

"Gentlemen," Osmanov drawls coolly. "I apologize, but it appears plans have changed."

"Where is he?" I bite out, earning me a heavy sigh from the Russian on the other end of the line.

"If I knew, I'd tell you. So, for now, it appears we'll need to reschedule."

"Tell us what asset you're hoping to acquire, or we're out," I threaten. Mac stands and glowers at me. But I'm done sitting around with my hand on my cock.

There's a pregnant pause. "Nothing of any significance, I can assure you. But it seems I'll need to find an alternative route to acquire it before it ends up in the wrong hands and things get a little ... messy."

"Anything to do with the Petrovs is significant in our eyes. Spit it out, or we're done."

The line crackles slightly before Osmanov says in a lower tone, "I'll be in touch if Ivan reaches out again. Otherwise, safe travels home, gentlemen."

And the line goes dead.

Twenty-Eight

Alora

Babies are terrifying. Their eyes are far too large for their heads, their bellies are too round for their bodies, and their personalities are volatile as fuck. One minute they're babbling and giggling. The next they're trying to send you to an early grave with their deadly diaper blowouts.

And Stella's baby boy, Finnegan, is no exception. And he's staring directly at me. Although, I have to admit, the little fucker is pretty cute.

I watch in awe as Finnegan stuffs his entire fist into his mouth. And not just his pudgy little fingers, but his whole damn hand, right up to his wrist. It's unnatural and only solidifies my theory that children are spawns of Satan. While Finn is trying—and succeeding—at eating himself alive, Lainey is twirling in the middle of the living room, a little wand in her hand and her curly, dark hair tied up into two pigtails on the top of her head. I'm willing to bet money there are little devil horns hidden within them.

"Here you go, sweetie," Harper, Zak's wife, says chipperly, holding a glass of red wine out for me.

"Thank you." I flash her a tight-lipped smile, watching out of the corner of my eye as she smooths her hand over her growing baby bump.

Between Stella's feral children and Harper's expanding stomach, I'm getting a healthy dose of birth control. Not that I need it, thanks to regular injections.

"Wine always helps me calm my nerves when Zak's away," Harper tells me, taking a seat on the sofa beside me. I glance at her belly again, and she huffs out a laugh. "Well, it used to, anyways. Six months sober and counting." She beams at me then pulls an old, tarnished coin out of her pocket and flashes it at me. "Got my sobriety chip and all."

I can't help but laugh at her cute sense of humor. When Liam informed me he was leaving for Russia and that I'd be cooped up in Stella's house with her children and Harper and the alien growing inside of her stomach, I nearly choked on my own spit. Rachel was easy to talk to because it was just her and me, and she reminds me of Liam in some aspects. But these two? I'm out of my league, even though they've both been incredibly welcoming and pleasant to be around.

Combine their complete awesomeness with my lack of ability to mesh well with other women, and you've got yourself a big old bowl of socially awkward soup.

Harper kisses the coin and tucks it back into her pocket. I get the sense there's a story there. Like the coin is a lucky token or something. But I don't ask because it's really none of my business.

Stella appears a moment later, curling up on the oversized chair beside the fireplace, wine in hand.

"So, Alora. You and Liam, huh?" She waggles her perfectly groomed brows at me, her hazel eyes twinkling with mischief I'd recognize anywhere as a curious smirk stretches across her face.

I take a sip of my wine, mulling her question around for a moment before responding, "Yeah. I guess so."

"I bet he has a massive dick," Harper blurts.

"Harper!" Stella chastises. "Impressionable young minds present."

Harper swats the air. "They've heard worse from their Auntie Harper. Anyways," she singsongs, tucking her legs under her. Her blue eyes are wide and hopeful when she asks, "I'm right, aren't I?"

I curl my lips between my teeth, suppressing my amusement.

She points a pink-painted nail at me. "Ah ha! I knew it." She leans back and sighs. "God, that's satisfying to know."

Stella cocks a brow at her best friend. "Wondered about Liam's dick for a while, have you?"

Harper rolls her eyes. "Don't tell me you haven't wondered too. The dude has major big D energy. I'm just glad he's finally laying some of that pipe, you know. Sewing his wild oats."

I nearly blow wine out my nose, pressing my hand to mouth to stop from spewing it everywhere.

"Now look what you've done," Stella says. "You're terrifying the poor girl."

I laugh and shake my head. "No, no. Please continue. I haven't had this much fun in a long time."

Both women stare at me, their expressions sobering.

"Well," Harper starts. "Get used to it. Because you're stuck with us now. No way is Liam going to let a catch like you slip away."

I swallow around the rocks in my throat. It wasn't a direct compliment, but it still feels nice to hear.

"Nope," Stella chirps. "I'd throat punch him if he did. And then we'd keep you for ourselves."

"So, keeping people runs in the Sweetwater family."

Both women burst out laughing, and I angle my head and watch in awe as they crack up.

"Girl ... you have no idea. These guys are fucking ridiculous at times."

"Harper," Stella warns again, shooting her a glare.

"Sorry. These guys are ducking ridiculous." Stella rolls her eyes. "Wild animals, I tell ya. Look at Joel." Harper gestures to Stella. "He was the world's moodiest dick, all big muscles and serious scowls and bossy as duck. Now?" She pauses for a thought. "Well, let's be real, he's still all those things. But he's a husband and a father and if somebody even so much as glances in Stella's direction, they'll be sleeping with the fish by sunrise. And Zak?" She says her husband's name all breathy, little hearts flashing in her eyes. "He was the king of douchebags for the longest time. But he staked his claim. Pissed all over his territory. And there's not a man in the world dumb enough to try to take what's his."

I nod in understanding because yeah, that's a pretty accurate description of both of their husbands.

"And Liam ..." Stella says from her chair, and I perk up. "He's all that multiplied by a thousand."

"Try a million," I murmur against my glass, taking another sip to ease my nerves.

Stella snorts.

"Oooh," Harper says. And I can't keep up with their banter. "Are you guys going to get married and have babies?"

I clear my throat, my eyes shifting downward as I spin the wineglass in my hands. "I don't think that's in the cards for us."

The room falls quiet, just the sounds of Finnegan's slobbering mouth sucking on his fingers and Lainey's socked feet pounding the floor.

"I mean ..." What the hell do I say to that? I shrug a shoulder, a weird feeling creeping into my chest and clawing at my windpipe. Sadness? Is that what the fuck this is? No. Impossible. "I have a lot of baggage. I'm not sure Liam and I could ever make this permanent."

"What kind of baggage?" Stella asks.

I stuff whatever feeling is ripping at my throat back down where it belongs and take a sip of wine in an attempt at stalling. But the two women just stare at me expectantly, and I guess I'm not escaping this.

"I don't stay in one place for very long. Never really saw myself settling down. Kind of a drifter and a bit of a free spirit. Commitment terrifies me."

Harper's lips press firm before she says, "Girl ... Same. But whatever crap you're carrying around with you ... it doesn't matter to Liam. He's clearly in love with you. Doesn't take a rocket scientist to see it. I bet if it weren't for all his own trauma, he'd have already spilled the beans and told you that."

My chest aches. And I think maybe I'm having a heart attack. Panic attack, more likely. But I stuff that down as well. Because I'm damn good at suppressing my feelings and forging on.

I huff out a phony laugh. "There's no way he's in love with me. It's only been a few weeks since we met, and we didn't exactly start our ..." I say, twirling my hand in the air and searching for the right word, "relationship off like most people."

Harper snorts and Stella laughs.

"What?"

"Oh nothing. Just another thing we all have in common."

I can't help the smile that breaks out across my face. Is this what it feels like to have friends to gossip with? Other women to relate to and share stories with? If so, I kind of like it. Could maybe even get used to it.

"I have an idea," Stella tosses out of left field. "I have to go to Casa del Sol in the morning to check up on a few things. Why don't you and Harper come with me? We'll make a day of it. Grab lunch. I'll even call the babysitter so we don't have any kiddos to lug around with us."

I glance at Harper again who's nodding eagerly, her brows pushed high and a bright smile splitting her face in two.

"What's Casa del Sol?" I ask.

"The rehabilitation center I opened after my mother passed away. It's a safe place for victims of trafficking and trauma to escape to and get the support they need. We offer classes and therapy sessions and give them the means to get back on their feet."

"Wow." I have no words. "That's ... You opened a rehab center for victims?"

"She sure did," Harper cuts in, her voice thick with pride. "You should see the place. It's amazing. So, what do you say? Girls' day tomorrow?"

I nod, a little bubble of excitement building in my chest.

"Yeah. Okay. That sounds fun."

Twenty-Nine

Alora

I BARELY SLEPT A wink last night despite the copious amounts of wine I consumed thanks to Stella tasking herself with topping up my glass every time it fell below half. Normally, I can kick a hangover within a couple hours of waking up and showering. But today my skull is throbbing like the bass of a techno club, my stomach is unsettled, and I have a severe case of hangxiety.

And even though I'd rather curl up in bed and die, I promised Stella and Harper we'd have a girls' day.

So here we are.

When Harper said Stella's rehabilitation center was amazing, she wasn't exaggerating. Casa del Sol, which I've learned means House of Sun, is a massive stone mansion perched on rolling acres of vast, vibrant gardens, meticulously manicured lawns, and a forest with well-groomed trails. There's another smaller building, although calling it small is terribly inaccurate, set back a few hundred feet behind the mansion—Stella's office, she told me, and a place where staff can spend the night if they'd like.

"On Mondays, we garden," Stella chirps, leading the way as Harper and I saunter behind her on the narrow stone path that weaves between flower beds. The bodyguard Liam hired trails a little behind. He's wearing a pair of dark sunglasses that hide his eyes, but I know he's scanning every inch surrounding us. "We let the residents choose what they'd like to plant. We have vegetable and fruit gardens, as well as flowers where residents can pick their own bouquets for their rooms. Harper and I mapped the beds out, then we took the ladies shopping for all the gardening tools and seeds they could ever need."

"Jesus," I murmur, glancing around the property. "This must cost a fortune to upkeep."

It makes my petty thefts and donations feel incredibly insignificant.

Stella glances over her shoulder to smile at me. "Uh huh. But it's worth every penny."

When we reach a clearing at the back of the property, I stop to take in the sight of the lily pad-covered pond, an old wooden swing perched along the shoreline and facing out at the scenery. A large weeping willow tree sits off to the side, its long, feathery branches reaching all the way to the lush, green grass. Frogs croak and crickets sing a little tune. It's heavenly. Peaceful. So quiet compared to the hustle and bustle of the city.

"Liam said you went to school for art," Harper says, taking a seat on the swing to give her feet relief.

"I did. Visual arts. Painting, specifically."

"Oh," Stella cuts in. "You know what would be amazing? If you taught a painting class here. The residents would love that. We'd supply everything you need: easels, paints, and brushes. And you'd be compensated."

Her enthusiasm is palpable, and I feel a little guilty for not sharing in it.

"Yeah, maybe." My response is vague, and a little dry. Not because the idea doesn't intrigue me—in fact, it sounds incredible—but because I'm not sure yet if I'm going to be around long enough to take her up on the offer.

Stella's smile falters briefly before she says, "You think about it and let me know. We'd love to have you. But no pressure."

We hang around Casa del Sol for another hour or so, Stella introducing me to some of her staff and the residents who have been living there for some time, before we hop into Harper's vehicle again and drive to a little hole-in-the-wall French bistro with the cutest outdoor patio. Hanging planters line the front of the covered space, colorful flowers and vibrant green ivy draping from the pots providing a false sense of seclusion from the outside world. The chairs and tables are all antiques, each one different from the rest, which only adds to the charm.

Stella leans forward between Harper and I and squints at the patio from her spot in the back seat, a small smile gracing her lips.

"It reminds me of the spot Joel took me when we were in Italy for Giulia's funeral," she says, a memory flashing behind her eyes.

The three of us clamber out of the SUV and take a seat at a small wrought-iron table. I wave at the bodyguard Liam insisted follows us around if we leave the house. The big brute gives a curt nod back and settles into a spot on the other side of the patio, allowing us privacy but still within a close enough distance that if anything comes up, he can reach us quickly.

When I glance around, my eyes migrating to the panes of glass separating the outdoor dining area from the inside of the restaurant, my gaze settles on a man seated inside in a window booth. He has thinning gray hair and a large hooked nose that would be hard to forget. Familiarity tugs at my insides, and I find myself staring directly at him, desperately clawing at where I've seen him before.

"You okay, Alora?" Harper asks from beside me, her hand settling on mine.

"Yeah," I rush out, forcing a smile. But it's a lie because I'm anything but okay. Unease is trickling into my bloodstream like an intravenous drug. It's the same eerie feeling I had when I walked down the hall at The Afterlife and met Ilya Petrov in the flesh.

Ilya Petrov.

Ever since I heard that name, I've been racking my brain, trying and failing to pinpoint where I recognize it from. But I've come up empty each time.

The waiter appears beside me, blocking my view of the man as he fills our water glasses and lays menus out in front of us. But I can't be bothered to open the leather binder and read a damn thing on the menu because right now, my focus is on peering around the waiter's body at the man sitting inside.

I swallow hard because now his obsidian eyes are burning a hole through my soul. I point my gaze downward and feign ignorance. When I feel his heated stare wander away from me, I chance peeking back over to find the booth empty.

My shoulders lower from my ears, and I release a shaky exhale and stamp down the unease, shifting my attention back to the conversation happening between Stella and Harper. They're discussing nipple cream and breastfeeding, and I immediately begin blocking them back out. When Harper rises, resting her hand on her bump and announcing that she needs to pee for the millionth time today, I offer to go with her. Because that's what women do, I think—travel in packs.

Stella remains at the table, the bodyguard watching her like a hawk. I wave at him and point at Harper's belly and mouth "bathroom."

He nods, folds his arms across his chest, and relaxes back into his seat. Harper and I wander toward the French doors that lead inside the restaurant.

"This place is so darn cute," she chirps, waddling through the doorway and moaning dramatically when the air-conditioned air meets her skin.

Just as we reach the mouth of the hall that leads to the restroom, I hear the doorbell chime. It's the slightest jingle of a bell, but it's no less alarming than a wailing police siren. I glance back at the doorway and freeze, every cell in my body crystalizing. My heart lodges itself into my throat, cutting off my airway as I stare at the well-dressed man in his sixties. Polished Italian leather dress shoes. Expensive suit. A flashy silver watch I'd recognize anywhere. Salt-and-pepper hair slicked back with not a single strand out of place.

It's the devil himself—Charles Gregory. My stepfather.

Irritation laced with slight panic kicks in, and I snatch Harper's hand and drag her down the hall. She releases a little yelp when I haul her into the bathroom and slam the door shut behind us, flipping the lock and flattening myself to the cool wooden surface.

"What's wrong?" she rushes out, her eyes flashing with concern and hand splayed protectively over her stomach.

"Use the washroom, Harper. Then we need to get the hell out of here. Like ... yesterday."

I begin to pace frantically.

What the hell is he doing here? Quaint little restaurants like this aren't his style because they're not pretentious and over the top. And I don't have the mental capacity for his bullshit right now. And I know for a fact he'll be irritated that I've ignored every single one of his attempts at making contact with me for the last two years.

"Why? What is it?" she asks, all the while taking a seat and relieving her bladder while I stare at the floor and rip at my hair.

"There's a man out there I know. And he's a horrible human being."

I chance a peek at Harper, noting the way her brows are furrowed, a vicious protectiveness sweeping over her features. She finishes peeing and flushes the toilet.

"A man," she says plainly. "Did he hurt you? Whose ass do I have to kick?" She folds her arms over her chest and pops a hip. There's not an ounce of fear on her face.

"It's nothing like that. And you don't need to kick anybody's ass today. We just need to get Stella and get out of here. I can explain in the car."

I instruct Harper to keep quiet then lead her back out of the restroom, my head rotating side to side and heart pounding violently against my ribs as we creep down the hall back toward the seating area. We stop to glance around the corner, my eyes immediately locking on the back of Charles's perfect head of hair. The asshole has always been obsessed with his image.

But what really causes my heart to stall is who he's seated with—the strangely familiar man.

Instincts flare wildly in my gut, and I position Harper at my side as we stroll calmly across the restaurant, keeping my face hidden from the view of Charles. When we break out into the heat of the high-noon sun, I bolt toward Stella and slap my palms on the small metal table she's seated at.

"We need to get the fuck out of here," I blurt, earning me some looks.

The bodyguard stands and reaches around his back, presumably for a gun. I shake my head at him then gesture that we need to leave. If he goes in there and confronts Charles, I'm royally fucked. The only option I have right now is to get Stella and Harper out of here and put as much distance between us and that monster as possible.

Neither of them protest, and I have to wonder if this drill is something they're familiar with. I don't bother asking. There will be time for that later.

We exit the bistro the same way we entered, and I practically throw myself into the passenger seat of Harper's SUV. But even after I'm safely seated behind the tinted windows with the bodyguard in the vehicle trailing behind us toward Stella's house, my guts are all knotted up, panic twining with something else.

"Okay," Harper begins, her fingers drumming on the steering wheel. "Spill the beans. What was that all about?"

Gnawing on the inside of my cheek, I contemplate her question for a moment. I could tell them the truth—that I hate my stepfather and am avoiding him. At the very least, they'll think my exit was a little too dramatic. It was, no doubt. After all, I do have a tendency to be a little extra at times. But they don't know him the way I do.

Just as I'm opening my mouth to speak, the screech of tires on asphalt steals my attention, and I squint out my passenger window.

Headlights appear from around a corner as a large white van barrels toward us. The driver behind the wheel guns the engine, pointing the vehicle straight at my side of the SUV.

I release a shrill scream and throw my body over Harper's stomach, all of my worst fears coming to life at once.

The impact feels like a bomb detonating. Metal crunches metal. Glass shatters all around, shards of it raining down on me. The buzzing in my ears is so loud that I can't hear myself think.

None of that matters though because before I can open my eyes to check on Harper and Stella, darkness seeps in around the edges of my vision, and everything goes black.

Thirty

Liam

MAC AND JOEL ARE both asleep in their hammocks, Zak's scrolling his phone, drooling over pictures of Harper, and Sloane's at the table, her eyes glued to her laptop. Despite the fact that Ivan Petrov didn't show up for his meeting with Osmanov, everyone seems relaxed.

Except for me.

I flip my switchblade opened and closed, the cold steel glinting in the dim lighting of the plane. I'm still dressed in my fatigues but relieved of my weapons, and my boots are wearing a hole in the plane floor from obsessively pacing.

I glance at Sloane, wondering briefly if I should ask her to pull up the security feed of Joel's house so I can see Alora's face. So I can confirm she's safe. Every natural instinct I have is telling me I should, but I promised Alora I'd give her some space as long as she promised to stick with Stella and not whine about the detail I hired to follow them if they left the house. I'd be lying if I said I believed her when she told me she'd obey.

"You alright, big guy?" Sloane asks, her gaze lifting from her screen and meeting mine. Concern is etched onto her face, and I hate that she can see straight through me better than anyone else on the team.

I nod once, then resume pacing.

My phone vibrates in my pocket, and I retrieve it at lightning speed, my heart skidding to a stop when I read the name flashing across the screen. I answer the call immediately.

"What is it?" I boom at the bodyguard.

When he begins spewing the details of what has transpired, all the blood in my body hardens to a poisonous sludge, filling my lungs and making it impossible to breathe. Rage rises like a riptide, a red haze clouding my vision.

And then a domino effect takes place. Zak's and Joel's phones chime next, and when they both take their calls to notify them their wives have been in a car accident, the air in the plane hums with thick, negative energy.

My monster roars, beating his chest and gnashing his teeth. My fingers coil around the arm of a chair and I hurl it across the plane. Everything goes deathly silent around me except for the whoosh of the blood in my ears and the chanting of my demons.

Not only was there a collision, but Alora's been taken, and I'm stuck on this fucking plane.

I can't get to her.

The ache in my chest is catastrophic as I reach for every object I can get my hands on and heave it across the aircraft. I faintly hear Sloane's voice in the background as she tries to calm me, but it's drowned by the screaming in my head.

I'm manic. Unstoppable.

The next two hours turn into a blur, dragging on for what feels like an eternity. All while Alora's getting farther away, less traceable by the second.

When the plane finally touches down, Zak and Joel head straight to the hospital to Harper and Stella. The detail I hired is on Bluetooth in my truck while I slam the gas pedal to the floor, my heart pounding in my chest as Sloane and I haul ass to the cafe the bodyguard said Alora began to act strangely in before the truck collided with Harper's SUV.

Apparently, it all unfolded within the blink of an eye. The bodyguard was trailing the women closely when the accident occurred. He skidded to a stop and bolted out of his vehicle, but by the time he had his gun drawn, Alora's limp body had already been pulled out of the shattered passenger window and tossed into the back of a cargo van. He opened fire at the vehicle, but they slipped away. I want to ring his fucking neck for not getting back in his car and chasing the van, but there were two more women in the SUV, and one of them was pregnant. So he made the choice to stay and get them to safety.

A flashback of the day we found Rachel in the bunker in Russia flashes behind my eyelids. But instead of Rachel's sad, hollow eyes looking up at me as I drop to my knees in front of her and pull her sickly thin body into my arms, it's Alora's big green ones. She's covered in track marks, and the butterfly tattoo on her ankle has been brutally carved out of her flesh.

"Pulling up the camera feed of the streetlight cams as we speak," Sloane says calmly from my passenger seat, her fingers flying over the keyboard of her laptop. She's in full huntress mode, and although I keep reminding myself that she's the best at what she does, it's still not good enough. No amount of reassurance can calm the turbulent storm violently churning within me. "Got it."

Sloane watches the footage, describing the vehicle that collided with Harper's. She does a search on the license plate and spits out a name—Robert Smith—an alias that I already know will lead us nowhere. She zooms in on the faces of the men who took Alora and begins searching for them via facial recognition software.

When my tires screech to a halt in the parking lot of the cafe, I tell Sloane to keep searching while I fly out of my truck and storm into the restaurant. I head straight for the hostess, praying to high hell she was on shift when Alora was here.

I pull a photo of Alora up on my phone and shove it in her face. The hostess recoils, her eyes wide and filled with trepidation.

"This woman was here earlier with two others. Do you recognize her?"

The hostess swallows, her brows pinched in concern as she stares unblinkingly back at me.

Lowering my tone to a less threatening level, I say, "She's in danger. And I need to find her. Do you recognize her?"

The hostess slowly moves her gaze to my phone, her eyes flaring with recognition. "Yeah. She was with a pregnant lady."

"Yes. Where were they seated?"

She points at a set of French patio doors. "Out there." I glance over at the patio. Just as I'm about to head out there to see if I can find anything, the hostess blurts out, "She looked scared," halting me in my tracks. "Her and the pregnant woman were headed to the bathroom. The woman in the photo paused and stared at a man who walked into the restaurant, then they raced down the hall and went into the washroom. When they came back out, the woman you're looking for seemed distressed. They scurried out to their table and then took off before the waiter had a chance to take their orders."

"The man that came in ... What did he look like?"

The hostess shuffles on her feet, seemingly hesitant to share this information. But as she studies my expression, she comes to some sort of conclusion and tells me, "He was tall. Average build. Kind of handsome with black-and-gray hair. He was dressed in an expensive-looking suit. He came in and sat down at a booth with another man. They left immediately after the women did."

"Are there any security cameras in here?"

She shakes her head, and I'm down the hall and busting into the ladies' restroom without another word. My eyes dart all over the space, but there's nothing here. No clues.

A sinking feeling, like I've stepped in quicksand and it's just a matter of time before I'm swallowed whole, takes hold. But I'll forge on. Because there's not a chance in hell Alora is going to be taken from me.

Heads will roll. Blood will flow. And my monster will feast off the flesh flayed from the bodies of anyone who lays a hand on my little thief.

Thirty-One

Alora

I'M LYING ON A beach in a little blue bikini, my toes buried in the sand and fingers curled around a sweating margarita glass. The sun is warm on my tanned skin, a soft breeze rolling in with the waves and causing the long grass scattered around the palm trees to rustle. I roll my head and glance over at the easel and paints set up a few feet from my lounge chair, a gentle smile gracing my lips.

Perfect.

A slight chill sends bumps scattering over my heated skin and I loll my head the other direction, watching with bated breath as Liam strolls leisurely across the sand. He's wearing nothing but tropical-print swim trunks that clash hilariously with his dark tattoos and severe expression. A pair of sunglasses hide his amber eyes, but I know his gaze is roaming over my body because it's burning hotter than the fiery ball hanging high above me.

Every step he takes toward me makes my heart beat a little faster. His lip twitches as he saunters behind me, his fingers grazing my bare shoulder before he leans over and plants a gentle kiss on the top of my head. I close my eyes and hum in satisfaction.

This is everything I've ever wanted. Right here in Mexico. Peace. Freedom.

Liam.

He withdraws and leaves my line of sight, and another chill rolls over me, this one different from the last. A sudden ache settles deep into the marrow of my bones. The lingering taste of the lime margarita on my tongue turns metallic, the coppery tang of blood flooding my mouth.

I attempt to stand, but my limbs are dead weight.

I pry my scratchy eyelids open and realize I was dreaming. I'm not on a beach in Mexico. And Liam's not here with me. Panic sets in and I suppress a whimper. I'm lying in the back seat of a vehicle, my arms bound behind my back and my brain throbbing against the inside of my skull like it's trying to escape my body. I can feel my pulse in every one of my fingers and toes, my eyeballs too.

I blink a few times in an attempt to bring my vision into focus, but a wave of nausea rolls through me, and I swallow the bile rising in my throat. A gruff male voice causes me to stiffen. He's not speaking in English, so I have no idea what he's saying, and that only causes my fear to intensify.

How long have I been out?

Without moving, I slide my eyes around, deciding to remain still and feign unconsciousness to use the little opportunity I've been given to formulate a plan. But I'm lying on my side, my face smashed into the back seat, so besides the aging brown stain on the faded fabric of whosever vehicle I'm in, I can't see a fucking thing.

When the tires hit a bump in the road, I jostle and turn my head just slightly, catching a glimpse of two strange men in the front, only the sides of their faces visible. I snap my eyes shut in a desperate attempt to recall how I got here. The memories flood in faster than my foggy brain can comprehend.

The cafe. Charles. The car accident.

A boulder lodges itself in my throat. Stella and Harper. The baby.

I'm not a religious woman, but in this moment, I pray to whatever god exists that they're okay.

Heat pricks at the corners of my eyes, but I will away the tears and force myself to focus. To stay strong. Because that's what Liam would tell me to do. He'd tell me to be smart and calculated.

He may or may not know I've been taken yet, but when he finds out, I know he'll rip the world apart to find me. And I need to make his search easier. Maybe I could leave him clues. Or try to stall.

The deadly panic attack building in my chest will have to fucking wait.

The car rolls to a stop, and I work to calm my breathing and relax the muscles in my face and body. When the door at my feet cracks open and I'm dragged roughly across the seat, my shirt riding up my stomach and back, I stamp down the natural instinct to struggle against my captor. Harsh sunlight blasts my aching skin, filtering through the thin flesh of my eyelids as I'm tossed like a sack of potatoes over someone's shoulder. My head bobs limply and more bile rises in my throat at the sudden jerky movements.

Don't vomit.

When I peer through my barely cracked lids, I see squares of cracked concrete moving beneath me. A sidewalk. I'm in a city.

Think, Al, think.

I take a chance—because what other choice do I have—and lift my head slightly. Judging by the run-down state of the buildings and the amount of garbage littering the streets, we're in the slums. I could scream for help. Surely someone would hear me. But I've lived somewhere similar for two years now, and I know that most residents would lock their doors and close their blinds and pray there's not a shoot-out right here in front of their homes.

We cross an intersection, and that's when I remember Sloane telling me she uses street cameras and facial recognition to locate people.

I lift my head again, every vertebrae in my spine and neck feeling seized, and look up at the traffic lights. Hope inflates in my chest as I make eye contact with the little black box attached to the overhanging lights. If there's ever a time to show my face, now is it.

I'm tossed into the back seat of another vehicle, this one reeking of stale cigarettes and something sour and rancid.

The two men hop into the front seat and begin exchanging words in their native language—Russian, I think—as I'm trans-ported to another location. I take inventory of the number of stops and every turn. The vehicle comes to a standstill and the engine cuts out. But this time, when I'm hauled out of the back seat, I make the mistake of wincing from the pain shooting across my ribs.

One of the male voices escalates, and something hard connects with my skull, sending me careening back into a black abyss.

When the fog clears from my brain and I begin to come to again, I wiggle my fingers and toes, slowly bringing awareness back to my aching body. But my wrists are bound uncomfortably behind my back, and I'm hunched over in a small wooden chair in the middle of an empty room. An uncontrollable tremor shakes my core, and I search around the dank, dark space for any signs of where I am. But there are no windows and nothing on the cinder block walls to give me any indication. The only light is from a single bulb dangling overhead.

My soul feels as cold and empty as this room.

A set of polished black dress shoes appear on the floor in front of me. I lift my head, which feels like a brick of cement being chipped at with a jackhammer, and peer into a set of cold, familiar eyes. All those well-constructed walls of mine bust open like a broken dam and a sudden wave of confusion blasts through.

"Darling stepdaughter. It's so nice to see you again," Charles drawls, his tone laced with venom.

When I peel my tongue off the roof of my mouth and wet my chapped lips, the faint tang of blood assaults my taste buds, and I shudder. A million burning questions flip through my mind like a Rolodex, but I can't form a coherent sentence.

Charles's clean-shaven face splits into a wide smile as he stares down at me, appraising me the way he so often did. His silent judgment is no less infuriating than it was when he was married to my mother. I've always been a disappointment to him. Nothing but a pitiful waste of intelligence and work ethic. His hopes of sanding me down and polishing me into a shinier version of myself evaporated before his eyes when I dropped out of school just before graduation. And ever since then, his distaste for me has grown exponentially.

But the feeling is mutual because I hate this motherfucker more than anything in the world.

He reaches out and touches my swollen cheekbone. I hiss at the contact, leaning as far away from him as my tired muscles will allow. Every bone in my battered body aches with a pain that has me wishing for death.

"Don't you fucking touch me," I sneer, imagining all the ways Liam would make Charles bleed if he were here right now.

Charles bares his pretty, veneered teeth at me, looking every bit the vile creature that he is. His polished appearance is nothing more than a costume he wears like a second skin to camouflage the demon within.

"You should be grateful you're still breathing, Alora." *For now* dangles on the end of his comment, but the words are never spoken.

I ignore his statement, desperate to know if Stella and Harper and her unborn child are okay. "Where are my friends?"

Deep-seated concern for their well-being seeps into my bones. I blink away the tears gathering in my eyes and stiffen my chin, refusing to show him the fear that's poisoned my system.

He swats the air and tsks. "They're not of my concern."

"Of course they're not. Because you're a selfish bastard who deserves to rot in—"

The back of his hand cracks across my face, my cheek searing with fire as my head whips sideways. Copper seeps into my mouth, and I know his ring broke my skin. I wad the blood and saliva on my tongue and spit it at his feet and sneer at him.

"What the hell do you want from me, Charles?"

He angles his head, a curious glimmer in his eyes.

"You haven't put the pieces together yet," he says in amusement, his shoes clacking on the dirty concrete floor as he thoughtfully paces the small space in front of me. "You're a smart young woman. I'm sure it'll come to you eventually."

I shake my head, squeezing my eyes shut and desperately trying to jam all the puzzle pieces in my mind together to create a bigger picture. But those pieces are skewed every which direction, and nothing really makes sense. There are too many holes. Too many missing components. And my skull feels as if it's imploding in on my brain.

No matter how hard I try to make sense of why Charles would kidnap me, I come up empty.

When Charles grows impatient with my struggle, he releases a long, exaggerated sigh and says, "The Petrovs, Alora. They are my clients."

The Petrovs. *Ilya Petrov.*

I recoil as another piece clicks into place. I recognized the name because my mother mentioned it in her journal. They were one of the clients she said she was concerned about him defending.

"The Petrovs? Are you fucking insane?" I squawk, my shrill voice causing my head to throb. I wince at the pain and press on. "They're human traffickers, Charles! How could you?"

"They certainly are, darling. The worst of the worst. But Ivan had ample funds to pay me handsomely for my services, most of which consisted of defending young Ilya." He sighs. "Such a silly little boy, he was. Always getting himself into trouble. Much like yourself." He stops pacing and stands in front of me, his shadow casting an ominous darkness that feels like a promise of what's to come. "Unfortunately, though, I've found myself wrapped up in their business dealings and have acquired some debt. Initially, I was going to simply pay them in cash. But then I got thinking ... Why sacrifice the money I've worked so hard for when I have another asset to offer up instead? One that requires little to no work on my part."

The chuckle that rumbles from his chest is dark and humorless as he shakes his head in disbelief.

"Imagine my surprise when only weeks after I gave Ivan the green light to take you, he calls me up to inform me that you lifted Ilya's watch right off his wrist in a casino then walked straight out the front doors and vanished. How you managed to slip away from them is beyond me."

"You sick motherfucker," I spit.

He laughs again, and it's manic and insane.

"You're very creative, Alora. I'll give you that. But you're also very naive."

He flashes me a dazzling smile. I don't need to ask why he's telling me all of this. I already know it's because I'm as good as dead. Liam's in Russia. Harper and Stella are god knows where. And I have no way of escaping. But as much as defeat has injected itself into my veins, I won't go down without a fight.

This isn't over.

"It's truly a shame that it has to end like this. But ultimately, we all win this way."

Except for me.

He strolls over to the table parked against the wall at the side and retrieves something. When my eyes dart to a familiar brown leather journal, disbelief causes them to bulge from my head.

"It was you," I sneer accusingly. "You broke into my apartment."

He swats the air. "Don't be ridiculous. I would never stoop to that level. I hired someone instead." He cocks a brow at me and pulls a lighter from his pocket. He flicks it open and ignites it, bringing the dancing flame to the tattered corner of my mother's journal.

"No," I yell in desperation. "Please don't."

His face lights up in satisfaction as he watches the only thing I have left of my mother go up in smoke. My heart shatters into a million pieces, tears leaking from my eyes and tumbling down my cheeks. When the flames eat up the remaining inches of paper, he tosses the blackened bones of the journal into a steel trash can and frowns at me.

"Time's up, Alora. Just as your mother's time was up. It's a shame she couldn't keep her mouth shut about my business arrangements. Always inserting herself into things that didn't concern her. Sadly, when she thought it wise to attempt to turn me over to police, I had no other option but to shut her up for good."

My heart comes to a screeching halt then cracks wide open at his confession. "Y-you killed her?"

He smirks, and I want nothing more than to drive a stake through his blackened heart.

"She left me no choice, darling. But I assure you, she went peacefully. Never felt an ounce of pain. I'm not sure I'll be able to say the same about you, though."

A door creaks open behind me, the hinges groaning as if they haven't been oiled in centuries. Charles's gaze moves past me, and he flicks his chin at whoever just entered the room.

He returns his attention to me, and his mouth turns down into a frown. "I'm very sorry, Alora. Truly. This isn't personal. Just business." He turns on a heel and walks away.

Cold. Soulless. Bastard.

The familiar man from the cafe appears before me, and that's when the final pieces of the puzzle fall into place. My body temperature plummets as the big picture comes into view.

Ivan Petrov was never going to meet with the leader of the Russian Bratva. He set that meeting up knowing Liam would leave me behind.

And now here he is, his obsidian eyes—the same bone-chilling black as Ilya's—boring into me.

And I know I'm not about to die. I'm about to suffer.

I wiggle in my chair, a trickle of warm blood trailing from my wrist to my palm, the plastic zip ties digging mercilessly into my flesh. I feel the droplet creep down my finger and plop onto the floor beneath me.

The bony claws of fear tap down my spine one vertebrae at a time as Ivan's weathered face splits into a wicked grin. He takes a step forward, and I squeeze my eyes shut and clench my jaw, preparing for a blow that never comes. Instead, he grips my bicep and drags me to my feet.

"Hello, Alora," he taunts in my ear, his breath hot and acidic and Russian accent thick. "Time to go."

"Where are you taking me?" I croak out, my voice shaky and hoarse.

He doesn't speak. Because words aren't necessary. I can tell by the crazed look in his eyes that wherever I'm going is where I'll spend my last waking moments. Where I'll take my final breaths. No doubt he believes I'm responsible for both of his sons' deaths.

My feet drag beneath me on the concrete floor, my body growing more and more sluggish as Ivan pushes me down a long, dark corridor. The walls are a dingy gray brick, the ceiling rafters exposed and windows coated in a thick film of dust. It looks like an abandoned factory of some sort—one plucked straight out of a horror film.

As much as I'm itching to run, I can't. There are too many factors in play. My hands are literally tied. I have no idea where I am or where the exits are. And Ivan has a gun pressed into my back, coaxing me ahead.

I refuse to be a trembling mess because I suspect that's what my captor wants. I'm not going to allow him the satisfaction, even though my insides are vibrating in fear of what's to come.

I hiss when he digs the gun into my spine and gives me another harsh nudge forward. If I survive this, which I've already accepted is highly unlikely, I'm going to rip this guy's tiny dick from his body and shove it down his fucking throat. Then I'm going to find Charles and do the same to him.

We turn right at the end of the hall, and a steel double doorway comes into view. The handles are chained together, a large padlock securing the ends. Ivan shoves me against the wall beside the doors.

"Move and I'll shoot you," he threatens, pointing the gun at my face.

He pulls a key from his pocket, and I eye the gun in his hand as he fumbles with the lock. Peeking around, I see no other exits. Nowhere to run but back where we just came from.

When the lock finally clicks, he unwinds the chain from the handles and tosses it to the side.

I glare at him as I prop myself up against the cool wall behind me, my body drained and legs threatening to give out. Another trickle of blood drips down my palm, and I'm reminded of my silly plan to leave clues. I know it's unlikely Liam will find what I leave, but I have to try.

Smearing the blood from my palm over my fingers, I remain backed against the wall so my body is blocking Ivan's view of my hands. I smear my blood across the wall, leaving a written message. I keep my breathing calm and my expression blank so Ivan doesn't grow suspicious. He's on a cell phone now, barking something out in Russian. Judging by the color of his neck and face, I'd say he's angry.

He glances over at me, and I still my working hands.

His lip curls, baring his yellow teeth, but he returns to his phone call. When he's done yelling at whoever was on the other end of the line, he grabs me by the bicep and hauls me outside and into the blinding light. I wince at the harsh assault of the high sun. When my pupils finally adjust, I take in my surroundings.

Besides the waiting sedan Ivan is shoving me toward, there's nothing but fields and asphalt. Nowhere to hide if I take off running.

Ivan shoves me ahead again, his gun digging into my back as we make our way across the abandoned parking lot.

Stumbling just before we reach the vehicle, I toe out of one of my shoes, leaving it behind on the pavement. I half expect Ivan to pick it up and bring it with us, but he doesn't. Instead, he steps over it.

"Keep moving," he grunts.

I do as instructed, one bare sole burning on the hot pavement with every step I take. But when the trunk of the car pops open and he gestures for me to get inside, a renewed sense of panic sets in.

"No way. I'm not riding in the trunk." I shake my head and glare at him.

"Get in," he snarls, and I shake my head again.

"Not a fucking chance."

He rolls his eyes as if I'm a petulant child pulling a temper tantrum, then grabs me and forces me in. I cry out in pain when I land roughly on my back, my arms still bound behind me and restraints biting into my flesh.

The urge to hoof him in the balls is strong, but it would only anger him further. And since he's the one with the weapon ...

"Where are you taking me?" I yell, spit flying from my mouth as I struggle to roll off my bound wrists and give my hands some relief.

But the trunk slams shut, casting me into total darkness. And that's when I begin to hyperventilate, a bitter dose of reality crashing through my bloodstream. I scream and buck and kick at the carpeted walls of the trunk, terror lodging itself into my throat and cutting off my air supply.

When the engine starts up and the car begins moving, I squeeze my eyes shut, tears tracking down my face. It's hotter than hell in here, and my body temperature is quickly rising. I keep swallowing the vomit bubbling up my throat, and my stomach is aching with the realization that this is the end of life as I know it.

My thoughts skip to my mother and her final moments. The coroner's report confirmed she died by suicide. But I now know that's not true. She was murdered by the man who vowed to love her forever. To protect her. Did she know it was coming? Or did she die under the false pretense that she could someday escape him?

When it dawns on me that I'll likely never know the full truth, I release a shrill cry as every emotion fathomable rips through me. Guilt. Fear. Rage. Sadness.

I'm so sorry, Mama. I'm so fucking sorry.

Thirty-Two

Liam

Darkness has consumed me. Every second that passes, my hope of finding Alora wanes.

"They switched vehicles," Sloane tells me from the passenger seat of my truck.

White heat flows through my body, igniting every sick fantasy running rampant in my mind. Whoever took my girl from me is in for a rude fucking awakening. The sounds of bones crunching. The blood-curdling screams. The disturbing suctioning noise my blade will make as it enters and exits their bodies, over and over again.

"Where?"

"East side." Sloane's mouth hooks into a smirk and she shakes her head in disbelief, turning the screen of her laptop toward me.

I glare at the monitor and my stomach clenches, what's left of my heart crumbling like dry mud.

Alora's limp body is slung over an unfamiliar man's shoulder, her head bobbing limply.

Until it's not.

She tilts her battered face upward and stares directly at the camera, as if she knows I'll be right here looking back at her. Her eyes are filled with desperation, and it only serves as gasoline to the fiery rage inside me.

I'm right here, little thief. And I'm coming for you.

"Your girl is smart. She's leaving us clues," Sloane chirps before returning to searching. "But I lost the vehicle just outside of the city at the last traffic light. Here." She punches an intersection into the GPS on my dash, and I gun it to the last known location Sloane tracked Alora to, gripping the steering wheel so tight my arms ache.

Sloane's laptop pings with an incoming message, and I glance over at her. She's smirking at the screen, and I want to throw my fist through the fucking dash. She peeks over at me with that shit-eating grin.

"Tell me you love me," she quips.

"Sloane," I warn.

"Come on. Say it. Tell me I'm the best and you don't know what you big, dumb idiots would do without me."

I groan, the air in my lungs growing stale as I hold it in. Sloane's fingers hammer on her keyboard as she types away, her concentration unaffected by the ticking bomb sitting right beside her.

Eventually she sighs and punches a different address into the GPS.

"Where are we going?" I snarl.

"To pay Charles Gregory a visit."

My eyes snap to hers.

"Alora's stepfather? Why?"

Sloane blows a bubble and pops it as I take the ramp onto the highway and gun the engine.

"Because there's reason to believe he's the pretty boy the hostess said was in the cafe. And likely the reason your girl was taken."

Ice crystalizes in my chest cavity as dark thoughts slither through my mind. Why would Charles do this? What if Alora's not with him? What if he's already dumped her somewhere?

I should have agreed to kill him the way Alora had asked me to despite the fact that it was an irrational request on her part.

"What makes you think this?" I ask.

Sloane shrugs. "I have a reliable source."

"Which is?"

She pops her gum. "You'll find out soon enough. But you need to have a little faith, big guy. She's going to be just fine. You have my word."

I want to press on. To hear what makes Sloane so certain that everything is going to work out. But I've known the team huntress longer than anyone on the team, and I trust her with my life. So I take her promise at face value.

Minutes tick on as I fly down the road, blowing through red lights and swerving around traffic.

When we pull up to the front of a ritzy hotel, those dark thoughts intensify.

"That's Charles's vehicle," Sloane tells me, pointing at a shiny, black Escalade parked in the wheelchair spot by the main entrance.

Entitled prick.

I barely have my truck in Park before I'm hopping out and aiming my gun, Sloane hot on my tracks as I approach the waiting SUV to find it empty.

"Seventeenth floor," Sloane tells me.

I eye her skeptically before moving boots through the front entrance and straight to the elevator lobby, jamming my finger into the elevator button.

We ride in silence up to the seventeenth floor, my heart hammering and irritation licking at my guts with a forked tongue as soft jazz music plays from the speakers overhead.

The second the doors slide open, Sloane and I are hauling ass down the carpeted corridor to the suite that Charles has allegedly rented for the evening. I press my back to the wall beside the door as Sloane knocks three times.

"Housekeeping," she singsongs, winking at me playfully as we wait for Charles to unlock the door.

The moment the door cracks open, I barrel toward him and grab him by the shirt, slamming him into the wall. I hear the door click shut behind me, and I know Sloane's standing close by.

"Where the fuck is Alora?" I bellow, my face a mere inch from his, his expensive cologne pungent and manicured hands grappling at my forearms.

His clean-shaven jaw hangs slack as he stares in utter horror back at the raging machine pinning him to the wall. I close my fist around his throat and press the shitty end of my gun to his temple, making him feel the cold steel against his flesh—an unspoken promise to end his miserable fucking existence.

Sloane appears at my side.

"You might as well spill the beans, Charlie boy. Because my very big, very angry friend here isn't really in the mood for pleasantries." She steps in closer and brings her mouth to his ear, whispering tauntingly, "And believe me when I tell you the gun in his hand is the least of your worries."

Charles wriggles like a worm on a hook then begins pleading. But it's all lies.

"Please. I don't know what you're talking about."

Coward.

I dig my gun in further and cut his airway off with my hand.

"Try again," I snarl.

"I-I don't know," he croaks out, the pulse in his throat thumping hard and fast against my fingertips.

But his heart won't be beating for much longer.

"Wrong answer."

I cock the hammer, reminding him who has the upper hand. But I don't need a gun to do what I intend on doing to Charles. I don't even need my fucking knife. Just my bare hands and the raw, uncut fury plaguing my system.

"Okay, okay," he chokes out, and I loosen my grip just enough that he can speak. "There's a Russian ... One of my old clients. H-he has her."

"A name. Now," I bellow.

"Ivan Petrov."

My blood turns to ice as my suspicions are confirmed. Ivan never showed for Osmanov because he had other plans. And not only did Alora's sick fuck of a stepfather collaborate with the Petrovs, he handed his own stepdaughter over to them. He handed what's mine over to them.

"Where is he?"

Charles whimpers again, my finger hovering dangerously close to the trigger.

The second the words leave his mouth and he tells me what I want to hear, I pull the trigger. Blood splatters my face, chest, and arms. Chunks of brain and fragments of bone coat the wall behind what's left of Charles's skull, dripping like thick sludge and making sickening plopping sounds on the floor.

I would have taken great pleasure in strapping him to my table and spending countless hours peeling the flesh from his bones. But the clock is ticking. And getting to Alora is the only thing that matters.

I drop Charles's lifeless body to the ground and stare down at him, my chest heaving with heavy breaths.

A feminine hand settles on my shoulder.

"I'll take care of surveillance in the truck. Let's go get your girl."

Thirty-Three

Alora

THE DRIVE IS LONG. Too fucking long. And my body is so slick with sweat that it's soaked straight through my jeans and tank top, my face hot and tears flooding my cheeks. I can hear other sets of tires on the asphalt as vehicles whoosh by, so I know we're on a highway and moving fast. I've tried to pull the trunk release, but it's been disabled. So every time the car rolls to a stop, desperation overwhelms me, and I kick and scream in hopes of someone hearing me. But all that does is exhaust me further. And if there's ever an opportunity for me to run, I need to conserve my energy.

We take a slow turn, and the vehicle stops. The engine cuts out a moment later.

I squeeze my eyes shut and will away this nightmare. None of it's real. It can't be.

An image of Liam flickers behind my eyelids. I can almost feel the rough pad of his thumb swiping my tears from my cheeks. I can almost smell him. Almost hear him telling me to keep my head straight and focus.

Almost.

When the trunk pops open and sunlight blasts my too-hot skin, I stifle a sob. I need to stay strong, even though all I really want to do is break. To shatter into microscopic pieces because I know Liam would pick every last bit of me up and put me back together.

Except he's not here to do that.

"Let's go," Ivan grabs me by the arm and drags me out of the trunk. The pain I feel everywhere is a reminder that I'm still alive. And as long as my heart is beating, I'll stuff my discomfort aside and focus on finding a way out of this.

I search around in desperation, immediately recognizing where we are as confusion tangles with the fear that's knotted in my stomach.

Ivan hauls me toward the emergency exit at the back of the cement building and bangs his fist on the door as I toe out of my second shoe, kicking it to the side in hopes Ivan doesn't notice I'm leaving a trail of evidence.

Just as my mouth pops open to ask another pointless question, the door creaks open, and I'm greeted by another unfamiliar face. The man in the door says something in Russian, his eyes flicking from my feet to my face then back down. He nods at Ivan then gestures for us to enter.

I'm shoved forward, nearly tripping over the small ledge up into the building as I step into the air-conditioned hallway. My bare soles sink into plush burgundy carpet. Black paisley wallpaper lines the walls, dim sconces dotting the length of the corridor and casting light down on the pattern.

We're at The Afterlife, and just being in a building I'm familiar with brings me a sliver of comfort. Glancing down the hall, I spot the black door that Liam took Ilya Petrov's life behind—the Champagne Room. My lids flutter shut, the memory of being locked in that room with Liam filtering back, soothing me for all of a split second. I take solace in being here. But that feeling is quickly wiped clean when Ivan's gun presses into my back.

When we walk into the empty lounge and I'm forced into a chair in the center of the open space, I straighten my spine and clamp my mouth shut, listening for any Russian words that I might recognize. My ears perk up at a familiar name spoken amongst the gibberish—Osmanov— just as a tall, broad man appears from the hall, seemingly out of nowhere, like a well-dressed ghost.

But this ghost is very fucking real. And Jesus, Mary, and Joseph. He's intimidatingly handsome with his glittering green eyes and sparkling white teeth. His suit is tailored to fit his obviously muscular body, and like Liam, tattoos creep out from under his sleeves and shirt collar. His gaze, cold and calculated, meets mine for all of a millisecond before fixating on Ivan.

When he pauses a few feet away and speaks, his voice is demanding and authoritative, and I'm left wondering who this man is. He reeks of power and money, but there's a mysterious aura surrounding him.

He looks to me again, and I shift uncomfortably in my seat, my arms aching from being bound behind my back for so long. I can no longer feel my hands, my ties having cut the circulation off at my wrists.

The unfamiliar Russian smiles at something Ivan says, then he switches to English, surprising me.

"We had a deal, old friend. But you didn't hold up your end. And you think this," he says, gesturing to me, "is how you'll repay me for the inconvenience?"

A deal? What deal?

"My apologies, Mikhail. But you of all people should understand my predicament. Both of my sons have been taken from me. I had no choice but to prioritize my children."

Mikhail. A meeting. It all makes sense now. This is Osmanov—the Russian Bratva leader that was supposed to help Sweetwater take down Ivan. But clearly Ivan doesn't yet know of those plans, otherwise he wouldn't be standing here in front of him. Hope trickles into my system knowing that Mikhail has previously cooperated with Sweetwater. But I'm quickly reminded that this man runs an organized crime group and that Liam doesn't trust him. And neither should I.

Mikhail begins to pace, slowly and thoughtfully, the backs of his knuckles scratching at his short beard. I know he's a certified genius. Sloane told me as much when I was locked in a truck with her while the guys met with him. And right now, I can practically see the smoke billowing from his ears as his brain works at an impressive speed.

"Do you take me for a stupid man, Ivan?"

Ivan shakes his head. "No. Of course not."

"Then don't insult me by feeding me lies. You neglected to show up for our meeting in order to take her," he says, gesturing to me, "as payment for her stepfather's debt. And when things went awry and your sons ended up dead, you prioritized revenge over our business relationship."

He pauses to stare at Ivan who looks like he's about ready to piss himself. I know the feeling. Because right now, my bladder is threatening to empty all over this chair.

"And now you're desperate to make things right. To save our relationship." Osmanov chuckles, and it's menacing. "And you think you can pass her off to me as an apology?"

Osmanov's eyes move to me again. He rakes them slowly over my body. It doesn't feel sexual. More like he's trying to make a decision about me. He smiles, and it's dazzling and terrifying all at once.

Ivan releases a small, suppressed whimper, like that of a scared child.

Osmanov sighs. "Nonetheless, I'll accept your offer," he tells Ivan. "But you will be penalized for wasting my time and resources."

Ivan's jaw ticks in irritation. But as powerful as Ivan Petrov is, he's no match for Mikhail Osmanov. So he feigns respect and lifts his chin.

"I understand."

Mikhail nods once, his attention once again flitting to me. I shrivel beneath the weight of his gaze. Then he winks at me. It's so fast and subtle that I'm second-guessing whether my eyes are playing tricks on me or if this guy is trying to send me some sort of signal.

He refocuses his attention on Ivan who's raking a hand through the five fucking hairs on his balding head.

"I hope you don't mind, but I've taken the initiative to draw the paperwork up in advance." He gestures to one of his men who steps forward and hands him a thin stack of documents.

Osmanov takes a seat at the table and waves a hand out for Ivan to join him.

I glance over at the main entrance of the club. Could I make it? No. Should I try? Debatable.

Minutes roll by as I assess the armed men hovering in dark corners. When Osmanov stands to shake Ivan's hand, I make a split decision and bolt for the door.

I hear Ivan shout, "Stop her!" just as I'm rounding the corner of the bar.

It feels as if everything that unfolds next happens in slow motion. The double steel doors of the main entrance fly open, harsh sunlight blasting my retinas and blinding me. There's some shuffling from behind me, then something big and hard slams into me, and I'm sent careening sideways, a shrill scream ripping free from my throat as my body hits the floor behind the bar with a nauseating smack.

I scramble up onto my ass, my arms still bound and pain radiating through every one of my battered limbs. Men are yelling, mostly in broken Russian. And when I look up, I realize it was Mikhail who body slammed me.

"Stay here," he orders before disappearing.

Maybe it's because I've been knocked out more than once today, but confusion takes hold. I shouldn't be grateful for Mikhail's assault, but I am, because if he hadn't thrown himself at me, then I would have been in direct line of fire of whoever just came busting through the doors and into the club.

I dig my heels into the sticky bar floor, pushing myself back until my spine connects with the bottom of the bar beneath the cash register.

There are gunshots. Many of them. Bottles shatter, shards of glass raining down over my head. I tuck my chin to my chest and squeeze my eyes shut, willing this moment to end and praying I don't catch a stray bullet in the cross fire. But with each piercing blast, the yelling fades. There are several thuds that I visualize as bodies hitting the floor, as if whoever just barged in here is pegging Russians off, one at a fucking time. My heart beats hard and fast, almost deafeningly.

And just as the last of the shouting ends, a large shadow appears at the end of the bar, a massive body clad in camo fatigues and a black T-shirt. My heart stalls, and my entire body floods with a tsunami of relief, wiping out every other emotion in its wake.

Liam.

Thirty-Four

Liam

TIME SUSPENDS ITSELF AS all the air in my lungs leaves in a heady whoosh. I blink several times, ensuring my eyes aren't deceiving me.

"Alora." I lunge myself at her, laying my gun on the floor as I drop to my knees and touch her everywhere, just to be sure she's real. When my fingers meet the warm, soft skin of her beautiful face, I close my eyes and breathe through the ebbing pain.

"Liam," she rushes out as I meet her tear-filled eyes. "I'm okay. I promise. Just a few cuts and bruises."

"You're okay," I parrot, because I need to hear her say it again.

She nods. "I'm okay."

Exhaling a relieved breath, I use my knife to cut the ties binding her wrists. Blood trickles from where the plastic dug into her flesh, and I stamp down the anger and focus on checking her over for any further injuries.

I plant a gentle kiss on her mouth, then topple back onto my ass, pulling her into my lap and burying my face in her hair, filling my lungs with her lemony scent. The low chant of my demons fades into the background as Alora's small frame melts into mine like warm butter, molding perfectly to me. Her head is tucked under my chin, her fists gripping my T-shirt tight as she stifles the sob I know my tough girl has been holding back.

When a loud crashing sound, followed by a series of colorful words spoken by a woman, echoes through the empty club, Alora perks back up.

"What's going on out there?" she whispers as I press a soft kiss to her forehead.

Mine.

"I brought Sloane."

She blinks up at me.

"Oh my god. Harper and Stella! The baby! They were ... Are they ..."

"They're fine. Everyone's fine."

Her shoulders lower from her ears and she drops her face in relief, more tears tumbling off her cheeks.

"Thank god." There's a pregnant pause where Alora mulls something over in her head. "Charles. He—"

"He's dead."

She doesn't budge. Doesn't so much as bat a fucking eyelash.

After a long, tense silence, she lifts her chin and says with finality, "Good. He killed my mother. I hope he rots in hell."

That sobers me completely. Sloane managed to somehow find out that Charles was responsible for Alora's abduction, but she never mentioned anything about Alora's mother's death.

As if she can hear my thoughts, she tells me, "She tried to do the right thing. But he ..." She swallows. "He stopped her."

"Hey, big guy. You good back there?" Sloane cuts in as she peeks over the top of the bar at us, a cocky smirk tugging at her lips.

I nod once then shift Alora in my lap and stand, keeping her in my arms and her feet off the floor and away from all the broken glass.

When I glimpse her bare feet, she tells me, "I was leaving you clues."

Pride enters her expression as I carry her over to a chair and set her down carefully. She winces, and I have to remind myself that Ivan Petrov is about to make every one of my most depraved fantasies come true.

When I stand to my full height and glance around, I spot him secured to a chair with thick, rough rope. I'm not entirely sure where it came from, but it doesn't matter. Sloane's hovering over him, whispering god knows what into his ear and making his eyes blow wide.

At the far side of the lounge, there are several bodies—all Ivan's men.

And seated at a booth, puffing on a cigar, is Mikhail Osmanov, a thin stack of papers on the table in front of him. He peels his gaze off Sloane's ass as she leans over Ivan and finds me glaring at him. His lip hikes up into a crooked grin, and he nods once at me then takes another puff.

"Good to see you again, soldier."

On the drive over here, Sloane told me Osmanov had reached out to her, informing her that Charles was working with Ivan and that he was due to meet him at The Afterlife, and that if we still wanted our shot at him, this was it. Of course, we were already en route and arrived a few moments sooner than Osmanov was expecting us. But it worked out.

Osmanov stands and saunters over to me, stuffing his free hand in the pocket of his slacks. He stops a few feet away.

"I trust you got everything you want," I say lowly.

"I always do." He takes another puff, his eyes sliding to Alora seated just behind me. "My apologies for scaring you," he says politely to Alora, and I ball my fists at my sides.

"It's okay," she responds in a shy tone. And the Russian prick smiles at her.

Cocky fucker.

But his attention swiftly returns to me, his smile fading. He gestures to Ivan. "Be sure to clean up whatever mess you're about to make. I want my club in tip-top shape for opening later this evening."

"Your club?"

"The Afterlife is under new ownership as of," he starts, glimpsing at the flashy silver watch slung around his wrist, "eight minutes ago."

He shoots me a tight-lipped smile, then turns on a heel and saunters over to Sloane. He stops directly in front of her, his green eyes glittering as he stares down at her. She folds her arms over her chest and smirks up at him, the same way she did when we met in a warehouse to retrieve Zak after Osmanov's men rescued him from Colombia.

"I'll be seeing you around, *malen'kiy psikh*," he says lowly to her.

"Catch me if you can, gangster," she chirps back.

Osmanov's lip twitches as he spares Sloane's cleavage one final glance, then he turns and walks out of the club, snatching the documents off the table on his way out.

Sloane turns her attention to me and winks.

"Sloane," I say with warning.

She rolls her eyes. "Don't worry about me, Liam. I'm a big girl and can take care of myself. You remember that, don't you?" She cocks a brow then saunters past me, hip bumping me on her way to Alora. "Come on, girl. Let's go raid the gangster's bar while your man finishes up here. I could use a stiff shot of tequila."

Thirty-Five

Alora

Liam's in the basement of Sweetwater's headquarters, which I've dubbed "the torture chamber," with Ivan, doing whatever it is he needs to do. I suspect there's a lot of blood and screaming. I know I should be disturbed by that, maybe even fearful of what Liam's capable of, but truthfully, I feel nothing at all about it. Especially with the knowledge of what Ivan put Rachel through, as well as countless other innocent women and children. Him, his shitty sons, and Charles can all burn in hell together for eternity.

Sloane and I are seated at the table in the kitchen. She pours two more shots of tequila from the bottle she stole from behind the bar at The Afterlife. We clink our glasses and take our shots, the alcohol burning my nose and causing my eyes to water. I slam the empty glass down and stare in awe at Sloane as she gets back to work cleaning and bandaging my wrists. She's so cool and collected, like all of this is just another typical day in her line of work.

"I want to be like you when I grow up," I tell her jokingly.

She smiles at me, angling her head slightly. "Trust me, girl … no you don't." When I don't respond, she asks, "You doing alright?"

I shrug. "Besides feeling like I've gone through a meat tenderizer, I'm fine."

Her expression softens and she grabs my glass, pouring me my third shot. I take it without hesitation, welcoming the buzz.

"I'm not sure what's going on in your head right now, honey," she says softly. "But I've been in some shitty situations in my life as well. And Liam had my back when I needed him. So believe me when I say I know you're trying to be strong when you really don't need to be. Because the man down there doing what he does is plenty strong enough for both of you."

Peeling my tongue off the roof of my mouth, I rasp out, "I don't want to burden him more than I have."

"Liam's solid, Alora. And once that foreskin he's peeling like a grape takes his last breath, I suspect the big thunderclouds he walks around with looming over his head will part way. And he's going to need a little sunshine. He's going to need you to lean on him so he still feels like he has a purpose. Liam's special that way. He lives to serve. So, when the men who have been tormenting him for years are finally gone and he feels like he's had his revenge, he's going to be …" She shrugs a shoulder. "A little bored, I think."

I slump down in my seat, suddenly feeling exhausted.

"Look. I'm not saying you need to be a weak little woman or anything. I think your stubbornness and independence are what Liam loves most about you." *Love.* There's that word again. Is love an accurate description of what Liam and I feel for each other? I'm not sure. But I can say with complete conviction that it's the closest I've ever come. "I'm just saying ... give yourself a break, alright? Rely on him a little. I know you'll be there for him when he needs it too."

I'm not sure why Sloane's telling me these things. But I get the sense Liam and her are closer than the rest of the Sweetwater family. And normally, where Liam's concerned, the little green monster inside me would be rearing its ugly head. But not with Sloane. Because what she said to me in the surveillance truck outside The Afterlife stuck with me. Her and Liam are like brother and sister. They've got each other's backs. And that's a reassurance for me, knowing he has someone who understands him and his darkness. Someone to look out for him when I'm not around someday.

I acknowledge what she's saying with a nod, then change the subject.

"So ..." I waggle my brows. "You and the sexy Russian mafia man, huh?"

Sloane snorts then swats the air. "Girl, that pussycat wouldn't know what to do with me. Besides, there's not a man in the world who's special enough to lock me down."

"Uh huh. Sure."

Sloane and I share a couple more silly grins before we take another shot of tequila.

And when Liam finally appears from the torture chamber, freshly showered and with a look of peace I've never seen on his face before, I know that there's no way he's going to let me go.

And the last piece of desire I had to run away forever splinters off and turns to ash.

I wake just as Liam's truck rolls to a stop. I don't know exactly what time it is, but the stars are all out. The exterior of the log home is lit by the warm glow of solar lights. It takes me a moment to straighten my spine and adjust in the passenger seat, every one of my muscles screaming in protest. My wrists have been cleaned and bandaged up by Sloane, but the tequila we drank is wearing off already, and so is the adrenaline, and I can feel every bump and bruise.

I glance over at Liam's profile, noting his tense expression. The relief that was there earlier is long gone, replaced by something else.

He puts the truck in Park and hops out. Even in the dark, I can see the intensity in his eyes as he rounds the hood and opens my door. I unbuckle my seat belt and turn to step down, but he's got me scooped up and is carrying me inside before my feet have a chance to hit the ground.

No words are spoken. Whatever we have to say to each other is conveyed with body language and eye contact.

He helps me undress, runs me a warm bath with salts, and tenderly cares for my injuries. His touch is gentle but unshakable. He's so solid and reliable, seemingly unaffected by the adrenaline rush he must have felt the last several hours. I watch his every calculated movement, my heart swelling with that frustrating emotion I can't seem to get a handle on. And when he carefully dries my body with a fluffy towel and tucks me into his bed, I have to forcibly stomp down the words I so desperately want to choke out. Words I've never said to a man before.

But the struggle doesn't last long because sleep comes for me almost immediately. And this time, I dream of my mother. Of her beautiful smile and soft hands. How she was the kindest human being I've ever known.

I wake sore, sad, and riddled with guilt for how I perceived her the last two years. How I was so sure she took the easy way out of her illness. How she left me behind to struggle all alone. How she was weak and pathetic.

The reality is she was incredibly strong and brave. Charles said she tried to go to the police—which is more than I've bothered to do. Between her and I, I'm the weaker one. I should have taken her journal to the cops when I realized what secrets it harbored. Maybe law enforcement wouldn't have done anything. Maybe a dead woman's written words aren't enough evidence of Charles's corruption to have put him behind bars. But the least I could have done was try.

Instead, I took off running the way I always do. I chose to turn my back and search for a fresh start somewhere else.

Swallowing the boulder in my throat, I decide with finality that I'm done running. I'm done fleeing reality and giving up when I think I've failed. Because the truth is, reality will find you no matter where you go or how well you hide. And failing is just proof that you're living.

Wincing as I sit upright, I climb out of bed—slowly and awkwardly—and go in search of Liam. I find him in the garage, his arm buried beneath the hood of my car as he works away at replacing my radiator.

He must hear the door creak open because he stands to his full height and turns to face me. His eyes are rimmed in darkness, and I know he hasn't slept.

"Hi," I rasp, taking a step forward onto the cold concrete floor.

I'm dressed in nothing more than one of his T-shirts, which practically swallows me whole. His eyes take inventory of the bumps and bruises covering my bare legs. His expression morphs into a scowl, the scar through his brow indicating he's unimpressed with my current state.

He sets the wrench in his hand down on the engine block and within a couple short strides he's towering in front of me.

"You should be in bed," he grumbles, and I can't help the smirk that tugs at my lips.

"So should you."

"I'm fine."

I roll my eyes. "No you're not. You're exhausted and need some sleep." His jaw slides beneath his short beard, but he doesn't speak. "Whatever you're doing can wait. Come to bed."

I clasp my hand in his and lead him through the cabin and back to the bedroom. He takes a seat on the edge of the mattress and watches me as I slip out of his T-shirt, baring myself to him. I know I'm a canvas of black and blue right now, but the way Liam's eyes roam over my body makes me forget all of it.

"Come here," he says lowly, gesturing for me to stand between his legs.

I step forward, feeling his warmth radiating off him in waves. He pulls me down into his lap and nuzzles into my hair. His lips skim up the side of my neck and to my ear.

"You're mine, little thief," he whispers. "In every way imaginable, and then some."

Instead of arguing like I normally do, I nod. "Okay."

He kisses me deeply, eliciting a moan from deep within my chest. It feels like all the pain and horror from the last twenty-four hours escapes in that moan, and Liam takes it as his own.

His hands skim over my curves, and he lifts me and lays me onto my back. His mouth leaves hot, wet kisses everywhere I'm injured before he lowers to his knees on the floor and laps at my wet center. My hands dive into his hair as he worships me with his tongue.

And when he slides one finger inside of me then adds a second, I come with his name spilling from my lips.

I'm still coming down from my orgasm when he unfastens his jeans and pushes inside me. He fucks me slow and deep, his eyes never leaving mine as he rocks in and out of me, finding his own release only after I've come a second time.

But when he's finished and lays down beside me and pulls me against him, I fall into another deep dream-filled slumber. And this time I dream of painting on the back deck of this very cabin while a shirtless Liam chops firewood in the backyard. Running around a playset that Liam built from scratch are two little girls. And lying at my feet is a black-and-tan dog, his eyes protectively fixated on the playing children. Liam props another log upright before glancing my direction and smiling.

And it's perfect.

Thirty-Six

Liam

I PACE THE EMPTY hall of Casa del Sol, my boots squelching obnoxiously on the polished marble floor. It's been a little over four weeks since Alora was kidnapped and I finished off the Petrovs once and for all. But that four weeks has been a rollercoaster of a ride. Every day is different. But I welcome the challenge of uncertainty because I know it means I get to spend that time with Alora.

I've been bringing her here every Wednesday and Saturday to teach a painting class to the residents. After which she sees one of the therapists Stella keeps on staff, to work through her traumas. I've also sought out some therapy for myself, thanks to Alora's impressive negotiating skills.

I won't go unless you do was her argument. And since I know she's stubborn enough to actually stick to that, I reluctantly agreed. But it's not the therapy that's made a dent in my mental state. It's knowing the world is safe from the Petrovs. Ivan's blood-curdling screams still echo in my ears. And it's fucking cathartic. The way he bled the same shade of red as every other human. The way his face lit with terror as I carved the initials of his victims into his flesh, although his canvas wasn't large enough to fit them all. The way the light dimmed from his eyes when he took his final breath. It calmed my monster. And I didn't hesitate to dole out the punishment I never had a chance to give Ilya. Ivan paid for not only his sins but for his spawn's as well. And I couldn't be more satisfied with my work.

But nothing holds a candle to the peace that falls upon me when I'm with Alora. When she stares up at me. Touches me. Kisses me.

As much as I want to give her the space she needs, I'm itching to be in there with her and holding her hand while she blabbers on about whatever's ailing her. Listening to her worries and dreams. Learning more about her past. I yearn to know every fine detail of what makes her the way she is—absolutely perfect. Joel and Zak would tell me I'm pussy whipped and headed toward marriage. And I wouldn't argue. Because I have every intention of tethering Alora to me for eternity.

The door cracks open and I stiffen, waiting in anticipation as Alora steps out from behind the confines of the therapist's office walls and sashays over to me. Her eyes are bright green and crystal clear, so I know she had a positive session today.

"Hi," she greets me with a gentle smile, and I relax a fraction at her light mood.

I take her hand, my thumb skimming the band of my Rolex that she still wears on her wrist everyday—it looks better on her anyways—and lead her through the mansion and outside into the high California sun.

"Say your goodbyes. We've got somewhere to be," I tell her, hating the feeling that washes over me every time I'm not touching her.

She cocks a suspicious brow at me before sauntering over to Stella and Harper. She takes her fucking time, chatting up a storm before saying goodbye. And I'm almost positive it's just to irritate me—something she enjoys doing.

"Where are we going?" she asks as she slides onto the back of my motorcycle and pulls her helmet over her head.

She's in a pair of black skinny jeans with tears in the knees, a cropped Led Zeppelin T-shirt, and a brand-new pair of Chucks that I ordered for her after she ditched hers while being kidnapped. And fuck me if it's not sexy as hell watching her perch confidently on the back of my Harley in an outfit that perfectly reflects her jagged take-no-shit attitude.

I slip on in front of her, and her arms instinctively wrap around my waist, her cheek resting on my back as I kick my bike to life.

"You'll see when we get there," I tell her before driving off the property and hitting the open road.

Alora melts against me, her fingers skimming gently up and down my stomach. But I'm a nervous wreck, and that's new for me. Where I'm taking her—what I'm about to do—is sacred. Something I never saw myself doing in my lifetime.

My hand finds her calf, and I give her a gentle squeeze. Having her on the back of my bike feels right. Like nothing else in this world matters. Just her and I. Forever.

We turn off onto an old dirt road, and Alora perks up and looks around. The sun is setting low beyond the horizon now, so the sky is the perfect shade of washed-out gray.

"Where are we?"

I don't bother responding because she'll see in a few minutes.

I slow my bike to a crawl, swerving around potholes and fallen branches. It's been months since I've been back here, but Rachel was just out here setting up for me, so I know there won't be any unexpected surprises when we pull up.

We take one final bend in the single lane drive, and Alora stiffens behind me.

"Oh my god," she rushes out in awe, and pride swells in my chest at her excitement.

We're on vacant land that's been in my family for generations, originally purchased by my great-grandfather and passed down the line from then on. It belongs to Rachel and me now, and we vowed to maintain its natural acres of forestry and the small clearing that we use for camping when the mood strikes.

Twinkly solar lights dangle from trees surrounding the open clearing, the bulbs casting a warm glow upon the ground beneath them. In the middle of the clearing is a firepit with two Adirondack chairs parked in front of it. Off to the side is a pitched tent. There will be more lights strung up inside of it, an air mattress, and heaps of blankets and pillows. There's a picnic table with a small vase filled with flowers. It's some weird, girly, aesthetic thing that Rachel insisted on. And I didn't argue because romantic gestures aren't my strong suit.

Beside the table is a large cooler filled with camping food, and a couple roasting sticks for the fire.

I would have come out here and set this up myself, but I haven't been able to leave Alora alone for the simple fact I'd go mental worrying about her. I know that uneasiness will eventually pass, and I'll feel comfortable leaving her side. But for now, it's not fucking happening.

When we park, Alora slips off from behind me and removes her helmet. I watch in rapture as she strolls lazily around the campsite, a small smile gracing her lips.

Fuck, she's beautiful. Even more so when she's happy and care-free.

"I've never been camping before," she tells me. "I asked my mother and Charles to take me when I was a teenager. But Charles thought he was too good for dirt and sticks and nature. And naturally, my mother agreed with him, and that was that."

It's a shame she's never experienced this before, but I'll be damned if I'm not satisfied that I get to be the one to give it to her. It's a privilege to be the man who builds these memories with her. One I won't take for granted.

She stops beside the pit and glances down at the ashes from the last fire I had out here.

"I've never even roasted a marshmallow before."

My legs carry me to her, and I pull her into me. Her arms slink around my waist, and she hugs me tight.

"This is amazing. Thank you," she murmurs against my chest. I hear her sniffle. She's crying. And I'm not sure if it's because she's thinking about her mother, or if she's happy to be out here.

I hook her chin with my finger and force her eyes up to mine before brushing my lips over hers.

"We can come out here as much as you want. Anytime. You just say the word and I'll drop everything and pack up what we need."

She grins, her green eyes twinkling with mischief.

"I like the sounds of it being a *we* thing and not just a *me* thing."

Exhaling the anxiety that's sitting like a ton of bricks in my lungs, I ask her, "How would you feel about the rest of our lives being a *we* thing?"

She blinks a few times and scans my expression for any signs of humor. She'll find none. And as she realizes I'm not joking, her grin dissipates.

"What are you asking me, Liam?"

I rake a hand through my hair and blow out a ragged breath. Words have never been more difficult to form. I lower to one knee and retrieve the small box from my back pocket that I had tucked away in my saddle bag, popping it open in front of her.

"I'm not asking you anything, little thief. I'm telling you that you've stolen more than just my favorite watch. You've got my heart, too. I'm at your mercy now. And the price you'll pay for that is agreeing to be my wife."

She blinks again, disbelief flashing behind her emerald orbs. And when she finally peels her gaze off my face and stares down at the ring I selected—a black teardrop diamond—all the blood drains from her face. And I wonder if I've royally fucked this all up.

"Liam, I ..." She's hesitating.

I snap the box shut and stand, my heart withering beneath the weight of her rejection. But she rolls her eyes and huffs out a dramatic sigh, confusing the fuck out of me.

"I wasn't finished," she tells me boldly. Her tiny hands grip my shoulders, and she urges me back down onto my knees. "Stay there for a second, would ya?" She begins pacing in front of me while I kneel silently before her. When she begins laughing manically, I begin to question whether the therapist she's been seeing has been any help at all. She comes to a standstill and smiles down at me. "You're the most impatient man I've ever met, Liam Davis. You're stubborn and bullheaded and irritating."

I open my mouth to speak. To tell her she's just as stubborn. But she presses a finger to my lips, silencing me. I cock a brow at her and wait for her to continue ripping me apart.

"I like this look on you. On your knees and at my mercy." There's a longer than comfortable pause where all I can hear is my heart slamming against my ribs. "So, yes. I'll be your wife."

I release a breath I hadn't known I was holding and pop the box back open, relief swimming with anticipation of what's to come.

"I'll happily worship the ground you walk on, sweetheart. Until my last breath and beyond."

I slide the ring onto her finger and stand again, scooping her into my arms and kissing her like it's the last thing I'll ever do. She moans and it's game on.

"I hear tent sex is amazing," she murmurs, then giggles as I carry her to the tent and make quick work of unzipping the fly and laying her down on the mattress.

We're both naked in record time, her wearing nothing more than my Rolex and ring. She's lying on her back, her mane of silky black hair fanned out around her like the most captivating midnight halo.

"Tell me you love me, little thief," I urge as my thumb slips between her pussy lips to massage her engorged clit.

She nods frantically and slides her hands through my hair, cupping my skull and pulling me closer. "I love you, Liam. I'll always love you. Through dark and light. Thick and thin. Always and forever."

I groan in relief and satisfaction then sink slowly inside of her hot, wet pussy.

"Good. Because I'm never letting you go."

Her back arches and breath hitches as she accepts every last inch of me. Gray light filters through the thin fabric of the tent, casting us in cool, muted tones. But her eyes shine brighter than two emeralds in the sun. I pump in and out of her at a tantalizingly slow pace, desperate to feel her clench around me and pull me in further as I continue to work her over, bringing her closer to orgasm with every deep thrust. And when she comes around my cock, my name falling from her lips like the sweetest of sins, I know I've found my dark angel, the one who's changed my life forever.

Epilogue

Alora

C ALL ME A CYNIC, but when I was a little girl, I never dreamed of wearing a poofy white dress on my wedding day. I didn't visualize a five-tier cake or live orchestra or lilies and roses. Because I always believed women like me—the jaded, bitter kind who found the male species simpleminded and self-ish—weren't built for marriage. In place of those dreams were plans to travel wherever the wind blew me and paint whatever spoke to my soul. I would live out my mother's dream, here in Mexico. I'd open a shop in her memory and romanticize my quiet little life every chance I had. And on the side, I'd dabble in petty theft to balance the scales of justice.

But all of that changed when the big, broody man standing before me—the one carefully enunciating every single word of his vows—stormed into my life like some sort of dark, all-consuming vortex. Liam is a wrecking ball who abolished my well-fortified walls and staked a claim to his territory. And although he's overly protective and annoying at times, I've never felt more empowered than I do when I'm with him. And now, a full year later, I get to marry not only my best friend, but a man I can depend on. One I can trust with my life. A man my mother would have been proud to call her son-in-law.

Tears spring to my eyes as I stare up at his ruggedly handsome face. Yeah, she'd have loved him.

I love him.

When the minister asks me if I accept, the two simple syllables that leave my mouth are nothing short of the God's honest truth.

"I do."

Relief swarms Liam's expression, and I barely have a chance to blink before I'm being pulled into a set of cannon-like arms and kissed until I'm dizzy with lust and my knees threaten to give way. The hooting and hollering of our guests is background noise, muffled by the beating of my heart. A heart that I've learned now lives outside my body in the form of another human being.

Because that's what Liam is—my heart. My soul. My every-thing.

Eventually, he releases me, and we're ambushed by all of our closest friends and family.

Family. A concept that's felt foreign to me ever since my mother died. But I've been welcomed into the Sweetwater family with open arms, and I couldn't be more grateful for each and every one of them.

Sloane appears beside me, her pale blue bridesmaid's dress a perfect fit and fire-red hair styled in soft curls.

"Congrats, girl. I'm so happy for you." She pulls me in for a hug before playfully nudging Liam's arm and beaming up at him. "You too, big guy. Now bring it in." She grapples at him and forces him into an awkward embrace. I can't help but stifle a laugh.

When she finally stumbles back from him, he scowls down at the half-empty margarita glass in her hand.

"Sloane," he says with warning. "How many of those have you had?"

"Only a hundred," she jokes, winking at me. But when Liam's jaw slides in irritation, she rolls her eyes and swats the air. "Relax, Liam. You know I'm perfectly capable of taking care of myself." She hiccups. "Besides, it's not every day one of you losers gets hitched. So, I'm celebrating." She whoops, then downs the remaining liquid in her glass.

When a waiter with a tray of drinks saunters past, she reaches for a refill and hands me a margarita as well, clinking our glasses in cheers. I take a greedy gulp, the tequila warming my chest and easing my nerves. Who knew your wedding day would be so chaotic.

"Auntie Sloanie," a tiny voice squeals from a distance. Sloane drops her gaze to knee height, and we watch in awe as Lainey, Joel and Stella's boisterous five-year-old daughter, comes bounding toward us. She pushes through the crowd like a tornado, a spitting image of her mother with her wide hazel eyes and dark curls. And she's looking cute as a button in her flower girl dress and sparkly unicorn tiara.

"Hey, Little L." Sloane spreads her arms and Lainey leaps into them. "You smell like candy and love, and I could just eat your little face."

Lainey giggles and squirms as Sloane tickles her ribs. "Did you see me, Auntie Sloanie? Did you see me throwing the flowers?"

"I sure did, honey. You did so great up there."

A bright, excited smile splits across her heart-shaped face.

"Better than Finn?" she asks, no doubt seeking approval from her favorite aunt.

"Well, now." Sloane straightens Lainey's tiara and clasps her pudgy little hands in hers. "That's not quite fair. You see, you and your brother both had a job to do. And his job was different from yours. So as much as you were the best flower girl I've ever seen, Finn was the best ring bearer I've ever seen. It's apples and oranges, L. They're not the same thing so you can't compare them. Do you understand?"

Her face pinches into a pout, and I can't help but smile. But when Liam leans into me and whispers in my ear, "I'm putting a baby in you tonight," I damn near choke on my drink.

Suppressing a silly smile, I tell him lowly, "I don't think it works like that. You can't just choose what day I get pregnant. These things can take time."

He grunts and pulls me into his side, his fingers finding purchase in my hip. I flush at the unexpected wave of heat that spreads between my thighs. Children still terrify me, and I'm still on birth control, but every day that passes, I find myself becoming more and more comfortable with the concept of being a mother. And I know Liam would make an incredible father and I could rely on him for support.

"In the meantime, we can practice making them." I waggle my eyebrows at him, and his lip twitches in amusement.

Harper cuts in. "Sheesh, you two. Save the dirty talk for the bedroom, would ya?"

An awkward laugh bubbles from my chest, and I take another sip of alcohol. Never in a million years did I imagine this would be my life. And it's all thanks to a series of strange, terrifying events that lead me straight to Liam. To my future.

"You remember our wedding day, don't you, kitten?" Zak murmurs to Harper, a crooked grin plastered on his stupidly charming face.

Harper giggles as a pink flush that I know for a fact is *not* from the hot Mexican sun creeps into her cheeks.

I lean toward Harper and Zak and whisper, "You know we can all hear you, right?"

Harper's smile vanishes and Zak's lips curl into a shit-eating grin. He chuckles and takes a sip of his whiskey.

"Speaking of weddings," Joel pipes up, slicing through the weird tension building amongst the group. He points his icy blue gaze at Sloane. "Looks like it's your turn to get hitched, Sloane."

Sloane snort laughs. "Oh, you boys know there's not a man on earth who could handle me. Besides, marriage is for lovestruck idiots like all of you." She pats Joel on the chest and shakes her head. "It'll never happen for me. I'm *untamed*."

As I glance up at my new husband, reveling in the light behind his amber eyes that was almost nonexistent when I met him, I recall the days I felt the same as Sloane currently feels. I was hyper-independent, uninterested in men and their empty offers. But now? Well … I only wish I had met Liam sooner so I could spend just a little more of my life with him.

Leaning into him and filling my lungs with his soothing signature scent, I return to my attention to Sloane and tell her with a smile, "Never say never."

THE END

Acknowledgements

WHERE DO I BEGIN? Writing this entire series has been an emotional rollercoaster. But this book in particular ... I don't even have words. My sweet, dark, twisted Liam has haunted my dreams for several years now. And I couldn't be happier that his story is now told. And Alora ... well, she holds a special place in my heart.

But writing is only half the battle of publishing, and I couldn't have done it without the love and support of so many incredible people.

To my girls Gabby and Cami ... I am so grateful to have found you. I owe my sanity to you both. Truly. Without you, I couldn't have found the perseverance or time to write. You're my rocks, and I love you and appreciate you more than words can express.

To my developmental editor, Kim, thank you a million times over for all of your incredible insight and honesty. Your attention to detail astounds me, and I'm so very grateful to have you on my team.

Kylie, my editor ... you are undeniably irreplaceable. Thanks to you, my stories are polished and beautifully edited. Thank you for being so thorough and efficient and putting up with my never-ending delays and procrastination.

To my family and friends (or at least the ones who know I write dirty, dark, fucked-up stories) ... I wouldn't have the grit to hit the publish button without you.

And finally, my ARC and street teams ... I quite literally would not be where I am without you. You guys are the real MVPs. I love you all.

Much love,

A.D. Wilde

About the Author

A.D. WILDE IS A Canadian author, born and raised in rural Ontario. When she's not reading or writing, she can be found hiking, road tripping to random North American destinations, or stuffing her face with carbs and wine.

Her favorite color is morally gray, her favorite MMCs are, at the very least, mildly psychotic and possessive, and her favorite FMCs are strong, stubborn and independent with a take-no-shit attitude.

A.D. is a mental health advocate, and encourages readers to always check the trigger/content warnings before diving in to any dark romance story.